"You're the only woman I want, Chelsea."

"When I started falling in love with you," she told him, "it felt like dying."

"And now?" he asked, his hands settling on her hips.

"Now I finally know how it feels to be alive. Not just parts of me, but all of them." Her long hair streamed over her shoulders as she shook her head. "I don't know to explain it. It's like you woke me up. Made me open my eyes."

The instant she whispered, "Make me yours, Eric," his fangs burst into his mouth so hard that it hurt.

His wolf prowled beneath his skin, brimming with instinct and the need for possession, but he had to make sure this was what she wanted, because once done, there was no going back. "Are you sure this is what you want, Chelsea?"

"I'm sure," she said a little breathlessly....

Books by Rhyannon Byrd

Harlequin Nocturne

#35 *Last Wolf Standing***
#38 *Last Wolf Hunting***
#39 *Last Wolf Watching***
#152 *Dark Wolf Rising***

Harlequin HQN

Edge of Hunger*
Edge of Danger*
Edge of Desire*
Touch of Seduction*
Touch of Surrender*
Touch of Temptation*
Rush of Darkness*
Rush of Pleasure*
Deadly is the Kiss*

*Primal Instinct
**Bloodrunners

RHYANNON BYRD

is an avid, longtime fan of romance and the author of more than twenty paranormal and erotic titles. She has been nominated for three *RT Book Reviews* Reviewers' Choice Awards, including best Shapeshifter Romance, and her books have been translated into nine languages. After having spent years enjoying the glorious sunshine of the American South and Southwest, Rhyannon now lives in the beautiful but often chilly county of Warwickshire in England with her husband and family. For more information on Rhyannon's books and the latest news, you can visit her website at www.rhyannonbyrd.com or find her on Facebook.

DARK WOLF RISING

RHYANNON BYRD

HARLEQUIN®

entertain, enrich, inspire™

Recycling programs
for this product may
not exist in your area.

ISBN-13: 978-0-373-88562-6

DARK WOLF RISING

This edition published by arrangement with Harlequin Books S.A.

For questions and comments about the quality of this book
please contact us at CustomerService@Harlequin.com.

® and TM are trademarks of Harlequin Enterprises Limited or its
corporate affiliates. Trademarks indicated with ® are registered in the
United States Patent and Trademark Office, the Canadian Trade Marks
Office and in other countries.

www.Harlequin.com

Printed in U.S.A.

Dear Reader,

The Bloodrunners series is one that's been near and dear to my heart since I first wrote *Last Wolf Standing* back in 2007, and I'm so thrilled to finally be bringing you Eric Drake's story. I love his smart-ass sense of humor, his bad boy ways, and the undying sense of loyalty he has for the people he cares about. But I never really understood how intriguing he was until I had to start playing around inside his head. Thanks to his bloodline, Eric is one of the most powerful Lycans in the Silvercrest pack, and yet, in the wake of his father's treachery, his entire world seems to be crumbling around him. That's when the feisty, all-too-human Chelsea Smart storms into his life...knocking the gorgeous werewolf right on his sexy backside. She's the last kind of trouble he needs, and yet, Eric finds himself fighting a temptation greater than any he's ever known.

Before I go, I just want to shout out masses of thanks for making the Bloodrunners a part of your lives. I promise there are more adventures to come!

Best wishes,

Rhy

For Crystall...

(aka Cici)

Sorry you had to wait so long, sis!

Love you lots!

THE BLOODRUNNERS' LAW

When offspring are born of a union between human and Lycan, the resulting creations may only gain acceptance within their rightful pack by the act of Bloodrunning: the hunting and extermination of rogue Lycans who have taken a desire for human flesh. Thus they prove not only their strength, but their willingness to kill for those they will swear to protect to the death.

The League of Elders will predetermine the Bloodrunners' required number of kills.

Once said number of kills are efficiently accomplished, only then may the Bloodrunner assume a place among their kin, complete with full rights and privileges.

THE DARK WOLF
A Dark Wolf bloodline is the purest
of the Lycan race.
They are the most primal and powerful of their kind.
Visceral. Predatory.
Creatures of instinct and hunger.

They are the potential for all things good and evil.

And when it comes to humans...they are a deadly
nightmare just waiting to happen.

DARK WOLF RISING

Something dark is coming...

Chapter One

Eric Drake had always believed that if there was one thing that didn't mix well, it was humans and wolves—which was why he had a bad feeling about the current situation. Or more specifically, about the woman.

Climbing out of his truck, he stared through the hazy glow of silver-threaded moonlight, struggling to make out the features of the female sitting behind the wheel of a sky-blue Volkswagen bus. A *human* female. And a ridiculous-looking bus. With a whimsical confection of puffy white clouds painted down its sides, the vehicle looked more like something that belonged on a laid-back, surfer-laden beach in Southern California, rather than the rugged terrain of the Maryland mountains. It was parked in a narrow field, just behind a small line of trees that hid it from the nearby road and any passing cars, which had obviously been the driver's intention.

Fortunately, a pair of Silvercrest scouts had discov-

ered the bus and its occupant while patrolling this private
stretch of road. It split off from the main highway a few
miles back, then slowly wound its way up toward Shadow
Peak, the mountaintop town the Silvercrest Lycans called
home—a fact which made this particular area exceptionally dangerous if you were human…and nothing *more.*

Eric didn't want to think about what could have happened to the woman if she'd put herself in the path of a
ravenous werewolf out roaming the dark woods in search
of prey. As a rule, his pack didn't feed on humans—and
those who did were marked as rogue wolves, hunted down
and assassinated by the Bloodrunners. But to find a defenseless human alone in the mountains while on the hunt
for fresh meat would be a temptation some might find difficult to resist. Despite knowing it was wrong, the dark,
destructive craving could all too easily overpower a Lycan's reason and sense of rightness.

The lady was lucky to still be sitting there in one piece.

Eric tried to get a good look at her, but even his exceptional night vision couldn't make out her features. Apparently uninterested in who had just arrived on the scene, or,
judging by the stiff set of her posture, too furious to care,
she sat behind the steering wheel with her face turned to
the side. A long, thick fall of brown hair covered most of
her profile, so that only the delicate tip of a small nose
could be distinguished, along with the soft-looking swell
of her lower lip.

Hell of a mouth, he thought, wondering exactly what he
was going to do about her. The situation obviously hadn't
improved since he'd received the call from Hendricks,
one of the two scouts who were on the scene. Her frustration seemed to all but fill the interior of the bus with
the weight of a thick, oppressive fog. With her shoulders
tight, back straight and arms crossed protectively over

her chest, she didn't appear ready to give in to their demands that she leave the area immediately, and go back to wherever she came from.

Drawing in a deep breath, he searched for her scent on the heavy mountain air, but the bus was sealed tight, windows up. Whatever trace might have escaped through the window as she'd talked to the scouts earlier had been carried away by the howling wind sweeping through the forest, rustling the new spring leaves upon their branches, bringing with it the damp, humid promise of a storm. They were common enough this time of year in western Maryland, and after flicking a quick glance toward the thickening, bruise-colored clouds that marked the midnight sky like blotches of smoke, Eric realized he was going to end up soaked if he didn't get a move on.

Shutting the truck's door with a sharp snap, he ran a quick visual on the nearby area. One of the scouts, a Lycan named Franks, stood near the driver-side door of the Volkswagen. The guy kept a wary eye on the woman as the wind whipped his shaggy blond hair around his gaunt features, while the other scout hurried over to Eric, launching into a hectic, breathless explanation, his words stumbling over themselves in his haste to get them said.

"I'm sorry again for bothering you on a Friday night, sir, but she refuses to leave the area."

"What has she said?" he asked, wishing he hadn't just smoked his last cigarette.

"She showed us a picture of a young woman and asked if we'd seen her. After we told her that we'd never seen the girl, we tried to explain that she can't stay here, but she insists that we can't kick her off the property, and I'm afraid we didn't know how to get her to leave without... um, that is, without..."

"It's okay, Hendricks," Eric murmured, trying to put

the younger Lycan at ease. "You know we want all territory infractions called in, so you've done the right thing."

The square-faced, spectacled Hendricks hadn't needed to finish his stumbling explanation—Eric knew exactly what the problem was. It had been impossible for them to get rid of the woman without getting physical with her, or betraying their secret. The newly appointed scouts were clearly on uneasy, unfamiliar ground with this young female who was too stubborn for her own good.

Taking a few steps away from his truck, Eric ran one hand back through his short scrub of hair, then over the scratchy surface of his jaw. What in the hell did she think she was doing? It wasn't safe for a woman to camp out by herself in the mountains, even if she *was* sleeping in her car.

Was she really searching for someone? Or was it just a scam? Given the whimsical bus, she could be one of those environmentalists looking to commune with nature, or whatever they called it. They'd had to deal with the type before. Or was she actually some kind of reporter trying to sniff out a story? God, the last damn thing they needed was a curious human snooping around the area. He and the Bloodrunners, the half-breed hunters whose job it was to hide the existence of their race from humans, as well as to hunt down those who turned rogue, already had their hands full working to get order reestablished up in Shadow Peak. Still mired in the process of forming a new government, the Silvercrest continued to deal with the emotional and physical wounds left over from the traumatic events of five months ago. Events that had left the pack without leadership, and reeling from a betrayal that had affected everyone from the adults who'd lost their lives down to the children who had been tragically orphaned.

Though once completely removed from the dealings in Shadow Peak, the Bloodrunners' newly established position within the pack's political structure put them in charge of Silvercrest security, with Eric working as the liaison between the pack and the Runners. After the recent treachery that had weakened their stability, courtesy of Eric's father and his savage plans to take over the pack, the Silvercrest had been left in a vulnerable position. It was a frightening time, and the wolves were all too aware of the aggressive nature of some of their neighboring packs—especially the Whiteclaw wolves, who lived to the south of them. As a precaution, Eric and the Runners had been taking turns supervising the night watch, any suspicious or unusual activities being immediately reported by the scouts to the one in charge on any given night. Since they'd begun rotating the shift, Eric had been involved in a variety of dangerous situations, and was for the first time getting a taste of what life as a Runner was like.

"Did she give you a name?" he asked, noting how uneasy the scout seemed. Hendricks's pale skin was flushed with color, his dark gaze repeatedly sliding from the ground to the sky, as if he was wary of looking directly at Eric's face.

"No, sir," Hendricks replied, slanting him a quick glance, and Eric struggled to keep his expression impassive. "To be honest, she's…well…"

"She's what?" he prompted, fighting down his impatience.

"She's not exactly what you'd expect from a human female. I could scent her fear when we found her, and yet, she absolutely refused to back down." Hendricks swallowed, the nervous movement visible in his throat. "She even pulled out a gun, saying that she'd shoot off our, um, manly parts if we dared to lay a hand on her," he admitted, his voice thick with embarrassment...and an unmistakable note of relief that he was still standing there, said manly parts intact.

Eric choked back a low bark of laughter, somehow managing to hide his smile behind his hand as he coughed. But his humor faded as Franks came over to join them, the scout's gaze swiftly focusing on something over his shoulder.

"Why don't you wait over here and let me talk to her alone for a minute?" Eric suggested, wondering if he had food stuck in his teeth. Neither Hendricks nor Franks seemed capable of looking directly at him—but then, there weren't many in the pack these days who were. Still, he'd expected better from these two, and he ran his tongue over his teeth just to be sure he was in the clear.

"Be careful," they replied in unison, looking relieved to be passing the situation to him.

The milky glow of the nearly full moon caught his eye as Eric made his way toward the vehicle, and his beast gave a lazy stretch beneath his skin, his senses quickening with a primal rush, eager...almost desperate to hunt. He'd been so busy lately he'd ignored his predatory hungers, which was never a smart move—especially for a bloodline as powerful as his. As a dark wolf, the product of two exceptionally pure Lycan bloodlines, Eric's natural cravings ran deeper than most, making the need for control even greater. He clenched his jaw, forcing the prowling animal deeper into his psyche. At the moment, he needed the calm, cool reasoning of the man—not the animalistic aggression of his beast.

But being cool and calm didn't seem to be on the agenda for the night.

As Eric approached the driver-side door, the woman shifted slightly, giving him his first clear view of her face, and his muscles tightened with a jolting, *slam-him-into-the-ground* kind of surprise. For some reason, probably because of how Hendricks and Franks were acting, he hadn't expected the woman to be so…well, *soft*-looking. Even attractive. But she was. She had the kind of beauty that crept up on a guy, making him want to keep staring… searching, noting new discoveries as he mapped out the finely sculpted contours, one by one. The full lower lip was only part of a lush, pink mouth that begged for the carnal aggression of a kiss…among other things. Things he had no business thinking about doing with a perfect stranger, not to mention a human one.

So get your bloody mind out of the gutter and stay focused! his conscience muttered.

Determined to continue his appraisal with a more critical eye, Eric searched for her first flaw, but failed to find one. She wasn't classically beautiful, but she was pretty, in a wholesome, appealing way. Her face was somewhat round, with a small nose and sweeping brows that arched over big blue eyes. Instead of making her look childish, the delicate features gave her an air of womanly innocence that would catch any man's attention. That made him want to be the one to corrupt her…to open those bright blue eyes to things that were warm and wet and undeniably wicked. To the harder, more primal angles of pleasure.

And there you go slumming around in the gutter again.

"Damn it," he muttered under his breath, wondering what was wrong with him. He hated to admit it, but she was affecting him in a way that made him want to turn around and get the hell out of there. It was more than just the dangerous, unwanted sexual attraction building inside him. Though that was bad enough. But for some inexplicable reason, he almost felt as if the human posed some kind of threat to him, which was ridiculous. *He* was the monster in this scenario, the thing to be feared in the silence of the night—not her. And yet, his chest felt too tight, his muscles coiled, ready to burst into movement, and he shoved his hands in his front pockets, his jaw so tight it made his teeth ache. Sweat broke out over his forehead and collected in the small of his back as he indicated with his chin that he wanted her to roll down the window, more determined than ever to get this over and done with as quickly as possible.

In response, she lifted one of those beautifully shaped brows and glared at him. Without so much as the flicker of a lash, Eric glared right back, letting her know he wouldn't be as easily cowed as the scouts. When she didn't budge, he made his tone as non-threatening as possible, knowing his size could be intimidating to a lot of women, and said, "I'm not going to hurt you, lady. I just want to talk."

She leaned a little closer to the window and ran her gaze over his tall form, working from his scarred hiking boots up to his short hair, then shook her head and raised her chin a notch higher. Eric choked back a low groan, thinking *why me?* Why couldn't his friend Jeremy have been stuck with this tonight?

"Look, I can be as stubborn as you are, so save us both the trouble and just roll down the damn window," he ground out, unable to soften the gruff edge to his order this time. He was uncomfortably aware of his wolf steadily prowling closer to his surface, taking note of her in a way that caused a deeper sliver of alarm to slip down his spine.

This time, she didn't shake her head in response to his…*request.* Instead, the crazy-assed woman narrowed her eyes and lifted one closed feminine hand. Then she very deliberately extended her middle finger.

What the…?

Eric stared…a little stunned, thinking there was something definitely not right about her.

Taking his hands from his pockets, he braced them on either side of her window and leaned forward, so close that his warm breath fogged on the glass as he spoke. "You can't stay by yourself out here in the middle of nowhere, so either turn this thing on and get the hell out of here," he said in a low, painfully controlled tone, "or start talking."

If looks could kill, Eric had no doubt he'd be drawing his last breath just about then. But at least he got the desired results. She uncrossed her arms, the scooped neck of her long-sleeved T-shirt revealing a shocking jolt of cleavage that was damn hard not to stare at. He forced his dark gaze back up to her face just in time to see her mutter something he couldn't quite hear, but could all too easily decipher on those sexy lips. Then she angrily reached for the window lever.

The second the window cracked open, he pulled in a deep breath, his razor-sharp senses searching…seeking. With her strange behavior, he'd half expected her to reek of alcohol or drugs, but he couldn't pick up a trace of either. Instead, she smelled…like a puzzle. Fresh and clean and delicious, but almost painfully complicated. Like something he needed if he wanted to figure out an answer, even though he didn't have a clue what the question was.

And it sure as hell isn't anything to do with me.

For a split second, Eric was almost disappointed by that particular truth. By the fact that his wolf didn't recognize that warm, mouthwatering scent as something that belonged to them. Something they were meant to own and claim and possess. But that was nothing short of insane. He lowered his arms and backed up a step from the bus, determined to put some distance between them. As well as knock some sense into his wayward libido.

That scent made him want to… *No.* He gave his head a hard shake, ignoring a bad idea that would only lead to an even worse situation.

She was the kind of trouble he didn't need. Or want. And once she drove out of his life, he'd forget her as easily as he forgot every other woman who'd ever stirred his interest. It was a given. A fact. He just had to convince her crazy little ass to get off the pack's private property, and that would be that.

Should be easy enough, considering how his species resided at the top of the food chain, and hers didn't. Even though she didn't know he was *different,* she would sense the predator in him. Would know this wasn't a safe situation for her to be in, the same way she'd naturally avoid a dark alley or a snarling, snapping animal. It was instinct. Simple self-preservation.

But as Eric stared down into narrowed eyes that burned like a heat-glazed summer sky, he knew, with his own gut feeling, that it wouldn't be that cut-and-dry. Knew she was going to be a pain in the ass, which should have bothered the hell out of him. But it didn't.

No, what bothered him was how much he and his wolf were suddenly looking forward to the challenge.

Chelsea Smart refused to take her glare off the man standing beside her bus. What exactly had she managed to land herself in? Something wasn't right, and while common sense demanded she get the hell out of there, her heart refused to budge, knowing this spooky mountain might prove to be her best chance at finding Perry. Not that her younger sister was a child in need of supervision.

At nineteen, Perry was old enough to make her own decisions—even if they landed her in a crapload of danger.

Unfortunately, Chelsea was afraid that was exactly what had happened. And with no one else willing to act as Perry's rescuer, she'd gathered what was left in her meager checking account, taken emergency leave from her teaching job in Virginia and hit the road in search of her only sibling. That'd been two weeks ago. Now she was almost out of money, low on gas and worn down to her last nerve, her frustration mounting with each passing moment.

The small pistol she'd bought three years ago rested in her lap, beneath the afghan she'd pulled over herself before the other two men had scared fifty years off her life, knocking on her window and waking her from a restless sleep. She resisted the urge to reach down now and stroke the cold metal for comfort, assuring herself that it was there. She could only assume this giant bulk of a man staring at her with dark gray eyes was meant to achieve what the other two had failed to do, and get rid of her. Hadn't he told her as much?

When he'd pulled up in a massive, black, testosterone-oozing truck, the engine rumbling obscenely loud in the eerie quiet of the forest, she'd looked away, not wanting to appear flustered or worried, even though she was a mass of churning emotion inside. She'd learned long ago how to bury her feelings beneath a calm, icy shield of indifference, which had been the only way to deal with her father's tyrannical rule while growing up. Though it'd been years since Chelsea had lived under his roof, some habits had become so deeply ingrained, it seemed it would take a lifetime to unlearn them.

Then again, she hadn't tried very hard to change, always finding it easier to avoid uncomfortable encounters simply by making it obvious that she wanted to be left alone.

But she hadn't been left alone tonight, and her worry and frustration were getting the better of her, to the point that anger rode the flushed surface of her body like a second skin. It was evident in her posture and her expression, and then she'd gone and actually shot the illustrious "bird" at this dark-haired stranger in a purely reckless display of temper. That was something she'd never done before... and would hopefully never do again.

The only thing that made her momentary loss of dignity bearable was the fact that the fascinating tower of maleness standing there, watching her, had obviously never mastered the art of masking his own reactions. From the moment she'd rolled down her window, emotions had been flitting across his rugged features like a montage of images flashed across a movie screen. Frustration. Shock. Irritation. Maybe even a touch of loneliness. They were all there, as well as something that looked surprisingly like lust. His glittering gray eyes had gone wide, then heavy, until she could barely see the mesmerizing color through the inky black weight of his lashes.

He was too tall, too rugged, and too damn good-looking, and he probably knew it. Add to that the obvious fact that he held some sort of position of authority in this area, and Chelsea knew he was the kind of guy she normally went out of her way to avoid. Of course, the last time she'd seen her sister, Perry had accused her of avoiding *all* men, making the snide assessment that she should either go lesbian or resign herself to being alone for the rest of her life. She'd told her sister to mind her own business, then changed the subject, but Perry's words had stayed with her, proving difficult to forget.

As a modern, educated woman, Chelsea knew, deep

down, that her cool attitude toward the opposite sex had been born from a soul-deep fear of ever becoming like her mother. Perry had dealt by immersing herself in the party scene, earning a reputation as the girl who would try anything at least once, whereas Chelsea had simply closed down, withdrawing, just like an oyster hiding within its shell. Despite her worldly views, she had little experience when it came to male animals, especially ones like the hunk standing so close to her bus…staring at her as if he couldn't decide whether he wanted to strangle her or eat her alive. His warm, utterly male scent, a seductive blend of heat and spice and the outdoors, was actually causing drool to collect in the corners of her mouth.

Amazing.

The whole "mouthwatering" reaction never happened to her, unless she was confronted by the scent of fresh baked brownies or watching a Gerard Butler movie. Despite her skeptical attitude toward the male species, even Chelsea had found herself a victim of the Scotsman's compelling sexuality.

But Butler had nothing on this guy. A quick flick of a glance over his body revealed a physique that was long and lean and powerfully muscled. The kind of body that would be hard and hot to the touch. That would ripple with muscle as he moved over a woman…as he moved *inside* her. Hard and deep and fast. Then hard and deep and…deliberately slow.

Giving herself a sturdy mental shake, Chelsea fought the urge to fan her face, and struggled to get her mind out from between the sheets and back on important things, like staying alive and finding her sister. But that was proving decidedly difficult to do, seeing as how she couldn't seem to take her eyes off him. God, what was happening to her? Were her hormones revolting, demanding satisfaction after being bludgeoned into submission for so many years? And if so, the timing couldn't be worse. Why now?

Unfortunately, she had a feeling the answer to that question was staring her right in the face.

Okay, so he wasn't her type, but he was certainly a pretty piece of eye candy, if one went for the rugged, alpha breed of male, complete with bulging muscles, tattoos and faded scars. Which she didn't, she reminded herself, while her body reached supernova levels of heat in an embarrassing, shocking, completely unforgivable act of betrayal.

His hard, sleekly muscled physique attested to what had to be an athletic lifestyle. Even his forearms were marked by ropey muscles and lean lines of sinew, his dark body hair lying flat against the deep, sun-darkened color of his skin. Without doubt, he was the most masculine thing Chelsea had ever set eyes on. He belonged here in the wild, rugged terrain of the forest, as if he were a part of it, completely at home within its primitive landscape.

As she watched him, he flexed his big hands at his sides, like he was working out a cramp, his arms rigid, powerful biceps stretching the seams of his black T-shirt. A fierce wave of tension emanated from him, blasting against her face like a hot wind.

And yet, despite the predatory intensity that surrounded him, all but oozing from his pores, she didn't fear him. Was the gun in her lap giving her a false sense of safety? Somehow, she didn't think so. Chelsea knew how she *should* be feeling, but there was something in his expression—something dark and uncomfortable— that said he was as wary of her as she was of him, and it bolstered her battered sense of security.

"Well?" she snapped, relieved by the waspish sound of her voice, having been half afraid she might actually purr at him when she finally located her ability to speak.

"Well what?" His voice was hard, deliciously deep and roughened around the edges.

She fought the temptation to roll her eyes, thinking they certainly grew them breathtakingly big around here, not to mention gorgeous, but obviously not too bright. "What. Do. You. Want?" she asked slowly, enunciating each word with patronizing precision.

He blinked, and then the corner of his mouth suddenly twitched, and a smooth spill of surprise warmed her insides at the fact that he'd reacted to her sarcastic tone with humor, rather than anger. Not that she wanted him angry, mind you.

No, all she wanted was for him to leave her alone, so that she could get some sleep, and then get on with her search…while doing her best to forget this fluttery feeling he'd put in her belly. It felt good, damn it—dangerously good—and that made her more nervous than his primal intensity ever could. Sexual desire was a dangerous trap that couldn't be trusted any more than the male species could be. She had to find some way to ignore it, no matter how good the rush in her pulse felt, as if she were stretching to awareness after a long, heavy slumber.

Part of her wanted to shout *So this is what it's all about!*—while the other part snarled *For the love of God, what kind of idiot starts thinking about having sex with a total, behemoth-size stranger?*

Apparently her kind, she realized, since she couldn't get the thought out of her head of what it'd be like to be covered by this sexy-as-hell hunk.

Thunder suddenly rumbled in the distance, signaling an approaching storm, bringing with it the crisp scent of rain. Chelsea glanced toward the swollen sky, and then softly, in a tone completely unlike her, she heard herself say, "It looks like a storm's coming. You wanted to talk, so talk, before it starts to rain."

He looked up, staring at the sky…at the moon, and when he lowered his head, once again trapping her in the piercing intensity of his stare, the look in his eyes burned even brighter, as though that silver gaze was somehow glowing, fired with heat from within. *Glowing eyes?* She blinked, shaking her head, knowing she needed more sleep. God, she'd been pushing herself so hard, she was getting delusional.

After what seemed like forever, he finally asked, "What are you doing here?"

The gravelly sound of his voice raised chill bumps on her arms, and she resisted the urge to reach out and smooth the deep furrows between his brows, then the harsh lines of frustration bracketing his sensual mouth. Instead, she reached up to the visor and took down Perry's picture, holding it up for him to see. "I'm looking for this girl. She's my sister. Have you seen her?"

He glanced at the photo that had been taken on Perry's last birthday. "No. Never set eyes on her before. She isn't here."

"Well, I'm not leaving until I've found her."

He drew in a slow, deep breath, taking a step closer to the bus, bringing the details of his ruggedly gorgeous face into a sharper focus. The ink-black hair, cut severely short, emphasizing that spectacular bone structure. The dark, mesmerizing glitter of those heavy-lidded eyes. The strong line of his nose, as well as the shadowed hollows of his cheeks. Each detail was almost painfully beautiful, and yet, perfectly masculine.

The air seemed to crackle between them, as if something was building…growing stronger, layer upon layer upon layer, each one gaining in intensity. Something powerful and electric that you couldn't see—that you could only feel…*sense*. His breathing grew deeper, his chest rising and falling as if he were exerting some kind of physical effort, when he only stood there…staring…watching.

The way he suddenly shoved his hands back in the pockets of his jeans caught her attention, and she could have sworn he was struggling for some kind of control over himself as he asked, "What makes you think your sister is here, on our mountain?"

Instead of answering his question, Chelsea returned the photo to the visor and posed one of her own. "*Our* mountain? What, you own it?"

He shrugged those impossibly broad shoulders, and her eyes snagged on the intricate design of the tattoo swirling over his right biceps, just visible beneath the tight stretch of his sleeve. It made her heart beat even faster.

"In a way, yes. This is private property."

A sick feeling swept through her stomach. "Your boy soldiers over there claimed the same thing, but I don't see how you can own an *entire* mountain. And I was on a public highway," she argued.

"Which you then turned off of," he explained, his voice a low, mesmerizing rumble, "and onto a private road." He arched one dark brow as he added, "I assume you missed the clearly marked signs when you exited the main highway a few miles back?"

"Must have," she said tightly, wondering what the hell she was going to do. "So what now? Are you going to waste your night trying to kick me out of here, or go back to wherever you came from and leave me alone?"

"I'm not going to *try* anything," he murmured, while something that almost looked like regret flickered through those beautiful gray eyes. "I *am* kicking you out of here."

With a tired sigh, Chelsea shook her head again. "I

was hoping it wouldn't come to this, but you aren't leaving me much choice. In fact, you're acting like a complete and total ass."

Then she lifted the pistol from her lap…and pointed the barrel right at him.

Chapter Two

Though there wasn't anything particularly funny about having a gun pointed straight at your heart, Eric had to fight the surprising urge to laugh at the human's audacity. A bullet wouldn't kill him, but it would still hurt like a bitch. He should have been furious that she was threatening him, but that wasn't the source of his anger. Instead, he was uncomfortably aware that the more she stood up to him, the harder it was for him not to pull her out of that goofy-looking bus and show her just how much danger she was courting here.

Running his tongue over the edge of his teeth, he said, "I'm thinking you probably hear this a lot, but you're too gutsy for your own good, lady."

She smirked, but didn't bother to lower the weapon. "Maybe I'll be more understanding if you just tell me what the big secret is. Why all the urgency for me to leave? Afraid I'll stumble across something I shouldn't?

Are you guys part of some religious cult?" Her brows lifted with curiosity. "Do you like to run around naked and worship the moon?"

"Something like that," he offered drily, still struggling against the driving urge to drag her out of the bus and take her to the ground, where he could press her into the soft, damp grass. Without doubt, she was a shock to the system. Instead of sharp angles to match that sharp tongue, the woman possessed a glowing, fresh-faced softness that made her look entirely adorable—and he had to fight back another grin as he imagined what her reaction would be if he expressed *that* opinion out loud.

Hell, knowing her, she'd probably shoot him the finger again. Either that, or just plain shoot him.

As if reading his mind, she said, "I'll put a bullet in you if I have to, though I'd rather not. Can't stand the sight of blood." She slowly lowered the weapon back to her lap, but kept her finger close to the trigger. "So don't tempt me."

"Wouldn't dream of it." His tone was even drier than before. "But you still need to get lost."

"You know, even if you succeed in making me leave—" her breasts swayed with a delicious jiggle beneath the tight green T-shirt as she shifted in her seat to face him "—I'll only come back."

She drew in a shaky little breath after making that rather forceful announcement, and for the first time since this bizarre confrontation got started, Eric managed to see past his frustration and lust, down to the exhaustion and worry haunting her gaze. And he didn't like it. What the hell had this woman gotten herself into? And why the fuck was he getting uptight about it? He damn well knew better!

"Do you have any idea how unsafe it is, what you're doing, coming to the mountains by yourself?"

She gave a negligent roll of her shoulders, then lifted her free hand to push that thick fall of hair behind her ear. "I came armed. I'm not stupid."

He flicked a dismissive glance at the gun in her lap, and a rude sound rumbled in the back of his throat. "It's a nice weapon, but isn't going to do you much good up here."

She arched one slim brown brow again. "And why is that?"

"Just trust me on it," he muttered, wondering if lightning was going to come down and fry him on the spot for the things he was thinking about doing to her. It was one thing for the Runners to take human lovers, seeing as how they were half human themselves—but Eric was in an entirely different situation.

"You can't stay out here in your car," he growled, the sudden pronouncement making her jump. "It isn't safe."

Carefully recovering her composure, she jerked her chin toward Hendricks and Franks. "Why? I won't go snooping where I don't belong. And no one was bothering me before those two showed up."

The headstrong woman had no idea how lucky that made her, and Eric wanted to keep it that way. "Save your breath and stop arguing, sweetheart. I'm not trying to jerk you around. You really can't stay here."

"First of all, I'm not your sweetheart," she snapped, obviously irritated by his choice of words. "And secondly, if you won't let me stay in my car, isn't there someplace in your town where I can get an…inexpensive room for the night?"

It was the hesitant way she'd said *inexpensive* that finally clued him in, making him wonder if she was sleeping in her car *not* because she was careless with her safety, but because she simply couldn't afford to sleep anywhere else. "I'm afraid not," he rasped, while something painful twisted in his chest. She was clearly in need of rescuing, and it bothered him that he couldn't be the one to do it. That he was more harm to her than help.

"Hmm," she murmured, and he could see the wheels spinning again in her head.

"Trust me," he said gruffly, "the best thing for you to do is to stay down in Wesley. It's only about an hour from here."

"Yeah, I know where it is." She looked away for a moment, chewing on that lush bottom lip, her gaze even more troubled than before when she finally brought it back to his. "You really think I can just go? That I can just give up and leave my sister to the wolves?"

Suspicion narrowed his eyes. "What the hell does that mean?" he demanded, watching her closely. Did she know what he was? What they all were?

"It's just an expression." Her voice was sharp, a slight frown settling between her brows. "I know she's in trouble, and I refuse to let it go and just sit at home wringing my hands, hoping a miracle will happen and some big burly man will step in to rescue her."

She her cut her gaze away again, but not before he caught the luminous wash of tears glistening in her eyes. *Aw, hell.* Knowing he wouldn't be able to take it if she broke down—that he'd rather have her angry than sad— Eric curled his lips and said something guaranteed to piss her off and get her back up. "Some big burly man, huh? I get it now. You're one of those women who has guy issues, aren't you?"

She snorted, shooting him a withering look from the corner of her eye. "Not any more than you have *women* issues."

"The hell I do," he drawled, aware that he was taking

some kind of perverse pleasure in verbally sparring with her. "I happen to like women just fine."

Her head tilted slightly to the side as she studied him. "I'm sure you like them when they're on their backs. Other than that, I doubt you have much use for them."

Eric gave her a slow, cocky smile and clucked his tongue. "Like I said…issues."

She opened her mouth, no doubt to make some cutting remark, but then quickly pressed her lips together, choking off whatever she'd been about to say. Judging from the color creeping into her face, he figured she'd probably just realized she was revealing more about herself with this particular interchange than she wanted to, while accusing him of being…what? A guy?

Yeah, he liked sex. What man didn't? Lately, Eric just didn't like how he felt after he'd finished it—as if there was something better that he couldn't reach. Something he wanted, but couldn't get his hands on. Which was exactly how he'd felt an hour ago, muttering a low apology under his breath as he'd rolled off Crissy Cowell's soft, warm body, extricating himself from her grasping arms as he'd turned his back to her and retrieved his cell phone to take Hendricks's call.

He'd felt bad about turning away from Crissy to answer the phone, but there was no denying that he'd been thankful for the excuse to remove himself from the Lycan's clingy post-coital embrace. Never one to cuddle, it wasn't the first time Eric had felt a piercing sense of relief at freeing himself from a woman's hold once their passion was spent—though it seemed that recently, no matter how physical the encounter, his body was left burning with a restless hunger for something more.

Not that there was anything wrong with Crissy, a well-respected pack female who owned the local garden center in Shadow Peak. She was nice, pleasurable and more than easy on the eyes. No, the problem was his and his alone.

A shrink would probably tell him he was psychologically punishing himself—perhaps even seeking some kind of screwed-up atonement for the destruction his father had caused, but Eric knew it was more than that. Still, guilt poured through his veins as steadily as his blood these days, until it felt as much a part of him as an organ or a limb—just a constant, sickening acceptance that his life would forever be tainted by his association with Stefan Drake: father, pack Elder…and psychotic son of a bitch.

The weight of the shame he carried in his gut over the horrifying events that unfolded five months ago had yet to lessen with the passage of time, and the Runners often told him he was working himself into the ground to pay for crimes that weren't his. But while there were some in the pack who had seemed to accept his innocence, Eric was aware of the accusatory sneers still sent his way…and he knew there were more than a few who blamed him all the same. For some, the sins of the father were often the hardest to forget…or forgive.

And yet, he was certain that this incessant hunger, this *craving* gnawing away at him from the inside out, had more to do with his future than it did with the past. Always one with a healthy sex drive, Eric had never before questioned his lack of interest in making a commitment to one of the women in his life. After being abandoned by his mother at an early age, he didn't need to be psychoanalyzed to understand the wounds that had been cut into his emotional fabric—but his commitment issues had never interfered with his enjoyment of the opposite sex. Even now, the problem wasn't that sex didn't feel good. Sex was sex, and it sure as hell didn't feel bad.

It just didn't feel…*right,* whatever the hell that meant.

And I sound like I'm losing my bloody mi—

"You know," the human murmured, interrupting his irritating train of thought…apparently unable to hold back what she'd wanted to say before. "I realize this may come as a surprise to you, but just because you're a guy who looks like God's gift to women doesn't actually mean that you are."

The second the words left Chelsea's mouth, a low, rich vein of laughter jerked from his chest, seeming to catch them both by surprise. Her toes curled inside her socks at the delicious sound, while her face burned with color as she realized what she'd just said.

Wow. I'm so smooth. Why don't I just shout it to his face that I think he's hot?

"Come on," he drawled after his laughter had died down, his mouth kicking up at one corner in the wickedest grin she'd ever seen. "You're judging me by my looks, and that isn't fair."

Maybe not, but Chelsea still wanted to curse at him for flashing her such an irresistible grin, the dimple in his cheek enough to make her groan. Not to mention the high-voltage sexual energy he was blasting at her, making her head spin. Given her lack of a social life, Chelsea knew her family and friends probably thought she was still a virgin, but they were wrong. She'd had sex. Not a lot, mind you, but enough times to know what it was all about. But her experiences had all been with cerebral types who were easily controlled and easily forgotten. She'd never played with a rugged, testosterone-laden male before, and she doubted she'd even know how to if she tried.

Her looks, or lack of them, had always made it easy to avoid *charming, oozing-sex-appeal-from-their-pores* Neanderthals like this guy, for the simple fact that they ignored her. No, that wasn't right. They simply didn't see her, as if she were a ghost. Something they looked right through. Not even a blip on their radar.

But this guy…*he noticed.* He was staring right at her, that strangely compelling gaze making her feel as if he didn't want to be looking anywhere else in the world. As if he saw her in a way that no other man ever had, and she resisted the urge to pull her shirt away from her skin, seeking relief from the blistering warmth sizzling inside her, despite the nighttime chill in the air.

And maybe she was just wasting both their time, keeping the argument going because she liked the look of him. Who said she couldn't start her bus, head down the road a ways, wait for them to leave, then turn around and come right back to find some other nearby place to camp for the night? According to the bleary-eyed girl she'd talked to at the strip club down in Wesley, Perry had only worked at the club for a couple of days before heading up into these mountains to stay with her so-called boyfriend. There was obviously a hell of a lot more to the story, but considering this was her only lead, Chelsea had to go with it.

She'd tried asking some locals in Wesley for assistance, thinking they could point her in the right direction, but none had been able to help. They knew of some private settlements in the mountains, but couldn't tell her where they were…or anything about the people who lived there. The whole situation was eerily unsettling, but she couldn't turn back now. She had to keep searching every small town she stumbled across up here until she found Perry, whether these guys liked it or not.

But that didn't mean she couldn't start with another part of the mountain and work her way back here—hopefully avoiding the gorgeous jackass watching her with those unusual eyes.

"Fine," she said, blowing out a rough breath of air. "Have it your way."

Surprise lifted his dark brows. "You'll leave?"

She allowed her own mouth to curl in a cocky smirk. "Yeah, I'll leave. But not before telling you how ridiculous you look with that red lipstick smeared all over the corner of your mouth. I hope she was a brunette. A blonde could never have pulled off that color."

He quickly lifted his hand, wiped at his mouth, then glared at the red smear on his fingertips. "Son of a bitch," he growled, scrubbing harder at his face. "Hendricks should have told me."

"It's all gone now," she murmured, taking pity on him. "You're clear."

He grunted something foul under his breath, then stepped closer and placed one hand over the window ledge, curving his long fingers over the door frame, as if he could keep her in place with that simple touch. "Where will you go?"

"*That's* none of your business," she said quietly, staring at those dark fingers, imagining them on her body… against her skin. Shaking herself, she set the gun on the passenger's seat, then turned the key in the ignition…but nothing happened. Just a sad, pathetic wail of sound from the engine, followed by a rapid clicking noise. Gritting her teeth, she turned the key again…and again, but with the same results.

Shit.

Without looking at him, Chelsea lowered her head to the steering wheel and prayed for patience. Nothing, not a single goddamn thing, had gone her way from the moment she'd started this miserable search. Why? She was trying so hard to do what was right, damn it—trying to help her sister…to get her out of what could potentially be a dangerous situation, especially after the girl at the club had said that Perry wasn't looking too good. So why this? Why was karma, fate or whatever the hell it was that controlled her destiny giving her a kick in the ass with every step she took?

It wasn't like her to be whiney, but she'd lost her sense of optimism so long ago, Chelsea no longer even knew what it felt like. Now all she had was this grinding, sickening feeling in her gut, and a bad case of nerves. Not to mention the sudden addition of ill-founded lust for the gorgeous jerk trying to get rid of her.

Talk about crappy timing.

Forcing herself to lift her head, she gave the dark-haired stranger a closed, expressionless look. "I don't suppose you could give me a jump start?"

He shook his head, looking as frustrated as she felt. "The problem isn't your battery."

"How do you know?"

"Because that clicking sound means it's your starter."

"Shit," she said for the second time, only this time out loud.

He muttered something rough under his breath again, then jerked his chin toward his truck. "Come on. I'll give you a ride down to Wesley."

She wanted to say, *"Are you crazy? What kind of idiot do you think I am, getting into a car with some guy I don't even know?"*

But the words stuck in her throat. Her options were more than a little limited here. The idea of staying in the woods had been scary enough when the opportunity for retreat had been available, but to be stuck out here in a broken-down car didn't strike her as smart, even though she had a gun. Then again, neither did driving off with Mr. Tall, Dark and Deadly Gorgeous. But if he was going to hurt her, he could have already done it. Right? The other two men, who were still waiting over by his truck, clearly submitted to his authority, as if he were some kind of superior they deferred to. She had the feeling that if he'd attacked, they'd have done nothing to stop him.

Which meant…what? Was she actually trying to talk herself into taking him up on his offer? She didn't have enough money for a motel room, but she'd figure something out. She always did, one way or another.

As if sensing her disquieting inner conflict, he wiped the scowl off his face and let go of her door, that warm, male scent pulsing off him the most interesting thing she'd ever smelled. "It's okay," he said in a low voice. "I won't hurt you. Just a ride into town, to a motel, and then I'll have your bus delivered to you in the morning."

"How can I get it fixed if I leave it here?" Not that she had the money to get it fixed, but he didn't need to know that. "Can't we just tow it behind us?"

"I'm going to call some mechanics I know and have them work on it here," he explained as if it was the simplest thing in the world to do. "They'll have it in running order by morning."

Wrapping her arms around her middle, she asked, "Why would you do that?"

"Consider it a fair exchange for the fact that I'm kicking you out of here," he offered with a strained smile. He clearly wasn't any happier about the situation than she was, and yet, he seemed determined to help her.

She didn't agree or disagree. She simply said, "It isn't smart."

A deep, almost silent rumble of laughter vibrated in his chest, and he arched one of those damn black brows again. "Neither was camping out in your car in the woods all alone."

"But at least I had a good reason for *that*."

He could have argued that she had a good reason for taking him up on his offer, as well. But he didn't. He just stared at her, the silver metallic of his eyes mesmerizing, like the liquid swirl of mercury in a vial—making her feel as if he could see right past her sarcastic bravado, down to the real woman huddling inside her skin. The one who was scared and tired and pushed to the edge of her limits. His cool air of command made Chelsea want to slap him, just as badly as she wanted to press her lips against that hard, utterly masculine mouth and find out if he tasted even half as good as he looked and smelled.

Pulling her lower lip through her teeth, she finally said, "If I accept, it doesn't mean that I owe you anything."

Instead of agreeing, he simply gave her a charmingly crooked grin that made her body react with ridiculous ease. "My name is Eric, by the way. Eric Drake. And you would be…?"

"Chelsea Smart."

He started to laugh under his breath, as if there was something *funny* about her name, but choked it off when he caught her glare.

"So, what's it gonna be, Chelsea?" He stepped back from the bus, shoved his hands deep in his pockets again and lifted his shoulders. "Will you trust me?"

The question was offered casually, and yet, she had the strangest feeling that her answer was somehow important to him. Which was crazy, seeing as how she'd never been all that important to anyone before, much less to a gorgeous man who didn't even know her.

What *was* it going to be?

She was acutely aware of each second passing slowly into the next…of each breath that expanded her lungs…

each hard, powerful beat of her heart that shuddered through her body.

Then she did something that she never did, and opened her door, putting her trust in another person. And not just any person.

No, for the first time in what felt like forever, Chelsea put her trust in the hands of a man.

Chapter Three

By the time Eric pulled onto the gloomy, rain-sodden streets of downtown Wesley, he'd managed to learn a bit more about the human than just her name and the fact that she had a prickly attitude. She was twenty-six years old, had just bought her first condo and taught Women's Studies at a private university in Smythe, Virginia. He'd also learned that she had spent the past few weeks searching for her younger sister, a nineteen-year-old named Perry, who also lived in Smythe…and whose party-girl lifestyle and recreational drug use had a habit of landing her in a variety of unsavory situations.

According to her roommates, Perry had suddenly disappeared a month ago, after hooking up with an amazingly hot guy at a weekend party. He'd fed her some bullshit story about how he really cared about her, but that his life was just too dangerous for a girl like her, and then skipped out. But Perry wasn't willing to give him up. After asking around about him, she'd learned he was heading to another party in a neighboring county, and she'd set off after him, determined to track him down. Then she hadn't come back.

When a few days had gone by and her roommates hadn't heard from her, they got in touch with Chelsea, claiming they were worried about their impulsive, risk-taking friend. Chelsea had been worried, too, while waiting for word from her sister…or a sign that she was okay and on her way back home. When her phone messages on Perry's cell went unanswered for over a week, Chelsea left Smythe and followed Perry's sloppy trail from one college party or nightclub to another, until her search eventually led to a strip joint right there in Wesley called Heaven and Hell.

Unfortunately, by the time Chelsea had arrived, Perry's short stint illegally serving cocktails in the club was already over. No one had been willing to talk to Chelsea or to give her any information, until she finally got lucky that afternoon and caught one of the girls, a hollow-eyed little slip of a thing named Maggie, on the way to her car in the parking lot. The girl had reluctantly divulged that a tired-looking Perry had hit the road after only a few nights at the club, when some guy she said she'd been looking for came in.

Apparently, the guy—a good-looking blond who Maggie had seen before, but whose name she didn't know—freaked out when he saw Perry working in the club. A fight started between him and the bouncers when he demanded Perry leave with him, but then they eventually told him just to get her out of there. She'd run in the back to collect her things, giddy with excitement, and told Maggie that her boyfriend was taking her home with him, to a place somewhere up in the nearby mountains.

And that was how Chelsea Smart had ended up in Silvercrest pack territory. Chelsea had left Wesley not long after talking to Maggie, determined to search any towns she found up in the mountains until she finally located her sister. When Eric asked why she hadn't bothered to go to the police, she told him she'd already tried that route, but there'd been nothing they could do to help. According to the officer she'd talked to back in Smythe, being stupid wasn't a crime. Perry was a legal adult who was apparently acting of her own free will, and until they had reason to believe otherwise, there was nothing the cops could do.

Considering that the private road he'd found Chelsea on led to Shadow Peak, and Eric was positive Perry wasn't in the mountaintop town, there were only a few other possibilities, and none of them were good for a human female on her own. Just as the road split off from the main highway, there was a turnoff to an old dirt path that wound its way over to the opposite side of the mountain, and into the territory owned by the Youngblood pack. Though the pack itself, a relatively small, peaceful group who kept to themselves, lived in a town that had been built on the western edge of their land, there was an even smaller settlement over the border in West Virginia where the Donovan family lived. Known for their corrupt business dealings, the Donovans had been asked to leave the Youngblood Lycan homestead in the late seventies—and yet, they hadn't been banished, seeing as how their Midas touch generated handsome profits for the pack.

As far as Eric knew, the Donovans had never set up shop in Maryland, keeping their various ventures in West Virginian towns that were closer to their pack lands. But he'd recently heard a few of the Runners say that the Donovans had been sniffing around Wesley the past couple of months, and the prickling at the back of his neck told him the family might somehow be involved with that particular club.

If he was right, there was a good chance Heaven and Hell was being used as a front for something far more sinister than peddling flesh. Over the years, there'd been rumors that the Donovans were involved with drug trafficking, among other illegal activities. From the sound of things, the guy that Perry Smart had hooked up with was probably associated with the family in some way, or they never would have let him walk out of there with the girl in one piece. And if that was true, then the odds were high that he wasn't a man at all, but a Lycan. One who, given the trail that Perry had followed, could very well be scouting out young women for the Donovan family to do God only knew what with.

All of which meant that Perry Smart had landed herself in some deep shit—and if Chelsea kept searching for her, she was going to end up in the same situation.

As he took the next right, she shifted in the passenger's seat of his truck, drawing his gaze, and he damn near couldn't take his eyes off her. The watery spill of light from the garish neon signs in that part of town played softly over her feminine profile and that long, wavy spill of hair. Though her attitude grated on his nerves, Eric had the strongest urge to fist his hands in that silken mass and draw her over to him. To press his lips against her pale, tender skin.

For some screwed-up, infuriating reason, it seemed that the more time he spent with her, the harder it was to keep his hands and his mouth to himself.

He grimaced at that unsavory realization, while adrenaline pumped through his system like a drug, making him restless, on edge—and yet, he didn't push the speed, trying to drag it out, making his time with her last. He knew he needed to get the hell away from her as quickly as possible, but there was a part of him snarling at the fact that the drive had gone by far too fast. There had been too many heavy silences, too many failed attempts to learn more about her. She'd been willing to tell him about her sister, and yet, for the most part, had remained stubbornly closed-mouthed about herself.

Not that there was any point in seeking the answers to his unasked questions. The human was going to walk out of his life as easily as she'd entered it. And that was the way it should be.

Unfortunately, his wolf had other ideas. The damn animal had sex on its mind tonight, when Eric knew that was the last thing he needed to be thinking about.

Though the rain had stopped falling nearly a half hour ago, it still lingered on the asphalt, reflecting the harsh colors from the oversized neon signs, so that it looked as if they were driving through an acid trip. "Are you sure you want to stay in this part of town?" he asked, casting an uneasy glance over the seedy storefronts and dark alleyways that lined the street.

"Yeah, this is good. Heaven and Hell is only a few blocks from here. I was thinking I should probably drop by there again tomorrow, just to see if Perry has recently tried to contact anyone she met there. If I'm lucky, maybe I'll even get a chance to talk to Maggie again."

Eric cut her a dark look. "I thought you said the place was a hellhole?"

"I did. A hellhole that disgustingly exploits women as sexual objects for the gratification of men, to be exact. But I'm still going back, for the simple fact that this is my sister we're talking about. Maggie might have remembered something more about the guy she saw Perry with."

"If that was the case, couldn't she just call you?"

She shook her head. "I suggested the same thing, but she wouldn't take my number."

Eric scowled, keeping his eyes on the road, wondering how he was going to talk some sense into her. He admired her commitment to helping her sister, knowing what it was like to want to protect your family. He felt the same way about Eli and Elise, his brother and sister. But the fool woman was going to end up getting herself killed.

Taking a deep breath, he opened his mouth, ready to launch into a lecture on how she needed to get her ass out of town as soon as she could, when she pointed to a flickering sign on the side of the road that read Melvin's Motel. "You can drop me off right over there. That motel will be great."

Uh, yeah, sure it will. And the Bates Motel was just a cozy little getaway...

Thinking she must be out of her ever-loving mind, Eric pulled into the lot—not because he planned on leaving her there, but simply because he wanted to be able to focus on the argument they were about to have without the distraction of driving. He was just slowing down to pull into a parking space, when the sign for the building next door caught his eye. It was a women's shelter, and he suddenly realized why Chelsea had chosen this particular establishment. She had no intention of getting a room at the creepy, sleep-with-a-knife-under-your-pillow motel, because she planned on staying at the shelter.

Like hell, he thought, knowing that too many things could go wrong with her half-baked plan. What if they didn't have room for her, or turned her away? She'd be left in the middle of Wesley with no car, no money and no goddamn place to go.

"Screw this," he muttered, gunning the gas. As he steered out of the parking lot and back onto the rain-slick road, she twisted in her seat, grabbing his forearm. It was the first time she'd touched his skin and his breath hissed through his teeth from the piercing jolt of awareness. It burst through him like a freaking detonation.

"What are you doing?" she demanded, her voice sharp. "Turn around and take me back there!"

He worked his jaw, ready for the argument that had already arrived, and so desperate for a cigarette he could have begged for one. "Forget it, Chelsea. I'm not leaving you there."

"You have to," she snapped, her anger coming through loud and clear.

Slanting her a hard look, Eric shook his head. "Save your breath screaming about it, because it isn't gonna happen. I'll find a decent place and get you a room. It won't be fancy in this part of town, but at least you won't be sharing the bed with a family of roaches…or worse."

"No way," she breathed out, pulling away from him, until she was huddled back against the passenger-side door. He knew from her scent that she wasn't afraid of him, but there was no doubt she was burning with bitter-edged fury. It pulsed from her small body in a hot, jagged wave. "I don't know who you think you are, but I'll stay wherever the hell I please. And I can pay for my own damn room!"

"No, you can't." The words were graveled and thick, his jaw so tight he had to force the words out past his frustration. "I know what you were planning. You were going to stay at that shelter back there, and I'm not letting that happen."

From the corner of his eye, Eric watched her send him a look that would have withered a lesser man. "It doesn't

matter what I was going to do, because it isn't any of
your business."

"It is now," he said with a harsh sigh, taking one hand
from the wheel to rub at the knots of tension in the back
of his neck, "whether you want it to be or not. So you can
take the gun you stashed in your bag and hold it on me if
you want to. Go ahead, if it'll make you feel better. But
I'm not going to back down about this."

"You arrogant bastard," she seethed in a choked voice,
the angry, electric pulses of her rage slamming against
him, filling the interior of the truck. It made her scent
thicker…richer, till he was damn near ready to howl from
this unusual craving he had for her. "Just who in the hell
do you think you are?"

"I'm the man who's trying to keep your crazy little
ass in one piece, no matter how determined you are to
put it in danger."

"That's insane!" she burst out. "Are you out of your
freaking mind?"

Was he? It certainly felt like it. This whole night felt
like a certain kind of madness. If she'd been his destined
life mate, then yeah, he could see getting this worked up
over her. But she wasn't. Hell, she wasn't even a Lycan.

Instead, she was something soft and breakable, and
Eric shuddered. He might be his father's son, but he did
not get off on hatred or pain. He wanted this woman badly.
Wanted her under him, pinned, at his mercy. But once he
got her there, hurting her wasn't what would drive him.
No, he wanted to smash through those damn prickly walls
of hers and break her open. Wanted her sweating and
clawing and screaming with pleasure, as animalistic in
her passion as he—

"Seriously, Eric. Why are you doing this?" Her voice

was tight, vibrating with tension as it cut into his thoughts. "It doesn't make any sense. You don't even know me."

He wanted to argue, to tell her how wrong she was. They might be strangers, and she might not be one of those women who loved to gush about themselves, but he was learning more about her with each second that went by. More about himself, too.

But she was right about it not making any sense. Thankfully, a Travelodge sign appeared up on the left, and while it wasn't the Ritz, at least Eric knew she'd be safe there.

The second he pulled into the crowded lot and parked the truck, she reached for the door, but he latched on to her arm, curling his fingers around the soft swell of her biceps. He was careful not to hurt her, but kept his grip tight enough that she couldn't break away. Before she could lash out at him with that wicked tongue of hers, he said, "I'm getting you a room."

She drew in a deep breath, as if searching for patience, and he tried like hell to ignore the way the sharp movement pressed her nipples against her shirt. Tried…but didn't exactly succeed, since it was obvious she wasn't wearing a bra.

"No, you're not." She glared at him as if he was something slimy that had crawled out of the drain. "You're not getting me anything. Do you understand?"

"Damn it, Chelsea. This isn't the time to be stubborn. Pride isn't going to keep you safe. It's going to get you hurt. I get that you hate to accept help from anyone, especially a man, but just let me get you a room and we'll chalk it up to an even trade for the fact that I kicked you off the damn mountain in the first place."

"We already did that with the ride to town. And the work being done on my bus."

"And this is just another part of what *I* owe *you*. Not the other way around. I swear."

She wasn't buying it, but he could feel the starch go out of her as she leaned back against the seat. Her breath soughed softly past her lips, their smooth surface glossy and pink and undeniably tempting. There was a danger there, the same way you weren't meant to stare too long at the sun. A beautiful view, but one you paid for with pain. Somehow, he managed to force himself to lift his gaze back to the dark, stormy blue of her eyes, and for a moment he wondered if she was actually going to say thank-you.

But, really, he should have known better.

"You know, Eric, it's high-handed, arrogant jerks like you who give your sex a bad name."

"Whatever. Just wait here," he grated, choking back his own anger as he climbed out of the truck. Christ, she had to be the most mule-headed woman on the planet!

A chime dinged as Eric jerked open one of the double doors at the entrance to the hotel, and a young guy behind the registration desk looked up from the comic book he was reading. "What's up?" he asked, staring at Eric from behind a pair of thick reading glasses.

"I need a room, just for tonight."

The transaction took longer than he would have liked, considering the guy moved as slow as molasses. Eric signed for the room with an impatient scrawl and grabbed up the card key, heading back out to the truck as quickly as possible, his breath jerking from his lungs with a sharp burst of relief when he spotted her through the passenger-side window. He'd half expected her to make a run for it—and was thankful she wasn't that impulsive. Or maybe she just wasn't done chewing him out yet.

Opening her door, he offered his hand, which she refused, glaring at it like it was some kind of insult. Instead, she hopped down from the seat without his help, careful to keep her body from brushing against his, though they stood so close he could have easily leaned down and pressed his lips against the top of her head. When she'd first climbed out of her bus, he'd been surprised by how petite she was, his height making him feel like a damn giant beside her. And yet, she wasn't scrawny. She was, in fact, deliciously proportioned, with a soft, curvaceous figure that made his mouth water, especially when it was so perfectly displayed by the hip-hugging jeans and that soft T-shirt. She kept tugging at its low neckline, as if wishing for more fabric to cover that delectable, shadowy view of her cleavage. Given her actions, Eric guessed she probably only wore the thing to sleep in, and hadn't meant for anyone to see her in it.

And I was lying through my teeth about wanting to get rid of her.

Grabbing the oversized backpack she'd brought down with her, she hitched it onto her shoulder, then turned back toward him, grabbing the card key that he held out. He wondered if she had any idea how hard it was going to be for him to leave her, instead of following her into that hotel room, where he imagined a queen-size bed was waiting. He could see the possible scenario in his mind as clearly as if he were standing beside the bed, watching it happen. Watching his larger body, with its tensed muscles and sweat-slick skin, taking her to the flowered quilt. Spreading her beneath him. Pressing his lips to the smooth heat of her flesh. Taking the taste of her hot, slippery sex into his mouth, onto his tongue, where it could imprint upon his memory. Hearing her husky cries as she came from his touch. Sweet. Wild. Undone and unraveled and outrageously beautiful.

Clearing his throat, Eric finally managed to scrape out some words. "The room number is 263. I'll have your bus brought here first thing in the morning, so that by the time you're up and ready to go, she'll be waiting. The keys will be left at the front desk for you."

"Fine," she murmured, rubbing her thumb against the smooth surface of the card key. Her gaze slid away, over the nondescript front of the hotel, then cut back up to him. "I appreciate the ride, the room and the fact that you're getting my bus fixed—but, I meant what I said before. This doesn't mean that I owe you anything."

"Actually, I've changed my mind about that," he told her, still fighting the urge to reach out, grab her and pull her against his chest…against his body. He wanted to know the feel of her, the heat. Wanted to have her unique scent wrapped around him, seeping into his pores. But it couldn't happen.

Instead, he had to do whatever it took to make her see reason.

Her slim brows knitted with irritation. "Excuse me?"

"You owe me your word that after you get your little ass up in the morning, you'll get it the hell out of town."

Her eyes rounded with a mixture of shock and indignation. "You can't force me to leave Wesley, Eric. Your mountain, maybe. But *not* this town. You don't have any power here."

He stepped even closer, scowling down at her, and forced himself to deliver the words he was hoping would save her life. "You stay, and you're likely to end up dead.

Listen to what I'm telling you, Chelsea, and don't argue for the sake of your grating little Miss Independent routine. Go home, and go back to work. Collect your paychecks, pay your mortgage on that condo you just bought and take care of yourself. When your sister wizens up, she'll come crawling back. But if you keep digging into things at that club, keep wandering around by yourself up in those mountains, you're the one who's going to end up in trouble."

Finally, he could see a shadow of fear creeping into her rigid expression. "Just what exactly is up there?"

He gave a hard, brief shake of his head. "Nothing you need to know about."

The scowl on his face would have terrified most men, but she simply glared right back at him. "So I should just be a good little girl and take your advice?"

"You *will* take it, if you know what's good for you."

"And if I don't?"

"You probably won't be around long enough for me to say I told you so. The best thing you can do is leave."

Her fingers tightened around the strap of her bag until her knuckles turned white. "How is that the best thing, when it means leaving my sister in the hands of this stranger and not caring about what happens to her?"

In a slightly gentler tone, he said, "I didn't say it was easy."

She blinked up at him, staring into his eyes with a sharp, intense focus, as if she knew there was more… something important he wasn't telling her. Taking a receipt from his pocket, Eric reached around her, into the truck, and grabbed a pen from the center console, then handed them to her. "Give me your mobile number."

"What for?" she asked with a heavy dose of suspicion.

"I'll look into some things, and if I do happen to run across your sister, I'll call you."

She hesitated for a moment, then quickly wrote down her number. With a slow shake of her head, she handed the slip of paper back to him. "You're so sure I'm going to do what you say, aren't you?"

"You'd be an idiot not to," he muttered, shoving the receipt back in his pocket. "And I have a feeling you're anything but."

She absorbed his words with a small nod, studying him for a moment longer, then shook her head again and held out her hand. Eric took it, closing his hard, roughened fingers around the tender softness of hers. It was a small, endlessly feminine hand, not bony, just cushioned and lovely and sweet. He wanted to pull it to his body and press it against his skin. Feel it hold him where he was hard…feel it grip him…the unwanted need making him restless, angry. With another scowl pulling between his brows, he released her chilled hand and took a hasty step back, hating the urgent feeling prickling beneath his skin. She was like a rash that he needed to shake, before the damn thing spread.

"Well, goodbye, Eric Drake," she said huskily, hitching the backpack higher on her shoulder. "It was certainly… interesting."

Eric gave her a jerky nod and clenched his jaw as she turned toward the hotel, walking away from him with a tired, but proud, confident stride. When he realized his gaze had snagged on the way those low-rise jeans hugged her ass, he muttered a blistering curse. Heading around to the driver-side of the truck, he quickly climbed behind the wheel and made his way back onto the road, gunning the engine.

He might not like it, but the truth couldn't be ignored.
No matter what demons she faced on her own, Chelsea Smart was a hell of a lot better off without him.

Chapter Four

Chelsea Smart needed to have her little backside blistered. And Eric was tempted to do it himself, just as soon as he managed to find her.

As he pulled into the parking lot of the Heaven and Hell strip club late the following afternoon, he didn't think he'd ever been so furious. There'd been an odd ache in his chest just moments before, when he'd driven past the Travelodge without spotting Chelsea's bus—which had been delivered to the hotel early that morning—in the parking lot. Though he'd known it was for the best, the idea of never seeing her again had been uncomfortably disturbing, a strange sense of loss weighing heavily in his gut. But instead of easing when he'd caught sight of that ridiculous bus parked in the *club's* lot, he was suddenly in a world of hurt. One much darker and deeper than before. One that was angry and hard and violent.

She'd blatantly disregarded his orders, and now the

headstrong little idiot was chin-deep in the kind of danger he'd tried to warn her about. *Son of a bitch.*

He'd mistakenly assumed that with her being a woman and him being a big, intimidating, dominant Lycan, it would be enough to make her realize she should listen to him, whether she wanted to or not. But he'd obviously been wrong.

After a long day of dealing with issues up in Shadow Peak, Eric had headed down to Wesley intending to visit the club to see if there was anything he could learn about Perry Smart's whereabouts, as well as to get a better idea of exactly what was going on there. He hadn't planned on having to save her older sister's stubborn ass, though that seemed the more likely scenario now that he knew Chelsea hadn't left town…but had done exactly what he'd told her *not* to do instead. Damn. He'd known she was willful, but still. The woman was downright destructive.

Pulling in a deep breath, he struggled for patience as he finished a pass around the two-story square, windowless building and parked next to her bus, trying to give himself time to come up with a plan, but the lingering traces of her scent inside his truck were still screwing with his head.

There were things *hidden* in that scent. Confusing things. Important ones. Things he needed to understand. He just…he couldn't quite catch hold of them, as if a strong wind kept whipping them out of his reach, like meandering whorls of smoke. One instant they would be so close, and in the next, *whoosh*. They were gone.

Climbing out of his truck, Eric dug his cell phone from his pocket, then reached into his other pocket for the receipt with Chelsea's number. The call went to voice mail after eight rings, and he ground out something that would have made his mother box his ears when he was younger. Whatever Chelsea was doing inside the club, she wasn't in a position to answer her phone, and a cold sweat settled over the back of his neck.

Her bus had been delivered to the Travelodge at six that morning. It was now five-thirty in the afternoon. Which meant she'd had eleven and a half hours to get into trouble. Nearly half a damn day to be bullied or threatened or whatever the hell else might have happened to her. Rape. Assault. Torture. The nauseating list was endless.

Muttering another gritty curse under his breath, Eric quickly scrolled through his contact list until he found the next number he needed.

"Burns here," said a deep voice, after only two rings. Jeremy Burns was one of the pack's Bloodrunners, and a serious badass with a warped sense of humor. He was also the husband of one of Eric's closest friends, Jillian, the pack's healer, which had put the two males on rocky footing when things had started heating up between Jillian and the Runner the year before. But as soon as Jeremy had accepted the fact that Eric and Jillian were nothing more than friends, he and the Runner had slowly become friends themselves. He knew he could trust the guy with his life, and with anything else he threw at him.

"It's Eric," he said, locking the door to the truck behind him. "I need to let you know where I'm at, in case I don't make it back to the Alley tonight." Bloodrunner Alley was a secluded part of the forest where Jeremy and the other Bloodrunners lived, and where Eric had been spending a lot of his nights lately.

"Well," the Runner drawled, "that's a hell of a way to open a conversation."

He scanned his surroundings to make sure no one was listening in. "Save the sarcasm for another time. I'm down in Wesley, in the Heaven and Hell parking lot."

Jeremy cursed, but didn't waste time demanding to

know what Eric was doing there. Instead, he asked, "You got weapons?"

"Yeah, but can't take them in with me. They'll have security at the doors."

The Runner's frustration was evident in the hard edge of his voice. "I should have known something was up when you started asking questions about that place this morning. Didn't think you were stupid enough to actually go down there on your own, though."

"What can I say?" he grunted, squinting against the last dying rays of the sun. "I needed something to do."

Jeremy snorted. "Yeah, well, next time just ask. If you're bored, I'll think of something to keep you busy. Jillian's gonna kill me if anything happens to you."

He started to tell the Runner that that's why he was calling—to make plans if something *did* happen—but Jeremy suddenly told him to hold on a second. Eric could hear him talking to someone else, relaying the situation, and then another voice came on the line. From the rough tone and lilting Irish accent, he knew it was Cian Hennessey, one of the other Silvercrest Bloodrunners. "I've got some information you might find useful, seeing as how you've decided to jump the gun on us."

Various possibilities of what the Runner might have learned ran through Eric's mind, and none of them were good. "I don't have a lot of time, Cian. Just get to the point."

"Well, after I heard about the woman you ran into last night, and that you were asking for information about that club, I thought I'd look into things for you. Made a few calls to some of my…" the Irishman gave a husky laugh "…let's just say some people who owe me a few special favors. But you're not going to like what I learned. You were right about the Donovans being involved with the club, but they're not the only ones. From the sound of things, the Whiteclaw pack has a finger in the pie, as well."

"The Donovans and the Whiteclaw?" Eric wouldn't have been more surprised if the Irishman had just told him that the NRA was partnering up with Greenpeace. As far as the Silvercrest knew, the Donovan family didn't like the arrogant, thuggish Whiteclaw clan any more than the rest of the Southeastern Lycan packs. "What the hell is that about?"

"Yeah, I know," the Runner murmured. "It sucks. All I can figure is that they have some kind of joint operation going on down there. The Donovans are obviously the brains and the money, the Whiteclaw most likely the hired muscle. And seeing as how they're all a bunch of assholes, it's not a comforting combination."

"No shit," Eric grunted. "Especially with them both so close to our land." The Silvercrest were still in a highly vulnerable position, thanks to his father's bullshit, and it freaked the hell out of him that the vultures were joining forces.

"Brody and I were planning on checking it out later," Cian said, referring to Brody Carter, his best friend and Bloodrunning partner, "but it sounds like you're beating us to it."

"No choice." Eric cast an uneasy look toward Chelsea's bus, his gaze moving over the whimsical confection of clouds. "She's here."

"She?" There was a significant pause, and then, "You don't mean the woman from last night, do you? The *human?*"

"Yeah. That's exactly who I mean."

Cian gave a low whistle. "Holy hell. That lady have a death wish or what?"

"Feels like it," he ground out, starting to make his way across the parking lot. "I'm getting her out."

The Runner's voice turned hard. "Don't be an idiot, Drake. You need to wait for us to get there. Brody and I can head down now."

"Can't—it'll take too long, and there's no telling how long she's already been in there. Can you put Burns back on?"

Cian ordered him not to do anything stupid, then handed the phone back to Jeremy. "Look, I don't have a lot of time," Eric said, "but I need to ask you guys for a favor. If you don't hear from me, I need the Runners to look after—"

"Dude," Jeremy cut in, "stop right there. If you go down, your sister will be looked after. That's a given. But keep in mind that I will track your ass to hell and put you through serious pain if you get killed. I will *not* be happy. You got that?"

A wry smile twitched at the corner of Eric's mouth. "What makes you think I'm not headed for heaven?"

The Runner snorted again. "The day they let a jackass like you past the pearly gates is the day those self-righteous pricks up in Shadow Peak stop looking down their noses at us."

They said a quick goodbye, and by the time Eric was slipping his phone back in his pocket, he'd reached the front of the club. Making his way down the concrete walkway leading to the entrance, he glanced up at the neon sign perched on the roof. The words *Heaven and Hell* glittered in the twilight with obscene brightness, pulsing like a heartbeat. *A fitting name,* he thought, walking inside, where a beefy bouncer sat on a black stool just inside the doorway. One quick sniff and Eric knew the guy was one of the Whiteclaw clan. The man drew Eric's own scent into his lungs, and narrowed his eyes suspiciously. "What's your business here, Drake?"

So the Lycan knew who he was. Good. He could use it to his advantage.

Anxious to get inside and find her, Eric deliberately ran his gaze over a tall, busty brunette who walked past the club's arched entryway, balancing a tray of shot glasses on one hand. "I'd think my reason for being here was rather obvious," he said, slanting the bouncer a knowing smile.

The guy snickered. "What's the problem? Can't get any in your hometown anymore, now that your old man turned psycho?"

Eric fought to hold his hard smile in place, but it wasn't easy. Slipping the bouncer a crisp hundred-dollar bill, he lowered his voice. "Let's just say that I'm bored with the usual fare I get back at home. If I was looking for something a little less…tame, would this be the place to find it?"

The Lycan didn't so much as bat a lash, but Eric knew he'd caught the guy's attention. The seconds stretched out while the bouncer's steely gaze bore into Eric's, looking for the trap. Finally, he gave a low grunt and moved off his padded leather stool. After checking him for weapons with a quick pat down, he told Eric to take a seat inside the club and order a drink, saying that someone would come by to talk to him within the hour.

Uncertain whether or not the bouncer had bought his story, Eric walked through the high arch that separated the entryway from the main room of the club and tried not to wince. But it wasn't easy. Why Chelsea's little sister would have ever been willing to serve drinks here, he couldn't understand. It wasn't as cheaply decorated as a lot of the clubs he'd seen, but there was no mistaking the heavy desperation that hung in the air. It slid against his skin like a damp, sickly caress, making the hairs on the back of his neck stand on end. He could only imagine how it made Chelsea feel.

Wanting to rip the place apart until he found her, Eric forced himself to slide into a chair at a table hidden in the shadows at the far side of the room, to the left of the raised stage where five glassy-eyed human females were slowly gyrating their naked bodies in time to the deep, throbbing rhythm blasting through the sound system. Despite the early hour, over a quarter of the tables surrounding the stage were already full, the clientele a mix of werewolf and human—a fact the humans were no doubt oblivious to. The Lycans seemed to come from a wide variety of packs, though he was thankful he was the only Silvercrest in the room. Eric recognized a few of the Lycans as belonging to the Whiteclaw clan, and suspected they were there to keep an eye on things. Either that, or to broker the deals for whatever illegal activities the Donovans were running at the club.

As he sat with his back to the wall and scanned the room, Eric had what could only be described as a seriously bad feeling. It didn't escape his notice that while the clientele were a mix of human and Lycan, the strippers and servers were *all* human females. And young ones, at that. It was like watching a group of baby seals unknowingly swim through shark-infested waters. A crap idea no matter how you looked at it.

The Whiteclaw, it seemed, were treading a dangerous line in their new partnership. Since the pack didn't have any Bloodrunners, any infractions of the laws that governed their kind were the responsibility of the nearest packs: the Silvercrest and Youngblood. If they were harming humans, deadly measures would have to be taken. If they were simply exploiting these women for money, then they'd be watched to make sure things didn't go too far.

And since the Donovans were a part of the Young-blood pack, there probably wouldn't be any help coming from that quarter. Rumor had it that the Donovans had been buying off the Youngblood Runners for years, lining their pockets with serious amounts of cash to look the other way. Jeremy and the other Runners had asked the Silvercrest pack's leadership to authorize an investigation into the matter too many times to count, but Eric's father had made sure the requests were always denied. Now it looked as though it would be an issue that came back and bit them in the ass.

Hell, at this point, Eric wouldn't have been surprised to learn that his father had been on the take, as well.

One of the servers finally approached his table, carrying an empty tray. She had an edgy, worried look about her, and a quick glance at the name tag pinned over her right breast had Eric leaning forward in his seat. His nostrils flared as he caught a faint trace of Chelsea's scent lingering on the girl.

"Maggie?" he said, before she could ask him what he wanted to drink. Her eyes went a little wide at the urgency in his voice, and he tried to dredge up what was hopefully a reassuring smile. "I'm not going to hassle you. I'm just hoping you can give me some information about a friend of mine. Her name is Chelsea. You spoke to her yesterday, about her sister."

The instant he mentioned Chelsea's name, the girl's face went white. "Please," she whispered, starting to tremble. "I can't—they'll hurt me if I let her go. I wanted to, but they—"

"Shh. It's okay," he told her, making sure to keep his expression easy, since he was the one facing the room.

But his pulse was rushing like a goddamn freight train. "Lean down toward me a little, like you're flirting. That's it," he murmured, hoping like hell he could get her to co-operate. "All I need to know is where she's at. Can you tell me where they've got her?"

Though she looked terrified, she managed to place one shaking hand on his shoulder, understanding the need to put on an act for anyone who might be watching them. "She's in a room in the back of the club. If you go to the men's restroom, there's a door at the end of the hallway, on the right. Go through it, into another hallway, and then use the first door on the left. That's where you'll find her." Her throat worked as she swallowed. "I don't know what it was, but Curtis and the others gave her something that knocked her out. I tried to wake her up, but she isn't moving."

Hearing that she'd been drugged made him want to howl with fury, but Eric forced a laid-back grin to stay on his face as he pressed her for more details. "Are any of the doors locked? Or alarmed?"

She shook her head a little. "No. I don't think so. But they've got a bolt on the room she's in. It's on the outside, so you'll be able to open it."

It was nearly impossible not to stand up and demand to know where he could find the bastards who had drugged her, then locked her in a room, so he could rip their fuck-ing throats out, but he managed to choke it back. Barely. "What about the back exit?"

"It's guarded like the front one. But I've heard that there are other ways to get out of the building."

"You mean like a hidden exit?"

Maggie nodded. "I don't know how many, but I've heard some of the other girls talking about them. I guess the owners use them when they want to get out without anyone seeing. But I don't know where they are."

"That's okay. You've helped me a lot," he said, determined not to lose control, even though he was seething inside at the thought of Chelsea being at the mercy of Curtis Donovan and his buddies. He'd never had much contact with Curtis, but he'd heard the twenty-something Lycan was a troublemaker. Whatever they had planned for her, it wasn't good.

"I'm going to get her out of here, Maggie. But whatever happens, don't tell anyone that we talked about her. As far as they need to know, if you're asked, all I've been doing is hitting on you. If you sense any trouble, get the hell out of here. In fact, if you know what's good for you, you'll leave this place and never come back."

Pulling her lower lip through her teeth, she said, "Yeah. I'm beginning to figure that out. No amount of money is worth this kind of crap."

"That's right. Now grab that half-empty bottle of beer on the table behind you, then throw it in my face and tell me to get lost."

She blinked down at him. "What?"

"Just do it. And act really pissed. If anyone asks, tell them I said something ugly to you."

Comprehension dawned. "Oh, I get it."

Tension coiled through his muscles with cold, dark purpose, his body burning with an icy rage. "Do it now, Maggie. I need to find her."

"Okay. But tell her that I'm sorry I couldn't do more for her." She took a deep breath, grabbed the bottle and flung the warm beer at him, then stormed away from the table, just like he'd told her to do.

Eric wiped the beer off his face as he moved to his feet, then plastered on a cocky smirk for the group of Lycans

sitting at the table to his right. "Guess she wasn't interested," he said to the males. They laughed, raising their
beer bottles at him as he walked by, heading for the doorway marked Restrooms. He scanned the club as he made
his way toward the door, looking for Curtis, but didn't see
him in the growing crowd. As soon as he went through
the doorway, he caught a subtle trace of Chelsea's scent.
The farther he went down the hall, the stronger that trace
became. Quietly opening the last door in the hallway on
the right, he gave a quick sniff, relying on his heightened
sense of smell to tell him if he was alone. He doubted
Curtis Donovan had left the club, and he wasn't in the
main room, which meant the Lycan was either upstairs or
somewhere back here. And Eric had little doubt the bastard would be armed. The smart thing to do would be to
turn and get the hell out of there, but it didn't matter. He
was willing to pay whatever price it took to get Chelsea
to safety. It might not make him smart, but at least he'd
still be able to face himself in the mirror if they managed
to escape in one piece.

Slipping into the hallway, he reached for the bolt on
the door to the first room on his left. His teeth ground together as he slid the bolt free, his heart hammering to a
deep, violent rhythm. He tried the brass handle, turning
it easily, and the door opened, a desk lamp on the far side
of the room illuminating what seemed to be some kind of
office. He immediately caught sight of Chelsea lying on
a short leather sofa against the back wall. She was curled
on her side, facing him, her long hair falling over her face.
She looked so small and helpless, and it was all he could
do to choke back a bloodthirsty snarl.

Rushing across the room, Eric dropped to his knees
beside the sofa and took hold of her wrist, checking her
pulse. It was slow, but steady, her skin chilled to the touch.

"What the hell have they done to you?" he grated, pushing her hair back from her face with an unsteady hand. He instantly noticed the purplish bruising under her left eye, and a primitive fury unlike anything he'd ever known caught fire beneath his skin. One that made him want to hunt down whoever was responsible for the injury and take them apart with his bare hands.

She was out cold and the door to the room hadn't even been locked. Any drunken asshole wandering the hallways could have stumbled across her and done anything they wanted. The bastards had struck her and left her completely defenseless—but then, they didn't care if anything happened to her. The only upside to the situation was that Curtis had no reason to think anyone would be coming after her, which would work to their advantage. If Eric could manage to get her out of the club without drawing any attention, he might actually start thinking that his luck was changing.

Pulling her into a sitting position, he propped her against the back of the sofa. "Chelsea, I need you to wake up." Her head lolled to the side, and he gave her a little shake. "Come on and open those blue eyes for me. Right now."

She made her first sound, a sleepy, muted little groan that reminded him of a child, and he shook her again. "Now, Chelsea. We've got to get out of here."

"Elric?" she whispered, and the word sounded slurred, no doubt an effect of the drug she'd been given. Her eyelids fluttered, and then slowly started to open, as if she had to pry them apart with sheer force of will. "How... How'd you *flind* me?"

"Chelsea, honey, look at me." He had to force himself not to grip her too tightly. "Are you hurt? Do you feel ill?" he asked, worried about how the drug might be affecting her.

"Um…one of them hit me, but I'm *oklay,*" she whispered, blinking up at him with the biggest pair of sky-blue eyes he'd ever seen. They were so clear and bright, shimmering with a thin veil of tears, though she wasn't crying. At least not yet. "Will you get me out of here?"

"I'm working on it, but we can't just walk out the way I came in." He pushed her hair back from her flushed face again, trying to gauge just how high she was flying. Her pupils were fully dilated, but she seemed to be finding it easier to focus on him. She even managed a little smile.

"Sure we can," she said, "if you help me walk. I'm a little dizzy, but no one will notice me."

He shook his head. "Chelse, you're not thinking straight. You can't just walk out through the front of the club. It's packed with people."

She tried to sit up a little straighter, that stubborn determination he'd witnessed the night before sparking in her gaze. "Trust me, Eric. It'll be *oklay.* Guys don't ever notice girls like me."

He stared…hard, unable to believe what she'd said. Not notice her? Was she blind? Either the drugs she'd been given were doing the thinking for her, or she truly had no idea just how…Eric struggled for the right word to describe her. How *beautiful* she was? *Enticing? Sexy? Unique?* Damn it, she was all of those things and more, the heady combination no doubt catching the attention of every man she came into contact with. If they didn't act on it, it was probably only because of that leave-me-the-hell-alone vibe she projected so well. But it didn't mean she hadn't been noticed…from the top of her glossy hair down to what were no doubt some adorable little toes.

Whether she believed him or not, Eric knew that who-

ever had helped Curtis Donovan put her in here would notice her the instant she stepped foot inside the club's main
room. Hell, they wouldn't even have to set eyes on her,
because there was no way that sweet, lush scent pulsing
from her skin would go unrecognized by a Lycan. The
second they caught a whiff of it, of *her,* the two of them
would be made, and who knew how many he might have
to face down while trying to protect her? No matter how
good he was at kicking ass, the odds of fighting their way
to safety weren't in their favor.

Scraping his fingers through his hair, Eric shot her a
dark look from under his brows. "You know, when I said
you weren't an idiot last night, I was wrong. Coming here
again has to be the stupidest thing I've ever heard of. What
did you do? March right through the front door, demanding to know what happened to your sister?"

Her eyes went wide. "You're mad at me, aren't you?"

"Mad doesn't even begin to cover it. Christ, Chelsea.
Were you trying to get yourself killed?"

"I'm sorry," she whispered. Her lashes glittered with
tears, then she blinked, and the salty moisture slipped
over her cheeks.

"You should be," he grunted, swiping at one of the
glistening tears with his thumb. He hated how badly he
wanted to comfort her, when what she really needed was
to have some sense scared into her. "You should have listened to me last night."

She sniffed, swiping at the tears herself. "I know. It
was *stlupid.*"

Eric exhaled a ragged breath. This was getting them
nowhere, except making him want to kiss that sullen pout
off her lips, and that was something they definitely didn't
have time for. They'd already wasted too much damn

time as it was. "Come on," he said, hauling her up into his arms. "We need to get out of here."

She clutched at his shoulders and gasped. "Why are you carrying me?"

With the soft, warm weight of her in his arms, his voice came out rougher than he'd expected. "Because you'll fall flat on your face if I don't."

"Oh. You're, um, probably right," she admitted with a wince, clutching at her forehead like someone with a raging hangover. "But you *dlon't* need to scream at me."

Despite the grim circumstances, Eric felt his lips curl with a wry grin as he headed toward the door. "I'm not screaming, honey. Your ears just aren't working right."

"No kidding," she grumbled, still holding her head. He noticed that the drug seemed to be affecting her in waves—one moment her speech would be relatively clear, the next she was slurring her words again—but he didn't know what it meant. Was she getting better, or worse?

"Wait!" she suddenly cried out, trying to look over his shoulder. "I need my backpack. They took it out of my bus."

Turning around, Eric scanned the room, then spotted the pack on the floor at the right side of the sofa. He headed over and leaned down, letting her scoop it off the floor. "Thanks," she murmured, clutching the pack between their chests.

"I need you to stay quiet now," he warned her, heading back across the room and using the arm under her legs to open the door. He took a deep breath, but couldn't scent anything or anyone in the hallway. Carrying her out of the room, Eric glanced right then left, trying to decide which direction they should go in. His gut instinct told him to head away from the muted, raucous blast of music coming from the main room of the club, so he turned left.

He could only assume that the hidden exits Maggie had mentioned would be located in the building's smaller outer rooms, like a private bathroom or a storage closet, where they would be less likely to be spotted, and he intended to search each one until he found a way out.

Walking at a swift pace, Eric hadn't taken more than a dozen steps when he scented another Lycan up ahead of them. Lowering Chelsea to her feet, he quickly shoved her into a small alcove, leaving her to stumble back against the wall, her backpack clutched in her arms, as he turned to face off against whoever was coming. He could hear her sliding down onto her sweet little ass, and felt bad when she gave a startled yelp of pain as she hit the floor, but there was no time to apologize. The asshole coming was a Lycan, which meant he'd scented them, as well. If he turned out to be one of Curtis's men who knew Chelsea had been taken prisoner, he was going to be a problem.

"Come on, you son of a bitch," Eric muttered, flexing his hands at his sides, his weight balanced on the balls of his feet. The Lycan came around the corner at the far end of the hall with a guttural snarl, knife at the ready, and launched himself forward with a powerful swipe that would have taken Eric's throat out if he hadn't swayed back to avoid the blow. He was definitely one of the Whiteclaw, the bald-headed giant standing at nearly seven feet tall and built like a friggin' juggernaut. At six-five, Eric was used to towering over others, but the top of his head barely came to the Lycan's chin. The guy looked like a juiced-up, 'roid-popping Spartan, hungry for blood.

Huh. Had he actually thought his luck might be changing? Stupid. That fickle bastard would always turn around and bite him in the ass, doing its best to take him down. He could only be thankful it was still too early for the behemoth to take his animal form, which always added height and muscle to a Lycan's physique. They could still release their fangs and claws before the rise of the moon, but both were strictly forbidden when near humans. Considering Chelsea was only a few feet away, Eric could only pray the bastard didn't break protocol.

Switching the knife to his other hand, the werewolf squeezed his right hand into a meaty fist and swung with more speed than Eric had been expecting. The punch connected with his jaw in a hit that could have easily sent him sprawling on his ass if he hadn't crashed into the wall, which was a pal, keeping him on his feet.

That was pathetic, he silently growled, pissed that he'd let the guy get in a shot. If Jeremy had been there, the Runner would already be laughing his ass off, mercilessly ribbing him for being such an idiot.

Time to end this shit.

The Lycan started to smirk, obviously thinking he was going to be an easy kill, and Eric brought his right leg around, knocking the knife from his hand and nailing the bastard in the ribs with a powerful sidekick. It doubled him over, but he quickly recovered, driving his shoulders into Eric's middle like a linebacker making a tackle, knocking the wind from his lungs. They hit the floor with a crunching thud, each grappling for the upper hand, landing punches that would have killed a human. The guy might have been bigger, but Eric was faster and more experienced—not to mention better motivated. Within seconds, he had the Lycan pinned facedown on the floor, hands trapped against the small of his back, Eric's right arm cinched tight around the male's throat.

"Where's the nearest hidden exit?" he demanded. "Tell me how to find it."

"Doesn't matter," the Lycan wheezed, his deep voice gritty with pain. "You can't win this. We'll kill her before we let you keep her. That nosey little bitch needs to be put down."

A thick, guttural animal sound vibrated in his chest, and for a moment Eric couldn't hear anything over the furious roar of his pulse pounding in his ears. His eyes narrowed with deadly purpose as he tightened his hold on the son of a bitch beneath him.

"No one touches the woman," he scraped out in a low, chilling voice, aware of something shifting inside him. Something feral and violent and savage that wanted the bastard's blood—but it wasn't his wolf. It was darker, deadlier, rising up from the depths of his being like a primordial beast surging up from the seething belly of an ancient, merciless god. His fangs burned in his gums, heavy and hot, while his claws seared beneath his fingertips, eager to draw a river of blood.

Taking a deep breath, he could scent the Lycan's fear in the air, and knew the male had sensed the darkness building inside him. Seeing through a red haze of rage, Eric lowered his mouth to the Lycan's ear. "No one—not a single one of you gutter-slime assholes—is *ever* going to touch her," he said in a soft, deadly slide of words. "Because I'm willing to do whatever it takes to see that she remains unharmed."

Then he curled his hand beneath the Lycan's chin, jerked it around with a powerful yank, and made his warning a fact.

Chapter Five

Blinking her gritty eyes, Chelsea tried to focus her wavering gaze, but it wasn't easy. Making it onto her hands and knees, she crawled a few steps forward, until she was able to peek around the edge of the alcove.

Holy...crap.

She blinked again, unable to believe what she was seeing. She'd been worried Eric was getting his ass kicked—but she needn't have been. He was standing in the hallway, hands clenched at his sides and his chest heaving, powerful muscles and veins bulging beneath the golden skin on his arms, while a massive, unconscious man lay at his feet.

From the look of things, Eric had been the one kicking ass.

She smiled, relieved to see that he was okay, even though she was finding it difficult to keep her thoughts straight. One moment everything made sense with perfect clarity, and in the next, she couldn't remember what they were doing there…or why she was finding it so difficult to concentrate.

"Eric," she said, her voice coming out as little more than a whisper. But he heard the scratchy sound, his head instantly lifting, hooded gray gaze locking with hers. "Are you okay?"

He gave a jerky nod, then reached down and swiped up what looked like a knife from the floor. The blade was long and gleaming, making the tiny hairs on the back of her neck stand up. It should have scared the bejesus out of her, but Chelsea felt strangely at ease as she watched him walk toward her, that lethal knife still clutched in his hand. For all his animal-like intensity, she was confident he wouldn't hurt her—that he'd do whatever it took to protect her.

She watched him with rapt fascination, thinking it was ridiculous, the way she hadn't been able to stop thinking about this man from the moment she'd walked away from him. That kind of obsession wasn't like her, and she didn't care for it. Wasn't comfortable with it. Didn't know how to handle it. She was scared to think about what it meant— but she wasn't scared of him. Yeah, her head might be spinning, but she knew her best bet of getting out of that place alive was the gorgeous hunk who'd just slipped the knife in his boot, and was now reaching down to grasp her arms, pulling her back to her feet.

She took a deep breath, loving the way he smelled as she kind of slumped against the solid length of his muscular body, her legs like noodles. She thought he might be saying something to her, but her head was spinning too quickly now to make out the words. She seemed to be floating in a warm, lackadaisical daze, her senses drowning in the feel of the man wrapping her in his arms.

It seemed so strange to think that they'd met only last

night. As mad as she'd been with him, it'd been so hard to walk away from him in that parking lot. There'd been a moment there, when he'd been standing so close to her, that she'd almost thought he was going to try to kiss her. Or suggest she invite him into her hotel room. But then he hadn't. Instead he'd gone all master and commander on her, his arrogance making her want to scream, reminding her too much of her father.

But…wait. Hadn't he kissed her after that? She could have sworn that he did. She'd been lying in her bed, thinking about him, and then he'd been crushing her beneath his hard, powerful body, taking her mouth in a deep, drugging kiss that had nearly caused her to go up in flames.

Or had that been a dream? she wondered, crying out as Eric suddenly shoved her back against the wall and turned to face another assailant who came out of nowhere. Damn it, she couldn't get her mind to focus enough to figure out what was real…and what wasn't, and cracking her head just now hadn't helped. She clearly wasn't thinking straight. After all, she thought she'd just seen this new opponent snap at Eric with a gleaming set of fangs.

Eric was standing with his back to her, his big hands locked around the other man's arms as they grappled for control. Somehow managing to stay on her feet, Chelsea braced herself against the side of the alcove with one hand, and reached out to tap his shoulder with the other. "Hey, Eric."

"Christ! Not now, Chelse."

She licked her lips, trying to focus on the back of his head. "But I *need* to ask you a question."

"It'll have to wait." His deep voice sounded a little breathless, and a whole lotta sexy. "I'm kinda busy here," he added, finally managing to shove the guy with shaggy blond hair against the opposite wall.

"But this is important." She frowned, unable to understand why he was being so difficult. "I just need to know if you kissed me last night…or if I dreamed it."

His head cut sharply to the side, his expression stunned as he looked over his broad shoulder at her, and the loss of concentration cost him. Big-time. The blond immediately brought his fist around, slamming it into Eric's nose with a sickening crunch. "Shit!" he snarled, blood pouring from his battered nose as he tore his attention away from her and back to the fight.

Wincing, she called out, "Sorry! You're right. We should *talp…talb…TALK* about it later!"

He grunted in response, and quickly got the jerk's front pinned against the wall, his arms twisted up at a painful angle behind his back.

"Where's the closest escape route?" Eric demanded, doing something to the guy's arms that made him give a bloodcurdling cry.

"Go down the hall, through the last door on the right," he wheezed. "It's a…a small storage closet. The latch on the left side of the shelving unit opens into a passageway. The door at the end opens into the bushes on the west side of the club."

Having gotten what he needed, Eric grabbed a fistful of golden hair and slammed the guy's forehead into the wall, knocking him out.

"What now?" she asked, watching the blond slump to the floor in an unconscious heap.

"Now we create a diversion." He headed toward what looked like one of those commercial fire alarms that public buildings and businesses were required to have. A second later, he'd pulled the lever and a jarring, head-cracking siren filled the building, warning everyone to evacuate the premises.

The next thing Chelsea knew, she was hanging upside down over his shoulder, but she couldn't remember how she'd gotten there. She rubbed her head, trying to think over the painful wail of the siren. Oh, yeah, he'd finished the fight, set off the alarm, grabbed hold of her and then started running.

They were actually going to make it! He'd saved her! Chelsea knew she should say thank-you. Be nice to him. But with the way she was hanging over his shoulder, she couldn't stop staring at his muscular backside long enough to put any words together, fairly certain that drool was collecting in the corners of her mouth. *Wow.*

Sure, he was gorgeous from the front. Mouthwatering, even. But she hadn't expected the back view of him to be just as stunning. His jeans hugged the long muscles in his powerful thighs, cupping his cute butt cheeks just right. It was the perfect view, and she wondered if his buns were as tight as they looked. She wanted to ask him, but knew he'd probably just yell at her again, seeing as how they were in the middle of an escape. And she was tired of being yelled at.

There was really only one thing to do...

With an eager grin on her lips, Chelsea reached down, determined to find out the answer for herself.

Eric Drake had had a lot of surprises in his thirty-five years, but feeling Chelsea Smart pinch his ass was definitely one of the biggest.

"What the hell are you doing?" he shouted, nearly tripping over his own feet as he carried her into the storage closet. The hinged door automatically closed behind them.

"Oops. Sorry," she mumbled, her voice too soft for a human to hear over the siren. But Eric heard her just fine. "My fingers, um, slipped."

They'd *slipped?* Christ, he didn't know whether to laugh or rush her to a hospital. The drug she'd been given was clearly having an overwhelming effect on her mental faculties. The woman he'd met last night would have *never* been caught pinching a man's backside. Chewing it out, maybe—but she definitely wasn't the type to fondle.

Considering the circumstances, he supposed he should be happy she hadn't reached around and copped a feel of his crotch. If that happened, it wouldn't matter how determined he was to save her. She'd probably find her sweet little ass braced against the wall and his tongue halfway down her throat, thoughts of escape replaced by calculations of how quickly he could bury himself inside her to the nearest nanosecond. Then they'd both end up dead, and he'd have no one to blame but his dick.

Which is why it's not...going...to...happen.

Forcing himself to concentrate, Eric found the lever that opened the hidden passageway, and carried her through it, relieved the blond hadn't jerked him around with false directions. The second they'd made their way through the exterior door and were clear of the bushes, he set her back on her feet.

"Hold on tight to me and hide your face with your hair," he told her, securing her against his side with his arm locked tight around her waist. He'd grabbed her backpack off the floor, and kept the straps fisted in his hand as they quickly moved into the crowd of evacuated customers that was gathering in the club's parking lot. Hoping they would blend in with the teeming chaos, Eric lowered his face to hide any lingering traces of blood from his busted nose and headed for his truck.

Twilight had given way to the deeper shadows of the night, the spring sky dark and storm-colored. He was careful to avoid the golden splotches of light shining down from the parking-lot lights, his senses on high alert as he searched for the animal scent of other Lycans. There was a group of them gathering off to their right, so he took her deeper into the crowd to their left, his pace quickening when he caught sight of his truck. Pulling his keys from his pocket with his free hand, Eric got the passenger-side door opened and lifted her into the seat.

"Get your seat belt on," he said, setting her pack by her feet before shutting the door and making his way around the front of the truck. After climbing in, he took the knife from his boot and stashed it in the glove box, then cranked the engine. Within seconds they were pulling forward, over a small dirt lot that lay between the club's parking lot and that of the convenience store located next door. He glanced at Chelsea, making sure she was okay.

"We made it," she whispered, her head lolling against the headrest, eyes closed. "Thank you."

"Don't thank me yet," he muttered under his breath as he steered onto the road, heading north. Using the back of his wrist to wipe the blood trickling from his nose, Eric kept an eye on his rearview mirror, checking to make sure they weren't being followed. Then he lifted his butt off the seat, reached into his front pocket for his phone and called Jeremy.

"What the hell took you so long?" the Runner barked, picking up on the first ring.

"What do you think? I had to go through one White-claw thug and a Donovan to get her out," he said in a low voice, watching Chelsea from the corner of his eye. She still had her eyes closed, which meant she'd hopefully fallen asleep. "The bastards gave her something that knocked her out. They had her locked in a damn room."

"Shit. They wouldn't have drugged her unless they'd

planned on keeping her. Do you think it has to do with the sister?"

Taking the next right, so that he wouldn't have to stay stopped at the red light, Eric said, "That would make sense. Wherever her sister is, they don't want her found. Either someone plans on keeping her, or she's already dead. In either case, the last thing they'll want is some woman stirring things up, drawing attention to the situation. So far the cops have blown Chelsea off, but if Perry Smart doesn't come back, there's a chance that someone might start listening to her. Whatever the Donovans and Whiteclaw have going on at that club, they don't want the cops getting involved."

"What are you going to do with her?"

"Hell if I know. I can't send her back home. They know her name and probably searched her wallet. By tomorrow morning, they'll have someone staked out at her home and her work."

"Then you need to keep her with you."

A low sound rumbled in the back of his throat. "Not a good idea."

"Don't be an idiot, Eric. She's in danger."

"I know that, damn it." He ran his tongue over his teeth. "It's just…complicated."

"Yeah." Jeremy's laugh was husky. "It always is."

"Look, I'll figure out a place where we can lay low for a while and call you with an update."

"What? No. You'll bring her up here."

Shaking his head, he said, "I can't take her into Shadow Peak, Jeremy. She's human." The woman had no idea that Lycans existed. Even if he weren't being watched like a hawk, there was no way in hell he could go bringing her into a town full of werewolves.

"Not the town," Jeremy muttered. "*Here.* Bring her to the Alley."

Eric ran the idea through his mind, surprised that it wasn't half bad. Unlike Shadow Peak, the Alley was at least a place where Lycans and humans lived together. It wasn't perfect, but it was the best option he had.

Still, he had to make sure that Jeremy understood what he was getting them into.

"If I head to the Alley, there's a good chance we'll be bringing trouble with us. The other Runners won't like it."

Jeremy snorted. "Bullshit. We look out for our own. Which includes you, in case you hadn't figured that out yet."

"And if I bring trouble?"

"Then we'll deal with it." He could almost hear the smile in the Runner's voice. "You know how much I like kicking ass."

There was no one Eric trusted more than the Runners, which meant she'd be safe. No matter how they felt about him, they would make sure Chelsea was protected. From the Donovans and the Whiteclaw. And even from himself, if it came to that. Which he really hoped it didn't. He just needed to keep his hands off her, and everything would be okay.

"If you're sure," he said, "then we're heading up."

"Just hurry. The sooner you get here, the better."

"You have no idea," he muttered, ending the call.

"Elric?"

He shot her a quick glance, before returning his attention to the road. "I thought you'd gone to sleep."

"Did I?" she asked around a small yawn. "I must have been dreaming. I thought we were talking about football. You were telling me about how Aaron Rodgers is the best quarterback in the league right now, and I was arguing that he didn't have anything on Peyton Manning. Then you accused me of liking Peyton 'cause he's cute."

Was she hallucinating? Jesus, what the hell was pumping through her system? He hated not knowing, frustration making his voice hard and rough, with more than a little of his wolf in it. "Damn it, Chelsea. Why couldn't you have just listened to me and stayed away from that place?"

"Dunno."

He gripped the wheel so hard he was surprised it didn't crack. "You got a death wish I don't know about?"

"I wasn't trying to get myself killed," she said softly, her gaze focused out her window. "I just wanted to ask them some questions. But they forced me into that back room and shot some awful needle in my arm, and then everything went... Hey, look at that! I just saw a purple kangaroo in that field over there!"

"Hell," he muttered, pulling his hand down his face. "You're as high as a kite."

Her head came around so fast he was surprised she didn't give herself whiplash. "I'm not high!" she gasped, sounding scandalized. Not to mention insulted.

The corner of his mouth twitched as he fought back a smile. "Honey, you're so baked you can't even see straight."

"I am?" She put both hands on her cheeks, her expression as woeful as a little girl who'd just lost her puppy. "That doesn't sound good."

"It's gonna be okay," he grunted, wondering when he'd become such a sap. "It'll probably start wearing off in a little while. But I need to go ahead and ask you some questions."

"Okay. I'm ready."

Eric grabbed one of the bottles of water he kept behind his seat, then handed it to her with the order to drink it.

After she'd taken a few sips, he said, "Did they ask you any questions before they doped you up?"

Nodding, she said, "A few of them did."

"What did you tell them?"

"Not much. Just that I was looking for Perry. And that you had kicked me off your land."

"You gave them my name?"

Her nose scrunched. "I think so."

Shit. Now he didn't know what the hell was going on. Had they kept her because of Perry...or because of him?

"Eric," she murmured, setting the water bottle in a cup holder, "I don't feel so good."

"What's wrong?" He could feel a frown settling between his brows. "Are you going to be sick?"

"No," she moaned, turning on her side and curling against the back of the seat. "I just can't stop...aching inside."

Fury swept through his veins like a blistering flame. "Where?" he rasped, terrified that she'd been raped and hadn't told him. "What the hell did they do to you?"

She shook her head, her long hair streaming over her shoulders. "It's not that," she groaned. "I think...I think it's the shot they gave me." The words were forced through her chattering teeth. "I'm...it's too much. I feel like I'm coming out of my skin!"

His jaw was clenched. "Where do you hurt?"

"Everywhere..." Her voice trailed off on a startled gasp, and he could scent the change the instant it hit her. One second she'd smelled of sexy female and exhaustion—and in the next, her scent exploded into something hot and wet and hungry. It hit him so hard he nearly drove off the side of the road, straight into a friggin' telephone pole.

"Chelsea?" he croaked, wondering what the hell was

going on. He could taste her escalating arousal on the air as if it were sitting in his mouth, on his tongue. Could feel it stroking over his skin like a physical touch. With each second that went by, her lush scent was getting thicker… richer, his wolf so turned on he was ready to howl.

"Eric, *Oh, God.* I'm burning up," she moaned, her tone needy and sexual, making him sweat. Then she reached up and started tugging at the buttons on her white, short-sleeved shirt, and he nearly died.

Hell, no. This could *not* be happening.

Cursing, Eric grabbed his phone again and quickly called Jeremy's number. "Change of plans," he barked, the instant Jeremy picked up. "I need Jillian. Now!"

"Hold on, man. I'll get her."

While he waited for the healer, Eric struggled with Chelsea's suddenly wandering hands, his eyes nearly crossing when she reached down and ran her palm over the blatant ridge that was trapped behind his button fly.

"Goddamn it. Stop that!" he growled, jerking her hand away from the most ill-timed hard-on he'd ever had.

Jillian's voice was suddenly coming through the phone. "Eric?"

Panting, he said, "Yeah, it's me."

"Listen. Cian just called Jeremy on the house line. He and Brody are almost in Wesley. Do you need them to meet you?"

"No! Tell them to head back home."

"You're sure?"

He imagined Chelsea trying to run her hands over a smirking Hennessey and nearly popped a blood vessel. "Yeah. If that Irishman comes within twenty feet of me right now, Brody's gonna be looking for a new partner."

"Um, okay. I'll pass along the message." He could hear

her telling Jeremy to call Cian back, and then she said, "Now tell me what's going on."

"It's Chelsea. Something's wrong with her."

"What do you mean?"

"She was shot up with something at the club, and when I found her, she was unconscious. Since she came to, she's been pretty much out of it. Then she started complaining about burning up, saying she was coming out of her skin, and the next thing I knew, her scent was off the charts."

"Does she smell aroused?"

He couldn't remember the last time he'd blushed, but he felt himself go hot around the ears. "Uh, yeah. Big-time."

"Eric, I think they've given her some kind of high-powered aphrodisiac."

Son of a bitch. He made a guttural sound deep in his throat, thinking of what those bastards must have had planned for her.

"Can you deal with it?"

"Deal with what?" he asked, distracted by the tempting thought of turning around, heading back to the club and ripping the throat of out every scumbag who had planned on touching her.

Jillian's tone was more forceful, demanding his attention. "Depending on how strong the drug is, she could end up in a lot of pain, Eric. I've heard of drugs like this before, and they're rumored to be very powerful. I'd tell you to take her to a hospital, but I don't think there's anything they'd be able to do. She's just going to have to ride it out, but the good news is that there shouldn't be any long-term effects to worry about. As soon as you can, though, you're going to want to get her someplace private, because there's a strong chance she's going to need help getting through it."

"Help?" Sweat chilled on his skin. "What kind of help?"

"The main thing is that you make her comfortable. Try to keep her calm."

He had to take the phone away from his ear for a moment as he struggled with Chelsea and those wandering, sanity-destroying hands of hers again. When she finally slumped back into her seat, her fingers busy undoing the rest of the buttons on her shirt, he lifted the phone back to his ear. "What exactly are you saying?" he asked, sounding breathless and pissed and completely freaked out. "Spell it out for me, Jillian. I can't have any gray areas here."

"Okay. If she needs to orgasm, then make her orgasm."

Aware of the tenuous hold he had on his control, Eric pulled off the road and into the lot of an abandoned gas station, his chest working like a bellows as he slammed the truck into Neutral. "Goddamn it," he seethed, forcing the words through his gritted teeth. "I'm not going to rape her!"

"That's not what I mean," she said, her tone deliberately calm. "And I understand what an uncomfortable position this puts you in, but she needs you right now. Her body is going to seek release again and again, until the drug is out of her system. If she can't make it happen on her own, then she's going to need your help. It won't require actual intercourse, though that's probably what she'll want."

Covering his eyes with his hand, he muttered, "This is a bad fucking idea."

"If you can't handle it, Eric, then you need to bring her to the Alley right away. I'm sure Cian won't mind—"

"Don't," he warned in a chilling tone, cutting her off. "Don't even finish that thought."

"Then stop acting squeamish and help her out," she

snapped, losing her temper. "You have no trouble screwing around with all those females up in Shadow Peak. I didn't realize you were too good to touch a human."

His breath left his lungs in a sharp, angry burst. "That's bullshit and you know it. I have no problem with humans. Just this one!"

"God, Eric. What the hell has you so uptight about this woman?"

"I don't know." He was careful to keep his gaze focused straight ahead, but he could see the snowy white lace of Chelsea's bra from the corner of his eye, and knew her feminine little shirt was now hanging wide open. "It's… She's…" He tried, but couldn't put his feelings where she was concerned into words. At least not any that made sense.

"Eric," Jillian said gently, and he tensed, knowing damn well she was about to drop another bombshell on him. "This isn't the kind of thing I would normally ask over the phone, but you don't sound like yourself. So I'm just going to ask. What is this woman to you?"

"What the hell's that supposed to mean?"

"Is she *yours?*"

His stomach churned. "No. My wolf didn't recognize her scent. But that doesn't mean it's a good idea to get involved with her."

"Well, the choice is yours. You can always call back and let me know what hotel you take her to, and then I can pass the information on to Cian."

And you know what Hennessey's like, his wolf snarled. *The Irishman would get such a kick out of this. He'd be more than happy to lend her a helping hand.*

"Jillian."

"Yeah?"

With a ragged sigh, he said, "Sometimes you can be such a bitch."

"But you love me anyway, right?" He could hear the smile in her voice.

"At the moment, all I want is to put you over my knee."

She gave a delicate snort. "Just be careful, and call me if you have any problems."

A gritty, humorless laugh surged up from his chest. "This whole goddamn night is a problem."

"You're going to be fine, Eric. Just trust your instincts."

"That's the *last* thing I trust," he muttered, disconnecting the call and shoving the phone back in his pocket.

Scrubbing his hands down his face, Eric struggled to get his thoughts into some kind of order, but it was impossible. Awareness of the all-too-human Chelsea Smart prickled across his skin like crackling sparks of electricity, his body vibing to a hot, jagged pulse of need. He could *feel* her, *scent* her, like the promise of something ripe and sweet, the husky cadence of her breaths the sexiest damn thing he'd ever heard. There wasn't a chance in hell he was gonna make it out of this with his sanity intact. The only thing he could hope for was that he could still look at himself in the mirror come morning.

You're making the right choice, his wolf rasped, its low tone thick with satisfaction.

"Shut up," he grated, knowing damn well the animal was looking forward to getting its hands on her. "I don't want to hear a single word out of you."

"What?" she murmured, mistaking the guttural words as being meant for her. "But I didn't say anything."

"I know you didn't, Chelse." He took off the hand brake and put the truck into Drive, heading back out to the highway. "I was talking to myself."

"Hmm. You want to know something? I can't believe

that you're here with me. That you saved me. I was so scared, but not anymore." She leaned over the center console, burying her nose in his throat, and he stiffened in shock when her tongue flicked against the hammering pulse throbbing beneath his skin. "Mmm," she moaned, "you taste so good. I want to put my mouth on you…all over you…"

Christ, God, Almighty.

The hairs on the back of his neck lifted, his muscles knotting like thick coils of rope. Jillian had told him to trust his instincts, but every fraction of instinct he possessed was telling him this was going to be the longest friggin' night of his life.

Hitting the gas, he wondered how long it would take before he lost his goddamn mind.

As Chelsea reached down, her small hand landing on his rigid thigh, Eric got his answer.

Not long at all.

Chapter Six

The motel room was decorated in pale shades of cream and blue—but the soothing color scheme wasn't helping him relax. Eric was still as restless and on edge as he'd been when he'd found the motel on the outskirts of town. Still thrown completely off balance.

And now he was stuck in this tiny space with a woman he wanted so badly he couldn't think straight.

With a hard, frustrated growl, Eric shoved his hands back through his short hair and locked his fingers behind his neck. She didn't deserve this, damn it. Yeah, she might be stubborn and bad at listening to sound advice, but she was a good person. She didn't deserve to be shoved into this kind of situation, and he was the last male on earth who should be laying his hands on her.

"Elric."

The slurred, whispered sound of his name made him flinch. Taking a deep breath, he turned toward the bed…

and the woman waiting there. He'd managed to get her to button her shirt back up before carrying her from the truck to the room, but it hadn't helped much. She still looked incredibly sexy, all rumpled and flushed, as if she were lying there just waiting for him to fall on her like a sex-starved animal—which was exactly what he felt like. It didn't matter how many women he'd bedded, or how recently he'd been with them. They hadn't been Chelsea, and that seemed to make a helluva difference.

He was pretty sure he didn't want to know why.

"It's getting worse," she moaned, holding her middle as if she was in pain. But her features were etched with sexual need, her heady scent thick with arousal. Whatever drug Curtis Donovan had given her, he had no doubt it was doing its job. Making her mindless with hunger. Making her as animalistic in her needs as he was.

"Is this…do I feel like this because of what they put in my arm?"

"Yeah." His voice was little more than a croak. "The drug won't hurt you, but it's an aphrodisiac. It's making you crave sexual release."

"I…yes…*crave*," she panted, moving onto her hands and knees and crawling toward him. Her eyes were glassy and bright, the deep blue reminding him of the sun-kissed surface of a lake. "You've got to hurry!"

"Damn it, Chelsea. You need to just take a second and think this through." He curved his hands over her shoulders as she rose up on her knees at the foot of the mattress, her own hands fisting in his T-shirt. "You don't want to do this," he said unsteadily, trying to hold her away from him without hurting her. "You don't even like me, remember?"

"Like you more than any other man I know." She leaned forward, nipping his chest through the soft cotton, sending him a hungry look from beneath her lashes. "Please…don't leave me like this. *Help me.*"

"Jesus," he hissed, his fingers tightening on her shoulders. "It should be any other man in the world but me here with you. I'm not good for you, honey."

She tilted her head back and stared up at him, her gaze slowly clearing, as if she was riding another momentary wave of lucidity. Her pink little tongue swept over her lips, and she seemed to be trying to calm her breathing as she said, "Eric, I know this sucks. And what I'm about to say probably doesn't make a lot of sense, but you're…you're the only guy I know who I'd trust, no matter where I was. Home. Here. On a freaking desert island. If this *has* to happen, I want it to be you."

"See?" His voice was raw. "That just proves it. You don't have a clue what you're saying."

"Trust me, I know. I'm just…just too desperate to let my hang-ups get in the way. But if it makes you feel better, I'm sure I'll be horrified that I said these things to you tomorrow. But only because I'll be embarrassed. Not because you helped me."

His nostrils flared as his own breathing turned ragged. "You're putting me in an impossible situation, Chelsea."

"*They* did this," she countered, starting to tremble. "Not you. Not me. I'm just trying to get through it."

If she'd been in her right mind, there wouldn't have been a force on earth that could have kept him from shredding her clothes, spreading her legs and shoving himself so deep inside her he could feel her soul. But this wasn't Chelsea's choice—she might have chosen him, but she sure as hell hadn't chosen the circumstances—and that changed everything. Shackled him in a way that he silently prayed would be enough. He couldn't afford to make any mistakes. One momentary slip of a claw or fang, and the consequences would be disastrous.

"Lie down," he rumbled in a low voice, reaching for one of her small, sneaker-covered feet. "Let's see if we can get you more comfortable. Okay?"

"Just hurry!" she panted, her voice cracking, and he could feel the need rising inside her. Could scent it on her skin. She caught her lower lip in her teeth, imploring him for help with her glistening eyes.

"Shh. It's okay. I'll…take care of you." *And probably lose my mind in the process, but hell, it's not like I was all that sane to begin with.*

If he had been, he never would have ended up in this kind of no-win situation, where every possible scenario and action seemed to make him a jerk. His stomach twisted, but he choked back his unease and turned his focus on Chelsea, determined to make it as easy for her as he could.

Tossing the shoe over his shoulder, he pulled off her sock and grinned down at the foot he held in his hand. "I was right."

"About what?"

He ran the pad of his thumb over her red toenails. "Your feet *are* adorable."

She smiled up at him with a wobbly, kinda shy curve of her lips as he dealt with the other shoe and sock, but he could see the pain building in her gaze, the normally bright blue bleeding into something dark and turbulent. "Take off my clothes, Eric." They were soft, almost silent words, but he flinched as if she'd shouted them.

"I can't." His voice was hoarse…tight, the phrase *No way in hell* looping through his head again and again. He'd get her off, because it was what she needed, but the more barriers he could keep between them while he did it, the better.

Stretching out on the bed beside her, he pulled her close, her back to his front as they lay on their sides. He wondered if she could feel the pounding of his heart thudding against her spine as he closed his eyes and curved a hand over her hip, slowly sliding it between her legs. She jolted at the intimate contact, even though she still wore her jeans. But Eric could feel the heat of her through the already-damp denim, his jaw aching as he gritted his teeth and fought to maintain control. Ignoring his own raging need, he buried his face in her silky hair and used two fingertips to apply pressure where she needed it most—rubbing…stroking…working that sensitive peak with every ounce of skill he'd managed to acquire over the years.

It didn't take long. She came hard and fast, her nails digging into his forearm as she held on, rocking against his stroking fingers while a sharp, keening sound slipped past her lips. But it wasn't enough. If anything, the orgasm seemed to rocket her body into an even deeper level of craving and pain. "I…I need *more. Please.* It hurts, Eric. I need…damn it, I need you inside me!"

He swore under his breath as he reached for the button on her jeans, his hand shaking as he worked down the zipper. Without giving himself time to think about what he was doing—how hard it was going to hit him—he pushed his hand under the elastic band of her panties and thought, *Oh, yeah…I am so going to hell for this.* Because at that exact moment, she shifted onto her back, spreading her legs, her knees falling toward her sides, and he couldn't stop his heavy gaze from locking on to the erotic sight of his hand shoved down the front of her pants. Tight white panties were digging into his thick wrist, dark curls tickling his palm as he reached deeper, stroking his roughened fingertips over the soft, swollen lips of her sex. She was tender and slick, like hot, wet silk, burning to the touch.

He stroked around the puffy opening to her body, then moved back up to the hard little knot of her clit, trying not to think about how incredibly soft she was…how wet. But it was impossible. He couldn't stop picturing how it would be if she wasn't human. No hesitation. No restraint. He'd have already spread her open and shoved his face against her, his tongue greedily lapping those hot, melting juices…with no thought to anything but making her come, making her scream.

"Inside me," she cried, pushing her hands down on his. "Now!"

Clenching his teeth, he rimmed the delicate, slippery opening again, thinking it seemed incredibly small as he pushed the tip of his index finger inside. Plush, sleek muscles clamped down on him, and he couldn't stop the feral growl that rumbled up from his chest, imagining what it would feel like to have her clasping onto his dick like that.

"You're so tight," he ground out, pushing in another fingertip, then working both digits deeper inside, his free hand reaching over their heads and fisting around one of the headboard's wooden slats. The wood groaned from the power of his grip, his fingers leaving deep impressions in the wood.

"You have such big fingers," she moaned, her head tossing from side to side, arms thrown over her head in a purely sexual pose of surrender. "Feels *so* good."

Ah, God, she had no idea. She was as tender and silky as a rain-slick petal, the mouthwatering scent of her sex the most addictive thing that had ever filled his head. He found her clit with his thumb, pumping his fingers as he buried his face in the pillow, fighting for control. Christ,

this was insane. Nothing was supposed to feel this good…
this *right*.

When she finally settled after another shattering orgasm, relaxing beside him, Eric ripped himself away from
her…the bed, and stumbled toward the bathroom at the
opposite end of the room. He slammed the door shut behind him, shaking from head to toe as he leaned back
against it, his breath sawing past his lips in a series of
rough, rapid bursts.

For two seconds, he fought the urge to lift his slick fingers to his mouth, then lost. Nostrils flaring, he shoved
them past his lips and nearly died, right there, in the cheap
little motel bathroom with cracked linoleum all around
him. He sucked on his fingers as if he'd been starved for
days, her succulent taste exploding over his senses like
something that could destroy him. It was *that* sweet…*that*
decadent…*that addictive*. A narcotic that tasted like it'd
been made especially for him.

His body ached, his hard cock pulsing with need,
throbbing with pain. He badly wanted to take matters
into his own hand and relieve the pressure, but knew it
was too risky. Once out, he might never get the damn
beast back in its cage.

Moving toward the sink, he pulled off his shirt and
tossed it on the counter as he turned on the tap, then
splashed his face with cold water. Lifting his head, Eric
stared in the mirror, no longer recognizing the face staring back at him. It was hard, etched with need, his eyes
glowing with the primitive hunger of the wolf, an unusual
rim of amber around the brighter silver that he'd never
seen before. He didn't know what it meant—but whatever
it was, it couldn't be good. Craving, dark and inhuman,
battered against his conscience like a hammer, fighting
to break him down…shatter his control.

You can do this. You can fight it. Just keep it the hell together.

At the same time, his wolf snarled for that reasonable voice to shut the hell up, urging him to act on the destructive craving clawing him to shreds on the inside, until he was amazed he hadn't bled out from the aggressive force of his hunger.

Just take her... It's what she wants. What she needs.

Opportunistic bastard! This wasn't what she wanted. She wanted to find her sister and be safe at home back in Virginia. She didn't want her life turned upside down by a bunch of strangers, and especially by him. They'd rubbed each other the wrong way from the very beginning. Not that it kept him from wanting her so badly his stomach was tied in knots, his cock so hard he could have hammered it through a bloody wall.

She cried out, the bleak sound muffled by the door, but he could hear the pain and need in those husky notes, and knew she was suffering again. It was time to stop hiding in the bathroom like a green-eared teen and get his ass back out there. He splashed another couple of handfuls of cold water on his face and the back of his neck, then shook the water out of his hair and opened the door. A pale wash of light shone from the bedside lamp, illuminating the hollows and curves of her feminine little body in the center of the bed…and Eric nearly fell flat on his face.

Holy…shit. Was she trying to kill him? Her white shirt was still buttoned up, all proper and prim—but she was completely naked from the waist down, her jeans and panties scattered over the floor, as if she'd literally thrown them off.

For a split second, he was frozen, held immobile by lust and hunger and things that were too primitive for most humans to understand. He wanted to bite her. Lick her. Take her under his body and trap her there…marking her in ways he had no business even thinking about.

She started to draw her knees up, and he quickly looked away, not trusting himself with the explicit view. Once he looked he would look his fill, and there'd end up being hell to pay. But from the corner of his eye, Eric saw her spreading her legs, revealing herself completely, and he couldn't have kept his gaze from locking on to that intimate sight any more than he could have stopped sucking air into his lungs. Heat crawled up his spine, curling around the backs of his ears, where his pulse was roaring like a fucking jet engine.

Christ. The woman was either trying to kill him or melt his brain into a useless lump of putty.

He tried to get some control over his ragged breathing, but it was impossible when he was staring at something so perfect and pretty. He had to choke back a primitive howl as he soaked in every lush, erotic detail. He wanted— *needed*—to feast on the tender perfection of her flesh until he was drenched in her, drowning in the blurring, liquid details, the data coming in too fast to separate, until lust was just a hazy, consuming cloud closing in around him, making it hard to breathe…to think.

So going to hell for this. So going to hell…

"Eric?"

"Please, don't…don't say anything," he rasped, rubbing his tongue over his teeth as he crawled onto the foot of the bed. A second later, he had his fingers shoved back inside that sweet, pink opening, his face pressed against her stomach, the low, animal sounds he was making muffled against her smooth, warm skin as the hem of her shirt bunched up beneath her breasts. He'd pushed his other arm beneath her, trapping her against him as he thrust his fingers into that plush, clenching sheath, spurring her into another one of those deliciously tight orgasms that made her scream. Her pleasure surged through him like a blistering rush of heat, a muscle pulsing in the side of his jaw as he gritted his teeth and tried like hell not to follow her over, spilling in his jeans.

When she finally quieted, Eric lifted his head, his body hard and burning as his heavy-lidded gaze instantly locked with hers. She was looking *right* at him, her blue eyes dark with passion, her lips swollen from the biting pressure of her teeth. She was the most beautiful thing he'd ever seen, her unique scent heady and rich, and he couldn't fight the need to have her intoxicating taste in his mouth again.

Holding that passion-wrecked gaze, Eric pulled his drenched fingers from the greedy clasp of her sex and brought them to his mouth, hungrily sucking them past his lips. Her eyes went wide with shock, as if she'd never seen a man do such a thing, and he growled low in his throat.

"You taste so damn good." The words were rough and raw. "I could happily keep my tongue buried in you for days, Chelsea. Weeks…months…and it still wouldn't be enough."

"Eric." She arched beneath him as if she'd suddenly been struck by lightning, her nipples pressing thick and tight against the front of her shirt, blue eyes glazed with need as she sank her teeth into her lower lip. *"Again!"* she cried, the next wave hitting even faster than he'd expected. Her body writhed beneath him as he caught the sudden head-spinning surge of her scent, and he quickly plunged his fingers back into that tight, slick heaven, giving her something hard and thick to break against.

But she wanted more. "I need you inside me," she moaned, her short nails digging into his sweat-slicked shoulders as she tried to pull him up her body. "Need you to make love to me. *Now.*"

"Goddamn it, Chelsea." His voice was little more than a guttural snarl as he shoved his fingers deep and held them there, letting her clench around him. "Don't do this to me," he choked out, squeezing his eyes shut as he lowered his head. "I'm trying to help you, baby, but I'm not… Damn it, I'm *not* raping you!"

She grabbed his head between her soft palms, tilting his face up. As he lifted his lashes, she whispered, "It's not rape when I'm begging you for it." She looked like she was burning with fever, her eyes bright, cheeks flushed with color. "Please, Eric."

His throat felt like he'd tried to swallow a boulder. "That's the drug talking. It's not you."

Red-tinged fury swiftly built to an inferno behind that sky-blue gaze, as if hell itself were burning in the heavens. "Damn you," she seethed. "This is *my* choice! Not yours! You don't get to tell me what I want."

"Damn me all you like," he grunted. "I'm still not taking you like that. Not for our first time."

She sobbed with defeat, her head falling back to the bed as she brought her arms up, curling them over her face. They were both hot and sweaty when she came for the fourth time, her arms falling limply to the bedspread, her body finally quieting as Eric crawled higher onto the bed and stretched out beside her. He lay on his side, facing her, memorizing the way she looked lying there all flushed and pink, her long eyelashes casting shadows over her cheeks as her breathing slowly mellowed.

He didn't know how much time had passed when she started to stir again, her dark gaze filled with determination as she lifted those long eyelashes and looked right at him.

"You've been so incredible," she whispered, rolling toward him and pressing her palm against the center of his chest, right over the heavy beat of his heart. Then her hand slowly started to make its way downward.

"It's okay, Chelse. You don't owe me anything," he groaned, catching her hand before she reached his navel.

A small frown settled between her brows. "But it hardly seems fair."

It was the hardest damn thing he'd ever had to do, but he somehow found the strength to say, "Let's just worry about you for right now, okay?"

As the night deepened outside the motel walls, Eric lost count of how many times he had to ease her through the pain. The drug kept mounting, each rise exhausting Chelsea…and taking him that much closer to the edge. Using one of the washcloths from the bathroom, he applied cool compresses to her sore flesh, making her drink countless bottles of water that he had delivered to the room. He even managed to get some crackers into her, though food wasn't what she ached for.

Just as Jillian had predicted, her body craved release, again and again, forging a level of intimacy between them that, despite all his years of sexual experience, Eric had never shared with another woman. He could say, without arrogance, that he was a good lover—but he'd never come close to focusing on a woman the way he focused on the intoxicating Chelsea Smart. His night became a lush, sensual tapestry of feminine textures and scents, his body attuned to the minute rhythms of her heartbeat, the quickening of her breath. He memorized her with the touch of his hands—knew the tight, cushiony feel of her sex and the slick heat of her pleasure by heart, imprinting the evocative details upon his mind the way a scientist soaked in data.

And yet, no matter how lost he was in her, the struggle never left him. Eric battled through the endless hours with nothing but sheer determination, never allowing the man or the beast to take more than was necessary. He wanted her so badly it was like a physical ache in his bones, breaking him down—but he never touched her with his lips... his tongue. Never took that slippery, melting sex into his mouth and drank his fill, though he was ravenous for that decadent, mouthwatering flavor that threatened to short-circuit his brain.

And he somehow found the strength to keep his jeans completely buttoned, no matter how many times she begged him to give her more. For that, Eric was fairly certain he deserved some kind of bloody sainthood.

The closest he came to losing control was when she became too sore for the touch of his fingers. Rolling to his back, he lifted her astride him, gripping her hips, and let her grind herself to completion against the thick, jutting ridge of his cock. She'd come so hard she nearly passed out...

And so had he.

"Shh. Just let me hold you," he murmured afterward, his arms wrapping around her in an unusually possessive hold as he pulled her down to his chest, her cheek resting above the heavy beat of his heart, her long hair streaming over his shoulder and arm. Her body was deliciously soft against his, her warm scent filling his head, giving him an unfamiliar sense of peace, despite the animal hunger still twisting and burning beneath his skin.

He was in a world of hurt, but he didn't want to move. Didn't want to leave her. Strange, considering how much he disliked cuddling with his bed partners. But he liked having Chelsea's curvaceous little body wrapped up in his arms, even when it was making him sweat. It felt...

comfortable. Warm and soft and sweet, and though he hadn't thought he'd be able to relax, he felt his eyes growing heavy...the tension leaving his muscles in a slow, mellow slide. It was so easy. So right.

For what felt like the first time in years, Eric surrendered to the moment...and slipped into the soothing darkness of sleep.

Opening her eyes to the bright morning sunlight, Chelsea said the first words that came to mind. "Oh. My. God."

"It's okay," Eric rasped from the other side of the bed. "Don't be scared."

Painfully aware of the fact that she was naked from the waist down under the sheet, she clutched the white cotton in a deathly grip and stammered, "I...I..."

"Take a deep breath, Chelsea. There's no need to panic."

From the corner of her eye, she watched as he stretched that long, muscular body, then lazily scratched at his chest and the dark shadow on his jaw.

What the hell have I done?

She stared at his hands, at those long, rugged fingers, and could remember the *exact* feel of them inside her. Could remember the harsh look of hunger on his face when he'd pulled them out, shiny and wet, and sucked them between his lips. He'd been greedy, softly growling, as if he couldn't get enough of the way she tasted.

He'd done it more than once—and yet, he'd done his best to keep things from going too far. Not that she'd been much help.

Now that the drug had worn off, he was probably worried she was going to accuse him of taking advantage of her, but she could remember enough from the night before to know that wasn't the case. If anything, *she* was the one who'd taken advantage of him. She'd played on his sympathy, begging him to help her.

God, if the bed could just swallow her whole, she'd have been eternally grateful. She had no idea what to say to him. How to apologize. The guy had saved her from heaven only knew what back at that club, had given of himself again and again to make sure she wasn't in pain, and she'd never even been nice to him. Had acted like a bitch most of the time she'd spent with him. Just because her emotions had been wrapped up in worry and fear during the short time that she'd known him didn't excuse her.

And even with everything that had happened, she didn't know if she could act any differently. Her wariness was a part of who she was, of how she'd been shaped. But she could start by at least telling him how sorry she was.

With a hard swallow, she tried again to force out some words. "I—"

"I didn't attack you," he said, cutting her off, his voice gruff.

She covered her face with the sheet. "I know you didn't. I…remember what happened," she choked out. In fact, she couldn't stop the images from flashing through her mind. Carnal. Intimate. Explicit. Her body shivered with remembered sensation, the tender flesh between her thighs sore from the endless hours of stimulation. He hadn't used her roughly—but she'd been insatiable, begging him to keep going…to keep making her climax, again and again and again, long into the early hours of the morning.

Her blood chilled as she caught a particular flash of memory—Eric above her, his handsome face darkened by an intimidating scowl as he'd made her come. He'd looked so…unhappy, and she cringed, unable to forget the rather important fact that he didn't like her.

Though he couldn't see her face, he must have sensed

that she was crying. "Damn it, Chelsea. Don't be upset. You didn't do anything wrong."

"I'm so embarrassed," she said, sniffing. "I can't believe I begged you… *Oh, God.* You should have just left me here!"

He gave a masculine snort that normally would have set her teeth on edge, but seemed somehow sexy to her when he did it. Then again, she pretty much thought everything he did was sexy. "You really think I would have just taken off and left you here in pain?" he asked, an edge of anger creeping into his voice for the first time that morning. "Christ, woman. I'm not *that* much of a bastard."

She peeked over the edge of the sheet. "Eric, you don't even like me. This—what happened last night—it couldn't have been pleasant for you."

He had the heels of his palms pressed against his eyes, but he lowered his arms and slowly turned his head to the side, locking that beautiful gray gaze with hers. "You're upset because you think I didn't enjoy it?" With each word, his eyebrows arched a little higher.

"I'm upset about a lot of things."

"Well, you can ease your mind on that score." He swung his long legs over the side of the bed as he sat up, one hand lifting to the back of his neck and rubbing at the tense muscles there. Her gaze moved appreciatively over his powerful shoulders and arms, before snagging on the dark, intricate tattoo that wrapped his right shoulder and biceps. She'd never thought of tattoos as all that sexy before, but she'd been wrong. Eric's tat was sexy as hell.

Blowing out a rough breath, he looked back over his shoulder, sliding her a heavy-lidded look from under his lashes. "It's obviously not the way I would have chosen to get a taste of you, but I enjoyed it," he said in a low, kinda gravelly rumble. "More than I should have, considering the circumstances."

"You can't have enjoyed it that much," she pointed out in a dubious tone, careful to keep her lower half covered with the sheet as she finally sat up. "You kept your jeans on the entire time." Even though she could remember repeatedly begging him to take them off.

"Yeah," he muttered under his breath, his tone dry as he turned his head forward again. "And now I need clean ones."

Color burned in her face at his meaning, making her want to duck back under the covers, but she couldn't manage to rip her gaze away from the beautiful, flexing muscles in his back and shoulders as he moved to his feet. He reached for the T-shirt that was lying over the room's lone chair, pulled it over his head, then cut her a wry look over his shoulder again.

"I haven't done that since I was…" He looked forward and scrubbed both hands over his face, his harsh sigh loud enough for her to hear. "Hell, I don't think I've *ever* done anything like that."

A soft burst of laughter slipped past her lips, catching her by surprise, and Chelsea quickly covered her mouth, mortified. "I'm so sorry."

She could only blink in astonishment as he turned around and slid her another one of those sexy smirks, before sitting in the chair and pulling on his socks. "It's okay," he told her, reaching for his battered hiking boots. "You can laugh if it makes you feel better. I'm tough enough to take it."

Watching him sitting there with the late-morning sunlight creeping around the edges of the cheap motel blinds behind him, Chelsea suddenly realized that her guilt was getting worse. She'd misjudged this man. Perhaps not completely, since he was, after all, a man. But enough to make her feel ashamed.

God, when she thought about what could have happened if he hadn't shown up to rescue her, there was no "probably" about it. The guy was golden. A freaking saint!

Swallowing the lump of regret in her throat, she raised her knees beneath the sheet, wrapping her arms around them, and stared at the foot of the bed. "I'm sorry about all that crap I said to you before. I was wrong. You're not a jerk. And the truth is that I should…I should have listened to you about the club. I can't…or *couldn't,* because of Perry. But I know you were only trying to keep me out of trouble. And last night…" She shivered, pulling her knees closer to her chest, and forced herself to find his gaze again…and hold it. "It could have been so bad without you. If you hadn't rescued me, hadn't gotten me out of there, hadn't helped me afterward…I don't know what I would have done." She paused to take a deep breath, then quietly added, "You're a good man, Eric. And I'm sorry for misjudging you."

His expression was so guarded, it was difficult to read—but there was a smile in his voice as he said, "Yeah, well, I'm sorry for calling you an idiot."

Her mouth twitched. "But you're still thinking it, aren't you?"

"No. I get what you're doing. Hell, I'd be doing the same thing, if I were in your shoes. I just can't stand the thought of you putting yourself in danger like that. It really pissed me off."

"I noticed," she offered wryly, thinking of the men he'd had to fight to get her out of there. "And while I'm at it, thanks for getting my bus fixed, too." She didn't know how he'd done it, but when she'd woken up yester-day morning, there'd been a note slipped under her door that said her bus was in the parking lot and was ready to go, complete with a full tank of gas.

She'd refused to think about how disappointed she'd been when she found that note. Grateful, yes. But there'd been an uncomfortable surge of regret, as well. Stupidly, she'd been hoping to get one more look at Eric Drake, thinking that he might bring the bus down himself. But he hadn't. And she'd thought that was it. Thought she'd never see him again.

And now, in a bizarre turn of events, she'd spent the entire night with his hands on her body, thrusting inside her, making her come with violent, scorching waves of pleasure over and over again, until that damn drug had finally worked itself out of her system.

Finishing tying his second boot, he looked up and said, "I'm afraid the bus is probably a lost cause at this point."

She sighed. "I figured as much."

"Don't waste time worrying about it right now. We'll figure something out. The important thing is how you're feeling. Does your head hurt?"

Rubbing her forehead, she said, "I have a bit of a head-ache, but it's not too bad. And my eye hurts from where one of those jerks hit me. Is it bruised?"

"Just a little. We'll grab you some aspirin on our way out of town."

She gave a slow blink, feeling like she'd missed some-thing. "Uh...where are we going?"

He leaned back in the chair with his hands resting ca-sually on his muscular thighs, his gaze disturbingly di-rect, as if he was getting ready to bark out an order that he expected to be followed. But all that he said was, "First, let me ask you this. Are you going to keep searching for your sister?"

She raised her chin. "Yes."

"And you're low on money, aren't you?"

She started to splutter. "That's not any of your—"

He cut her off. "It's a waste of time for you to get embarrassed. It won't help anything, and I need you to be honest with me. How were you planning on paying for the search?"

She looked away for a moment, then back at him, shrugging her shoulders. "I decided yesterday that I was going to have to ask my parents to loan me some money. I've never had to do it before, but I put every cent to my name on the down payment for my condo. So all this *chasing down Perry* stuff couldn't have hit at a worse time. They really don't care about her one way or another, but I'm hoping they won't say no. If they come through, then I'll hopefully be able to hire someone who can help me track her down. If not, I'll sell some stuff and keep looking for her myself."

He leaned forward with his elbows braced on his parted knees, hands hanging loosely between his legs. It was one of those purely masculine poses that would have looked ridiculous on a woman, but fit a rugged guy like Eric to perfection. "Chelsea, you need to think about what's happened. There's a good chance I'd be signing your death warrant if I leave you here to deal with this on your own. And we need to make sure that you're doing okay after the effects of the drug."

Trying to hide her fear, she said, "I don't need any medical attention. I'm fine. And you've already done enough to help me, Eric. More than any other man would have, that's for sure, and I truly appreciate it. But this isn't your problem."

The brackets around his mouth deepened, his gray eyes glittering with streaks of silver that must have been a play of the light. "Those men from the club last night—they're not going to let you just walk away from this. They more than likely searched your wallet, which means they now know your name, your address. They have the kind of connections that will let them get to you if they want to, Chelsea, even if you decide to run."

"But you can stop them?"

He nodded. "With the help of my friends."

She licked her lips, then carefully said, "I don't understand."

This was the part Eric had been dreading. The part where he had to persuade her that taking off with him was her best possible option, and not a scenario right out of some B-rated horror flick.

With a tired sigh that no doubt matched some dark smudges of exhaustion under his eyes, he said, "I want you to come up to the mountains with me. I can keep you protected there."

"Would we be staying in the town where you live?"

"Not quite. Some friends of mine live with their wives in some cabins that aren't far from the town. It's the most secure place I can think of to take you. And not only will they help keep you safe, but they'll be able to help us figure out what's happened to your sister."

Tears glistened in her eyes as she asked, "What do you think has happened to her?"

"I don't know much more than you, Chelse. But based

on what Maggie told you, I think she's with a guy who has ties to the men who drugged you."

"Oh, God," she whispered, turning as white as a ghost.

"I hate to say it, but you need to be prepared for the worst—for the fact that Perry might already be dead."

Her throat worked as she swallowed, lashes fluttering as she tried to keep her tears from falling. "You think that's why they tried to keep me?"

"It could be. Or she could be somewhere they don't want you to find out about. And if she *is* still alive, coming with me is your best chance at getting her back."

For a moment, she just sat there, staring at some distant spot over his shoulder as she slowly rocked forward and back, the furrow on her brow telling him she was deep in thought. "What do you think it means?" she finally asked, bringing her worried gaze back to his. "The drug they gave me?"

Shaking his head, he said, "Nothing good."

"That's what I'm afraid of." She shuddered, looking scared, and it was an expression Eric knew he would probably see again before the day was over. If he took her to the Alley, the others would insist she be told the truth about their species. It should have bothered the hell out of him, since there was a chance she might never come within ten feet of him again, once she knew what he was. But that wasn't what was tying his insides into knots.

No, what really had him on edge was the fact that she'd be living right under his nose. There'd be nowhere for him to run, no way for him to escape, and he rolled his shoulder in a restless motion, feeling as if there was a cage closing in around him, trapping him inside.

Damn it, he should have never come down to Wesley. Should have never—

Yeah, and where would she be? his wolf asked.

Trapped, some other Lycan's plaything, at the mercy of his twisted instincts?

No, he couldn't have let that happen.

So it's time to suck it up and deal.

He choked back a snarl, irritated by the animal's gloating tone. It was getting exactly what it wanted, which was more time to figure out the puzzle. More time with the human…time that was going to drive him out of his bloody mind.

How the hell was he going to get through this without begging her for another taste? One he knew damn well might end in disaster.

Why? You made it through last night without hurting her.

Yeah. And maybe he'd just gotten lucky. Maybe he'd—

"Eric?"

The sound of her voice jerked him from his thoughts, yanking him back to the moment. "Yeah?"

"Where were you?"

"Sorry," he grated, scrubbing his palm over his stubbled jaw. "I was just thinking."

Her head tilted a little to the side, the look in her blue eyes deep and curious. "What about?" she murmured.

Moving to his feet, he said, "We can talk about it later. Right now, we need to get going. Are you coming with me?"

He could feel her following him with her gaze as he moved around the room. "Are you sure your friends are willing to help?"

"Yeah, I am. But it's going to take some trust on your part," he said, gathering her jeans and panties off the floor and tossing them in her lap. "Can you manage that?"

With a scarlet blush burning in her face, she clutched the clothes to her chest and took a deep breath. "I can try."

"Then let's hurry and get out of here," he muttered, hoping like hell that he wasn't making the biggest mistake of his life as she ducked back under the sheet to get dressed.

Chapter Seven

To Eric, driving up to the Alley felt like a journey into the Underworld, with him starring in the infamous role of Hades. The deeper they went into the forest, the sharper his awareness of their differences became. Of his true nature…and her inherent vulnerability. If he wasn't careful, there would be hell to pay—a single lapse in concentration or control bringing disastrous consequences. He felt as if he was tempting fate…thumbing his nose at rational, sane behavior. But his damn options were so limited. If he left her in Wesley, God only knew what kind of trouble she would get into…or what kind of trouble would find her.

No matter how he looked at it, the Alley really did seem like her best bet at surviving this nightmare—so long as he could keep himself on a tight leash.

Since they were both starved, they'd grabbed some breakfast sandwiches at a fast-food place before heading out of Wesley, as well as two large, steaming cups of coffee they were still sipping from, long after they'd made short work of the food. "So what was the story with the bus?" he asked, rolling his window down a little to let in some fresh air, since her scent was still seriously screwing with his head.

"What was wrong with it?" Tucking one leg under her body, she turned in her seat to face him. "It was… adorable."

"Adorable, huh?" Eric slid her a laughing look from the corner of his eye. "That's not exactly the image I think you'd go for. Did you have to buy it after losing a bet or something?"

"Not exactly." Pushing her hair behind her ear, she gave a low laugh. "To be honest, I was feeling a bit…rebellious, when I bought it."

He arched a brow. "Yeah?"

"I loved the bus as soon as I saw it, but only because I knew how much my father would hate it."

"And that was a good reason to buy it? Annoying your father?"

This time, when she laughed, there was a touch of bitterness to the husky sound. "You have no idea."

"You might be surprised," he murmured, thinking they just might have something in common, after all.

"Oh, yeah? Is your father a world-class bastard, as well?"

"He was." Just thinking about Stefan Drake had his insides twisting. "But he died five months ago."

"Oh." Her voice was soft. "Should I say I'm sorry?"

He snorted as he shook his head. "Only that it took so long to get rid of him."

"That bad?"

Giving her words back to her, he said, "You have no

idea." And he wanted to keep it that way. "What about your own?"

He could feel the force of her gaze against the side of his face as if it were a physical touch—could sense the rise in her tension like it was his own. For a moment, he didn't think she was going to answer, and then she turned her head forward, staring out the windshield, and said, "He's...not a nice man. Hateful. Angry. The biggest misogynist you could ever imagine. He can't even be bothered to worry about what's happened to Perry." The quiet words vibrated with a low frequency of rage. "When I called to tell him and my mother that she was missing, he actually said that it served her right for leaving home and that he hoped she got what she deserved."

Eric shot her a sharp look of disbelief. "And you thought this man would be willing to loan you money to keep searching for her?"

She gave a tired shrug. "Not without a long, drawn-out fight. And I probably would have had to sign over the deed to my condo."

"You'd have been willing to do that?"

When she nodded, he said, "She's a big girl, Chelsea. Why do you feel so responsible for her?"

Turning her head toward him again, she gave him a disappointed frown. "You have a sister. Wouldn't you feel responsible for tracking her down if she went missing?"

"I would." He almost tacked on a *But I'm a guy,* and caught himself just in time. There was no telling what she would have done to him if he'd made such a sexist comment. "But you've gone above and beyond the duty of a sister. There's a story there. That's all I'm saying."

She looked away again, and it was a moment before she started to give him an explanation. "There's a big age difference between me and Perry," she said in a quiet, kind of halting voice. "I left for college when she was only eleven. She was so upset, but I promised that I'd stay close, so I could be there for her if she ever needed me. But I didn't, and I wasn't."

"You were young," he murmured, understanding now that her actions were driven by the powerful combination of love and guilt. "You can't be blamed for wanting to get away from home and starting a life of your own."

"That's no excuse," she said, shaking her head as she wrapped her arms over her middle. "I knew what life was like with my father. How intolerable it was. It just…it felt so good to be away from him. I couldn't stand going back…so I didn't. Not like I should have."

"And so you and Perry grew apart?"

"Yeah." She sighed, then said, "I finally came back to Smythe last year, to be closer to her. But things have been so busy at the university, I've barely seen her since I started teaching."

"Women's Studies, right?" He kept his eyes on the road as he steered around a low-hanging branch from one of the forest trees, then slid her a wry grin. "What exactly is that, anyway?"

"We study the role of feminism in modern society, looking at social paradigms and how they relate to women, with a focus on how women are objectified and subjugated by men."

"Sounds intense," he remarked, making a mental note never to let his sister within twenty feet of this woman. There'd be no freaking living with her.

Obviously on a roll, Chelsea said, "Heaven and Hell is a perfect example of how women are diminished to the role of sexual objects in today's society."

"Can't argue with that." Feeling the need for a smoke, Eric reached for the pack of cigarettes he'd bought the day before and lit one up. After taking a few deep drags, he said, "But what I don't get is how your sister could have stomached working there."

"You wouldn't think it was so surprising if you knew Perry. She craves adventure. This is probably all some big adrenaline trip for her. She'll think it's all been a huge laugh, until she ends up dead in a ditch somewhere," she finished sourly.

They rounded the next bend in the road, and the conversation was suddenly forgotten as Chelsea leaned forward in her seat, staring through the windshield at the cabins up ahead that were just visible through the trees. "Is this it?"

"Yeah, this is the Alley."

"It's an unusual name."

"I've never really thought about it," he lied, knowing damn well that the name came from the racial slur "back-alley mongrels" that someone from the pack had once applied to the half-human Runners who lived there. He took another slow drag on the cigarette, needing it to calm the tension that was steadily building in his system.

"I mean, I always think of alleys as being dark and creepy. But this place is gorgeous."

Eric had to agree. The Alley *was* stunning, built in a secluded, slightly sloping glade and surrounded by the wild, natural beauty of the forest. It housed the Runners' individual residences, since they lived separately from the pack. There were ten cabins in all, though Runners only lived in six of them, with Eric taking the seventh. And thanks to some hard work, they had all the modern amenities there in the Alley, from power to hot water and high-speed internet access, just like they did up in Shadow Peak.

He parked the truck beneath the shade of an oak tree,

beside one of the rustic, porch-fronted structures. "This is the cabin I use when I'm here."

Climbing out of the truck, Chelsea took a deep breath of the crisp, fresh mountain air, her eyes a little wide as she took in the surreal setting. Sunlight filtered into the clearing through the leafy trees, casting dazzling splotches of gold across the grassy carpet. It was like something out of a fairy tale, which sent a shiver of unease down her spine. Fairy tales always came with monsters, and she couldn't help but feel that there was something *unnatural* about this strange, primordial place.

"What's wrong?" he asked, obviously noticing her shiver as he came around the front of the truck to join her.

"I don't know. I just get the feeling that there's something...different about this place." Turning to face him, she asked, "What is it you said your friends do again?"

"They hunt a lot, among other things."

A frown wove its way between her brows. "You mean animals? Or people? Are they like bounty hunters?"

"You could say that," he drawled under his breath, avoiding her gaze as he flicked his cigarette into the damp grass and crushed it out with the tip of his boot.

"Hmm. I seem to be *saying* everything, doing all the talking, while you're being evasive."

Bringing his gaze back to hers, he said, "Look, I know there's a lot I need to explain. I just need you to be patient a little longer for me. Can you do that?"

"I guess I can try," she muttered, wishing he would just talk to her now, rather than later. What was he waiting for?

As he held her stare, something primal and hot burned in his heavy gaze, the gray of his eyes looking impossibly bright in the dappled sunlight. "I promise that you're safe here, Chelsea. I wouldn't have brought you here if you weren't."

"I just don't like not knowing what's going on. Especially given the circumstances. I mean, I don't even really know you."

"And despite everything that's happened," Eric said in a low voice, "you still don't trust me, either. Do you?" He couldn't help but feel a little bitter about that, considering everything he'd done to protect her.

She got that pinched look that some women got when they were pissed. "That's not fair."

Eric snorted. "Yeah, well, life's like that. And you're old enough to have realized it by now."

"What's wrong with you?" She sounded baffled, and maybe even a little hurt. "Why are you acting like this?"

Because he was stupid, that's why. Even though he knew anything between them was a nightmare in the making, his freaking feelings were hurt by the fact that she wasn't happy about being stuck with him. He could see it in her eyes…hear it in her voice. And she was going to be even less happy when she learned what he was. It wouldn't be right to keep it from her, with her staying here, and he wouldn't do that to her. But he knew what it would cost him. Knew the wedge would be driven even deeper between them, and it pissed him off, tapping into some growing pool of anger that churned inside him.

He was losing her before he'd ever even had her, damn it, and it made him want to throw back his head and let out a long, furious, bloodcurdling howl.

Not that he could explain any of that to her. She'd probably just shoot back some smartass comment about how he must have missed his meds, and he figured he could do without the humiliation.

"Come on," he grunted, jerking his chin toward the cabin. "I'll show you around inside."

He grabbed her pack from the truck, and they made their way up the porch and through the front door, into an open living area with high ceilings, the dining room and kitchen sectioned off from a large sitting room by a row of low bookshelves. The floors were hardwood, the walls painted the color of pale cream, with sturdy, rugged leather sofas and chairs.

Eric couldn't take any credit for the decorating, since it had all been Elise's doing—but he enjoyed the way Chelsea's eyes widened, her jaw dropping a little as she looked around the place.

"The bathroom is in the back, between the master and guest bedrooms," he told her, setting her bag down by one of the coffee-colored sofas. "Clean towels are under the sink. And there should be plenty of hot water, if you want to take a shower. I can grab mine later."

"Thanks."

"Are you tired?"

"Exhausted," she admitted, covering a small yawn.

"Well, after your shower, you can lie down for a while and rest. Feel free to choose the master or the guestroom. But don't go outside without me. I've got to run out for a while, so just wait for me to get back."

Caution crept into her gaze, and he could detect a sliver of fear in her mouthwatering scent. "You make it sound like I'm some kind of prisoner."

"Not at all," he said, shaking his head. "I just need to bring the others up to date on what's going on, and I don't want you wandering around getting lost. I'll send Torrance over to keep you company."

That sliver of fear began to bleed into angry frustration. "I don't need a babysitter, Eric. And who is Torrance?"

"She's the wife of a friend named Mason. They live in one of the cabins here. You'll like her, so be nice."

"I always am!" she snapped, looking thoroughly insulted, her pale cheeks flushing with color.

He didn't even bother to comment. He just snorted again.

"Though you're being exceptionally rude—" she glared as she picked her pack up, settling it on her shoulder "—I'm still going to say thank-you again. For what you did last night."

Her prickly tone goaded him into deliberately riling her. "Not necessary," he drawled, giving her a slow smile. "You don't ever have to thank me for making you come, Chelse."

If he hadn't been so irritated, he would have thought her reaction was priceless. She stumbled back a step, big blue eyes going all wide and shocked again. "I meant for *helping* me at the club," she said after a moment, each word formed with slow, careful enunciation. "And you *can* be such a jerk!"

"Yeah. And you can be an uptight little bitch." His gaze followed her stiff form as she stormed across the room. "We sound perfect for each other!"

"You wish!" she shot back over her shoulder. A second later, the bathroom door slammed shut, and Eric stood there in the middle of the floor with his arms crossed over his chest, wondering what exactly had just happened.

He wanted nothing more than to follow her into the bathroom, and right into the damn shower, but forced himself to make a quick change into some clean clothes, before heading back outside. It was necessary to put some distance between them, since each moment he spent in her company took him that much closer to the edge. Christ, the woman already had him acting like a friggin' idiot!

As he headed down the sloping glade, he caught sight of the Runners and three of their mates standing on Mason Dillinger's front porch, each and every one of them watching him, as if they'd been waiting for him to make an appearance. For a moment, he wondered what the hell they were all doing, just hanging around together in the middle of the day, then realized they'd probably planned to get together for lunch so that they could gossip about *him*.

"Where's the human?" Jeremy called out, a bottle of beer clasped in one hand, while his other arm was wrapped around Jillian's waist, holding her close to his side.

Hands shoved deep in his pockets, Eric made his way over to the cabin. "She's grabbing a shower."

Brody Carter stood near his wife, Michaela, his auburn hair hanging loose around his shoulders, while Cian lounged in one of the rocking chairs that had been placed to the left of the front door. The others were all either sitting in wicker chairs or standing with one hip hitched up on the porch railing, like Mason.

Keeping the chair rocking with one foot, the other perched on his opposite knee, Cian lifted his nose and sniffed at the air as Eric got nearer to the group. A deep sound of appreciation rumbled in the back of the Runner's throat, as if he'd caught the scent of something good. "Damn, Drake. Your human smells tasty."

Eric stopped in his tracks on the bottom porch step, his hands fisted in his pockets, and cut a narrowed-eyed glare at the grinning Irishman. "Don't even think about it, Hennessey."

"Think about what?" Cian asked, arching one ebony brow. "How good she smells?"

"About *her*," he forced through his gritted teeth. *"At all."*

The Runner threw back his head and laughed. "Oh, man, this is too classic."

Eric slid a dark look toward Brody, who appeared to be fighting back a smile. Damn traitor. "Shut your friend up, Carter, before I do it for you."

"Aw, come on," Cian drawled. "I'm your friend, too. You just have to learn to put up with me." A lopsided grin kicked up the corner of the Runner's wide mouth, his voice a little softer as he said, "And it's easier if you just give in."

"There's nothing to give in to," he muttered, something about Hennessey's tone telling him he wasn't going to like where this conversation was headed.

"S'that right?"

Eric could tell the Runner was no longer talking about the two of them. He was talking about him and Chelsea. "You need to back off, asshole."

A sharp burst of laughter rumbled in Brody's broad chest. "Come on, Drake. You can't blame Cian for the yearning state of your heart. It's written all over your pretty face. He's just calling it like he sees it."

Eric's lip curled as he snarled at the grinning Bloodrunner. "Her goddamn life is in danger. That's the only reason she's here. My heart has nothing to do with it."

"Hmm, I don't know," Brody murmured, slowly stroking his jaw as he played up his study of Eric's belligerent expression, his deep green eyes shining with humor. "I mean, you *do* look like you've been bitten by the love bug, man. Big-time."

"Piss off," he grunted as he headed up the steps, looking forward to knocking the stupid grin right off Brody's face. Just because he'd said similar words to the Runner when he'd been fighting his need for Michaela didn't lessen his anger, though he knew he was feeling more frustration than anything else.

"Enough!" Mason barked, the gruff command at odds with the crooked grin on his face as he stepped in front of Eric, blocking his advance. Looking at the others, Mason said, "Let's take this inside before the poor guy blows a fuse."

"It's at times like this that I wonder why I put up with you," Eric muttered, following the others inside as they all made their way to the kitchen.

"You talking about me?" Brody asked with an expression of mock devastation as he leaned back against one of the counters, a grinning Michaela at his side. "I'm crushed, man. Crushed."

"I'm talking about *all* of you," he snapped, which had the crazy jackasses laughing and slapping him on the shoulder, as if he was meant to enjoy their ribbing when his goddamn life was being turned upside down.

"So bring us up to date, starting from the beginning," Mason said, once everyone had made it inside and cold sodas had been passed around, along with a few cold beers. "Jeremy filled us in as much as he could, but I want to make sure we're all on the same page."

Crossing his arms over his chest, Eric leaned back against a counter and told them the story, starting with the call from the scouts on Friday night, then taking them through to that morning, without any unnecessary details about the effects of the drug Chelsea had been given... and what he'd had to do to ease her way through them.

"So you just left her at the Travelodge in Wesley on Friday night and drove away?" Mason asked, the corners of his mouth dipping with a frown. "You didn't think to put a set of eyes on her?"

"No." He grabbed his beer off the counter, took a long

drink, then wiped his mouth and said, "To be honest, it never occurred to me that she wouldn't listen when I told her to get her little ass out of town."

Brody laughed. "You're such an alpha, Eric. You think too much like a wolf. But she's human. A stubborn one, from the sound of it. She doesn't think like pack."

His response was wry. "Trust me, I noticed."

"So now that she's here, what's the plan?" Cian asked, propping the kitchen chair he was sitting on on its back legs. That was one of the things Eric had noticed about the Runner once he'd started spending so much time at the Alley. The guy was always in motion, never quite managing to sit still.

Before Eric could answer Hennessey's question, Mason said, "You're going to have to trust her with our secret. We don't allow humans to stay here without knowing."

"If her sister is where I think she is," he said, shrugging his shoulders, "she's going to learn the truth eventually, anyway. Might as well be now."

"Are you going to do it?" Brody asked.

"Hell, no. She doesn't exactly trust me."

This time, it was Cian who laughed. "Smart girl."

"Who, then?" Mason asked.

"Torrance, if she doesn't mind," he replied. "I thought it might be best, since she's human and still pretty new to our world." Part of him felt like a coward for not doing it himself, but his gut told him this was the kindest way for Chelsea to learn the truth about his species.

"I don't mind," Torrance said with a smile, her green eyes soft with understanding.

"Take Jillian with you when you go over," Mason murmured, pride and protectiveness burning in his gaze as he spoke to his wife.

She nodded. "Good idea. And I'll take Michaela, too."

"I'll stay here," Carla Reyes, the lone female Runner, murmured, speaking up for the first time. "The last thing this woman needs is me there freaking her out."

Her partner, Wyatt, snorted from his place on Eric's right. "Yeah, you *are* pretty freaky, ReyRey."

Carla replied with a sharp smile, looking ready to go for blood, but Mason put the conversation back on track before things got out of hand. "Then that's settled. Torry, Jillian and Mic will go over and talk with Chelsea this afternoon. Which brings us to the next problem."

"Figuring out what we're going to do about the idiot assholes running things at that club," Jeremy supplied, his gruff tone making it clear what he thought of the situation. He sounded as ready to kick ass as Eric felt, but this wasn't a situation they were going to be able to charge right into.

"Jeremy's right," he said. "But first, we need to know exactly what we're dealing with." Pushing away from the counter, Eric hooked the empty chair in front of him with his foot and joined those who were sitting around the kitchen table. "We need to find out why they have all those human girls working there, and what the hell they're doing with the drug they used on Chelsea. We also need to find out if the Youngblood pack has finally washed their hands of the Donovans. That might explain their partnership with the Whiteclaw."

"Either that," Wyatt offered, his dark eyes hard with worry, "or they're looking to beef up their numbers because they plan on making a move against us. The whole goddamn region knows we're ripe for the picking."

"Shit," Brody muttered, pulling a hand down his scarred face. "We could have handled the Whiteclaw or the Donovans on their own, but they're going to be a pain in the ass together. We should have seen this coming."

Mason shook his head, a disgusted look on his face.

"We've been so focused on keeping the pack together, we've lost sight of what's happening around us. We've been worried about the troublemakers who wander onto our land, when it's the ones controlling things beyond our borders that we need to be focusing on. The ones plotting in the background. It could turn out to be a mistake that ends up costing us."

"It's more than likely already costing those girls at that club," Eric said grimly, finishing off his beer with a final swallow. "We need to know what's going on down there. And to find out what's happened to Chelsea's sister. Whoever the girl is with, it's someone who has a connection to that place."

"Wyatt and I can get a surveillance group on the club," Carla said, "but it would help if we could get to someone on the inside of the operation. Is there anyone we can talk to from either the Whiteclaw or the Donovan family who might give us some answers?"

Sayre Murphy's soft voice floated in from the hallway. "You could ask Sophia Dawson."

Jeremy sighed as he shot a chastising look toward the empty archway. "Sayre, what have I told you about eavesdropping on Bloodrunner business?"

A second later, his sister-in-law came into view, an impish grin on her face. At eighteen, she still looked more like a girl than a woman, though it was clear she was going to be a stunner, with those blue-gray eyes and all that curly, strawberry-blond hair. Eric pitied the poor boys up in Shadow Peak who would no doubt lose their hearts to the waifish girl.

"I didn't mean to overhear," she explained, "but Torrance said I could use the computer in the office, and your voices just drifted in. If you didn't want to be heard, you shouldn't have been talking so loud."

Looking as if she was fighting back a smile, Jillian said, "Sayre, what did you mean about Sophia?"

Pushing her hands in her pockets, the girl propped her shoulder against the archway. "She was dating this guy from the Whiteclaw pack last summer. His name is Brandon something or other."

"What happened?" Cian asked, and from the corner of his eye Eric could see that the Runner was watching Sayre like a hawk about to go in for the kill.

Sayre's grin faded as she shifted her gaze over to the Irishman. "She broke things off because he started giving her the creeps. Got too serious on her."

"She got commitment issues?" Cian murmured, locking his hands behind his dark head as he regarded her with a hard, steely stare.

With a shrug, she said, "I can't say, Hennessey. You'd know more about that than I would."

Cian scowled. "I've never laid a finger on Sophia Dawson."

Sayre gave an exaggerated gasp. "Wow. You mean there's actually a woman in this state over the age of eighteen who you haven't nailed? I'm shocked. But I was referring to your own commitment issues. I figure it takes one to know one."

The kitchen went unusually silent, everyone seeming a little stunned by the strange interchange between the womanizing Runner and Sayre. Finally, Mason cleared his throat and said, "What does everyone think of Sayre's suggestion?"

In Eric's opinion, the idea had potential. If Sophia went to see Brandon in Hawkley, the Whiteclaw pack's hometown, she might even be able to get close to Perry, if that's where the girl had been taken. Sophia and Perry were close in age, and lived similar lifestyles from the sound of things, despite the fact that one was human and the other a Lycan. They might meet up by chance in the town, or even be introduced, depending on how willing Brandon was to cooperate.

They all weighed in with their opinions, the consensus seeming to be that so long as Sophia didn't do anything to put herself in danger, their best bet of getting some quick intel was to send her to Hawkley to question this Brandon guy.

"Okay," Sayre said. "I'll call Sophia and ask her if she can come down to the Alley in the morning. Just watch out for Max. He's going to be pissed if she agrees." Max Doucet was Brody's nineteen-year-old brother-in-law. He was also a human who had been changed to Lycan by a rogue wolf, and a soon-to-be Runner in training.

"They're not dating now, are they?" Michaela asked, looking concerned. Considering the fact that Sophia had a reputation for being a party girl who often got involved with the wrong crowd, Eric didn't blame her. He knew exactly what it felt like to be protective of a sibling. Especially one who had known their share of grief.

"Not yet," Sayre replied. "But it hasn't been for lack of trying. Max likes her. A lot."

Leaning back in his chair, Eric rubbed one hand against the edge of his jaw. "I think I should pay the Whiteclaw a visit, as well. Explain what I was doing at the club."

"Oh, yeah?" Jeremy asked, lifting his brows. "And what explanation will you give them for the dead guy you left behind?"

Eric rolled his shoulder. "I'll just make it clear that I had unfinished business with the human and he got in the way."

"I gotta hand it to you, Drake. You are one ballsy son

of a bitch," Wyatt murmured, slapping him on the back as he headed toward the refrigerator for another beer.

"I also think we should have Monroe run a trace on Perry Smart's number." Monroe was a Fed whose sister was married to a male from the pack and a good friend of the Runners. "I doubt it'll turn anything up, since they're probably expecting it, but it can't hurt to try."

"If you get me the number," Mason said, "I'll call Monroe."

Eric gave him a nod. "I just have to get it from Chelsea."

"Good. And now that we're done with that for the moment…" Cian drawled, lowering his arms as he leaned forward and braced his elbows on the table. He settled his dark gaze on Eric. "Let's get back to the juicy topic of the day."

"Yeah? And what would that be?"

"*You,* boyo."

With a tired sigh, Eric scrubbed his hands down his face, wishing the Runner would leave him the hell alone. "You can cut down on all the drama, Hennessey. Chelsea Smart is *not* my mate."

The Irishman lifted his brows. "You sure about that?"

Wyatt snorted. "I think he'd be able to tell if she was."

"Would he?"

Wyatt rolled his eyes. "From what I've been told. Didn't your mama ever teach you about scent recognition?"

"That's how it works for the rest of us, yeah. But who knows with a dark wolf? Those feckers are weird. I mean, just look at the one we have right here."

Eric responded by flipping the Runner off, which had all of them laughing.

"Ah, Drake," Cian murmured, balancing his chair on its back legs again as he tipped his beer at him and grinned. "This is gonna be so much fun to watch."

Chapter Eight

After a long, scalding shower to soothe her sore muscles, Chelsea had snuggled up on the queen-size bed in the guestroom and crashed. She didn't know how long she'd slept, but it was dark outside when she finally pulled herself out of bed.

As she made her way back to the bathroom to brush her teeth, she was still a little stunned by how beautiful Eric's home was. When he'd told her about the Alley, she'd imagined wilderness living, but the cabin was fully modernized, with gleaming hardwood floors and a rugged décor that looked like something out of a Pottery Barn catalogue. And the techno gadgets she'd seen when she passed by his office were all upscale and current. She still wasn't quite sure what he and his friends did for a living, but whatever it was, they sure as hell weren't hurting for money.

With her brush in hand, working out the tangles in her

hair, Chelsea made her way from the bathroom, down the hallway, and found three women sitting on the sofas in the living room. They all moved to their feet as she entered the room, making it clear they'd been waiting for her. A petite redhead with big green eyes introduced herself as Torrance, explaining that she lived there in the Alley with her husband, Mason, who was a friend of Eric's. The beautiful blonde was named Jillian, and Chelsea thought the name sounded familiar. With a warm smile, Jillian told her that she was married to Jeremy and they lived in the cabin nearest to Eric's. The last woman was a stunning brunette who was married to a guy named Brody, and the couple also had a cabin there in the Alley.

"It's nice to meet you all," Chelsea said, feeling a little stunned. They were so beautiful they made her feel like a frumpy schoolmarm.

Torrance perched on the arm of the nearest sofa. "Eric tells us you're a professor."

"That's right," she replied, thinking, *Oh, God. I really am a schoolmarm!* "I teach Women's Studies at the university in Smythe."

"Wow," the one who'd introduced herself as Michaela remarked with a friendly smile. "That sounds so interesting."

"It is. Though I have a feeling it's not nearly as interesting as things around here," she murmured, getting the uncomfortable feeling that these women had been sent to the cabin for a reason—and not just to make friendly chitchat.

"Yeah," Jillian drawled, tucking a strand of blond hair behind her ear. "This place is something else. In fact—" she gave Chelsea a sheepish grin "—that's actually what we're here to talk about."

"Oh?" Chelsea felt a sickly smile settle on her lips, wondering what in God's name they were about to tell her. Was this one of those freaky love communes? A religious cult? Some kind of underground militant movement ready to take over the world?

"Let's get some coffee on first," Torrance said, no doubt sensing Chelsea's panic. "I think we're going to need it."

Michaela gave a smoky laugh. "It might take something stronger, Torry."

"A bottle of wine, then?" Torrance asked, heading for the kitchen area that was all decked out in terracotta stone and stainless-steel appliances.

"I think we left a nice red here the other day," Jillian said. "Just grab that and I'll get the glasses."

When they were all settled back in the living room, wine in hand, Torrance, who was sitting with Michaela on the opposite sofa, started the conversation. "First of all, how are you doing?"

Chelsea took a deep breath, trying not to be nervous, and said, "Pretty well, considering the circumstances. Eric's not exactly the easiest person to get along with, but I owe him for saving my life last night."

Jillian, who was sitting beside her, gently patted her knee. "Be patient with him, Chelsea. He's had a hard time of it lately. So if he comes off a bit rough at times, don't hold it against him."

She wanted to ask for details, but held back, since it felt wrong to be doing it behind his back. But once she found out what the big secret was, she knew there was a possibility that her opinion might change. If something weird was going on here, she was going to want to know everything that she could.

Setting her wineglass on the low coffee table, Torrance leaned forward, resting her crossed arms on her knees, and carefully said, "Chelsea, it's important that you know we're all here for you, and we all want to see your sister make it out of this safely. But to do that, there's something we need to talk about."

"All right," she whispered, wetting her lips, painfully aware of her pulse coming faster…and faster, roaring like the engine of a train that just kept gaining in speed, shooting down the tracks with no concern for either her safety *or* her sanity.

Please, God, don't let it be anything weird. Or scary. Or creepy…

Torrance took a deep breath, then quietly said, "I know this is going to seem like a strange question, but what do you know about Lycans?"

She blinked, not certain she understood. "You mean like in the *Underworld* movies? The werewolves?"

A soft smile touched the corner of the redhead's mouth. "Yes. That's one interpretation."

Chelsea wet her lips again, surprised to find that they felt a little numb. No matter how nice these women were, she had a really bad feeling about where this was going. "I know that they're not real."

"Actually, they are."

Another slow blink, her chest aching as her heart began to pound to a hard, jarring rhythm. "Excuse me?"

"Eric and the others," Torrance told her. "They're Lycans, Chelsea."

She quickly shifted her gaze to Michaela and Jillian, hoping to see a grinning face so that she'd know this was just some kind of stupid joke—but they were both watching her with expressions of worry and determination. If she asked, they would both tell her that the words Torrance had just uttered were totally and completely true.

Ohmyfreakinggod…

Panic had her throat feeling tight, as if strong hands

were wrapped around it, squeezing her air off. "You're serious, aren't you?" she gasped, panting, unable to control the violent tremor that was shooting through her arms and legs. "This…this isn't a joke, is it?"

She would have loved to think these women were just delusional, but then wouldn't Eric have warned her? And she couldn't quite get the feeling out of her head that she'd seen something at the club when Eric had been fighting the guy with the blond hair. An inhuman flash of fangs? And then there was the way Eric's gray eyes sometimes seemed to glow with an unnatural light. She'd been telling herself that she must have just imagined those things—but that no longer seemed the case.

"I'm sorry, Chelsea," Jillian murmured, gently rubbing her back, as if she were a child who needed comfort. "I know it seems scary, but it's going to be all right. From everything that Eric has told us about you, we know that you're strong enough to handle this. There aren't many who know the secret, so we're placing a tremendous amount of trust in you by revealing the truth. Just take a deep breath and try to calm down, okay?"

She could feel herself nodding, and while her thoughts continued to churn in a dizzying swirl of confusion, she listened as the women explained about the Silvercrest Lycan pack that lived up on the top of the mountain, in the town called Shadow Peak. Then they explained about the Lycans they believed were involved at the club, and finally about the five men and one woman who lived there in the Alley. About how they were half human, half Lycan hunters whose job it was to protect the secret of their race from the human world, as well as to hunt down any wolves who turned rogue and became a threat to their human neighbors. They even told her why the Runners lived separately from the pack, explaining about the social divide that had always existed between those who were "pure-bloods" and the half-breed Runners.

"And Eric," she said, her voice tight with strain, "he's one of the full-blooded Lycans? A pure-blood?"

"That's right," Jillian told her, refilling Chelsea's glass.

She took a deep swallow of the wine, needing it to warm her insides, while trying to wrap her head around everything they'd said. "But he's friends with the Runners? He stays here in the Alley?"

Jillian nodded. "Unlike a lot of the Lycans in Shadow Peak, Eric's never bought into all their elitist nonsense. He really is a good guy, Chelse. If he wasn't, I promise I'd tell you." A grin touched the corner of Jillian's lips. "After all, we women need to stick together, right?"

She downed the rest of her wine, set the glass back on the table and exhaled in an audible rush. "Okay," she breathed out, bracing her elbows on her knees and dropping her face into her hands, "just let me think for a minute."

"Take all the time you need," Torrance told her. "We'll be in the kitchen when you're ready to talk."

Chelsea listened as they walked away, still struggling to stay calm, and hoping she could find a rational way to accept and deal with this new strange, mind-boggling reality she'd been presented with. More than anything, she knew she couldn't afford to get hysterical, though the idea was certainly tempting. But if this was the world that Perry had gotten her stupid little ass mixed up in, then she was going to need Eric and his friends' help. She couldn't handle something like this on her own. It was too unfamiliar—too unknown. She was out of her depth, and she knew it. So she had to slip over the customary freak-out period she normally would have allowed herself, and face reality like a big girl.

She might cry herself to sleep tonight out of sheer emotional exhaustion, but damn it, she wouldn't fall apart before then.

Hoping her legs would keep her steady, Chelsea moved to her feet. She ran her fingers through her drying hair, smoothed them over her shirt, then reached for her wineglass and carried it into the kitchen, where she could hear the three women quietly talking.

"Is there any way to kill them?" she asked, joining the women at a small, but beautifully polished breakfast table.

Torrance frowned. "Are you planning on trying to off one of them? Because we'll definitely take exception to that."

She shook her head, her fingers nervously twisting the stem of her glass as she said, "I just want to know what I'm dealing with. Do silver bullets work?"

The recessed lighting in the high ceiling made Michaela's dark hair look midnight-blue as she reached over and patted her hand. "This isn't a movie, Chelsea. Bullets can slow them down, no matter what they're made from, but they don't kill them."

"What does?"

Torrance still looked cautious. "Why do you want to know?"

Michaela slid an understanding look at her worried friend. "It's okay, Torry. She's not looking to murder anyone. She's just scared."

"You don't need to be," Jillian told her, going to the fridge and grabbing them each a bottle of water. "Not of Eric and the Runners. They're golden. They'd die before letting anything happen to a woman or child. But to answer your question," she said, sliding back into her seat and twisting the cap off her water, "a Lycan *can* be killed if they get cut up too badly and bleed out. But the only way to really make sure they won't heal from their wounds is to snap their spinal columns or remove their head from their shoulders."

"But deaths from bleeding out don't happen often," Torrance added. "Jillian is a miracle worker."

"What do you mean?" Chelsea asked, opening her water and taking a drink, the cold liquid feeling like heaven in her dry throat.

Pushing her hair behind her ear again, Jillian slid her a wry look from the corner of her eye. "I'm the pack's Spirit Walker."

It must have been clear from her expression that she didn't understand, because Michaela said, "She's like their holy woman, Chelsea. Their healer."

Realization slammed her between the eyes like a two-by-four. "You're…one of them?" she wheezed, coughing, thankful she hadn't just taken another sip of water, since she'd have spewed it all over the table.

"My parents are both Lycan, so yes, I'm one of them," Jillian said in a friendly, but matter-of-fact tone, as if she'd just admitted that her parents were members of Costco, instead of a shape-shifting wolf pack. "But as a Spirit Walker, I can't take the shape of a wolf."

"Oh." Chelsea pulled her lower lip through her teeth, but couldn't think of anything else to say. She never would have guessed that the beautiful blonde's parents were werewolves. But then she never would have guessed that Eric was one, either. Oh, she'd known he was alpha and rugged and more than a little primal—but only in an athletic, purely masculine, sex-god kind of way. The idea that he might grow fangs and claws and howl at the moon had never even crossed her mind.

"I know it's a lot to take in right away," Torrance murmured, "but you'll get used to it."

She gave a short, dry laugh and shook her head. "Oh, I doubt I'll be here long enough to get used to it."

Jillian's brows lifted with surprise. "Really? Eric's going to let you leave here unprotected?"

"Eric doesn't have any say in it," she replied a little more sharply than she'd intended, but the idea that she needed his permission set her on edge. "Once I've got Perry, we're going home."

Torrance's voice was soft. "And what if Perry doesn't want to go home? It sounds like she's pretty crazy about this guy she went after."

Chelsea felt a little sick inside. "I don't know," she admitted, not wanting to even consider that gut-churning scenario. "If that happens, I'll just have to do whatever it takes to make her see reason."

"You know those men from that club could be watching your condo," Jillian pointed out. "It won't be safe for you there."

"Then we'll find somewhere else to stay. But we both have lives to get back to. We can't stay here forever."

Jillian looked as though she was going to argue, but a quick glance from Torrance stopped her. Instead, they talked more about the Runners while Michaela reheated the lasagna they'd brought over for her dinner. While she ate at the small table, the women told her stories about the men they'd fallen in love with, and it became clear that even though the Runners were fiercely protective and possessive, they weren't overbearing about it. Instead, they were true partners, giving back as much as they took, and if even half of what the women said was true, it was obvious that they were incredible husbands. They were also madly, desperately in love with their wives.

After the delicious meal and a hot cup of coffee, Chelsea found herself relaxing to the point that she could finally enjoy herself. Torrance, Jillian and Michaela were wonderful women who sounded like they had found themselves some equally wonderful men. Chelsea didn't believe it happened often—but it clearly seemed to have happened for these three.

"Before we go," Jillian said, after they'd decided it was time to call it a night, "I just want to tell you that you're in good hands, Chelsea. Men don't come any better than Eric." She must have read something in her expression, because her tone turned wry as she added, "I know he's probably acted like a bit of a jerk at times, but I think he's just being defensive. It's clear that there's some kind of connection between the two of you, and I'm sure he's been worried about how you were going to take the truth about what he is. He's probably been thinking that once you knew, you wouldn't go near him again."

The words put a strange ball of warmth in her chest, her mind looking over their interchange that afternoon with new, startled eyes. "But he seems so confident," she murmured. "Arrogant, even."

Jillian laughed. "I know, but then he's an alpha. Arrogance comes second nature to guys like him." She grinned, saying, "And I know it might seem like it at times, but *alpha* isn't a synonym for *asshole*. Keep him in his place, but just…do me a favor and cut the guy some slack every now and then. I love him like a brother, and I want him to be happy."

"He's lucky to have you," Chelsea said, truly meaning it. "All of you."

"And we're lucky to have him." Jillian started to make her way outside, but stopped at the door to look back and say one more thing: "Just remember that you have him, too, Chelse."

* * *

Taking a long, satisfying drag from the last cigarette in his pack, Eric decided he'd wasted enough time wandering through the forest and headed back to the Alley. He'd tried to stay focused throughout the long afternoon, while Chelsea had slept, but his thoughts had kept fixating on the human. On how she was feeling and if she was sleeping well. On whether or not she was still pissed at him for acting like an ass when they'd reached the Alley. On how it would feel if he was ever lucky enough to get her in his bed. He'd actually spent a lot of time thinking about *that,* even though he knew it was something that shouldn't happen.

Then, as the hour had grown late and he knew she'd probably woken up, he couldn't stop thinking about how she was taking the news from Torrance, Jillian and Michaela. The worry was driving him out of his friggin' mind.

Thankfully, he caught sight of Jillian the moment he entered the Alley, just as she was heading up the front steps to the cabin she shared with Jeremy. She turned as soon as he called her name, a small smile on her lips when she saw him. "Hey, you."

"How'd she take it?"

Tucking a pale strand of hair behind her ear, she propped her shoulder against a porch beam and said, "Better than I thought she would. I think it's going to take a while for her to get comfortable with the idea, but she has an open mind. She'll be able to accept it. She just needs a little time to process everything that she's learned."

"But she's okay?" he asked, stubbing out the cigarette with his boot and shoving his hands in his pockets. "She isn't freaking out?"

"She's doing fine. We got some wine in her, then fed

her some lasagna, and gave her some coffee. But she's still tired. I think the drug was pretty hard on her system. We only just left, but she's probably already out for the count again in your guestroom."

"Oh. That's, uh, good, then."

Jillian gave him a knowing smile, as if she knew exactly how disappointed he was that he wouldn't get the chance to talk to the human again until tomorrow. "I like her, Eric. She's got backbone."

"What does Michaela think?" Though human, Michaela had the ability to read others' emotions—a skill that had come in handy for their group during the nightmare with his father.

"Mic says that she's worried and scared, but that she has a lot of inner strength. She also has a good heart—we think it's just been a little bruised somewhere along the way. She tries not to get too emotional about the people who are close to her, but it isn't because she's cold or uncaring. It's just the way she tries to protect herself from being hurt."

"She craves control," he murmured, thinking it was another thing they had in common. But while Chelsea wanted to protect herself from the world, Eric worried about protecting the world from himself.

Softly, she said, "She thinks you're going to let her go back home."

His wolf seethed, snarling with fury and frustration inside his head, but he simply gritted his teeth and said, "When this is over, she has to. She shouldn't be here. Humans and wolves don't mix."

"Whoa." Jillian's brown eyes went wide. "Is that your father talking?"

"I'm not a racist," he ground out, while a muscle started

to pulse in his jaw. "But for those like me, it isn't safe. You know that."

"And what about the Whiteclaw and the Donovans?"

His voice was getting harder. "I'll deal with them."

"For her?"

"Because they need to be dealt with," he growled, shoving his hands deeper in his pockets before he did something stupid, like put his fist through a tree in a childish display of temper. Jillian would never let him live it down.

"Eric, why can't you just admit the truth?" Her head tilted a bit to the side as she studied him. "You want her."

A grim smile twisted his lips. "Yeah. But is it for the right reasons, or the wrong ones?"

Frowning, she said, "I don't believe this. You're worried about what happened with your dad, aren't you?"

"Wouldn't you be?" he asked, his tone dry.

"Eric, you can't keep doing this. You've got to have faith in yourself. You're your own man. He doesn't have any hold over you."

His gaze slid away, focusing on the dark sway of the trees as the wind rustled through their branches. "You sure about that, Jilly?" he asked in a soft, almost silent rasp.

"Completely. But you need to stop distancing yourself from everyone and take a chance on finding happiness."

"If you're talking about finding a woman," he murmured, cutting her a wary glance, "I'm not looking for a relationship."

"And maybe it's about damn time you did." She sighed, her tone softening. "You'd make an incredible mate, Eric. And a wonderful father."

The surprising sentiment snagged his attention like a fish hooked on a line, and he mentally chewed on it, intrigued by the flavor. A family? Marriage? He didn't care for it, but the idea was definitely something to think about, if for no other reason than the fact that he *had* noted the differences between his life and the life that a few of the Runners had recently found for themselves. During the build-up to his father's maniacal plans, three of the lucky sons of bitches had found their life mates. They were now so blissed-out in love it was hard to look at them and re- member what they'd been like before, almost as if the hol- lows of their lives had been filled with…with something he didn't even know how to describe, a sense of belonging now replacing the bitterness they'd carried not so long ago.

Was it really a woman, then, that he was craving? Was that what had made him so restless and edgy lately? Christ, he hoped not.

If that's it, I'm screwed, he thought, a deep-rooted scowl slowly spreading over his face like a shadow fall- ing over the ground, while a fresh burst of frustration roiled through him with the searing, blistering burn of a flame. After all, what were his odds of ever finding her— the woman who was meant to belong to him, body and heart and soul? He already knew all of the women in the pack and not a single one of them carried the scent that marked them as *his.*

As if she could read his mind, Jillian said, "You're not going to find what you need up on the top of this moun- tain, Eric. Those women aren't right for you."

He didn't like it, but she had a point. The pack females he'd been with over the years didn't complain. Didn't de- mand. Didn't expect anything from him. They didn't… *hell,* they didn't even know him. Not a single one of them. He'd spent his whole life growing up with those women, but he wasn't a flesh and blood man to them. He was a dark wolf. Something not to screw with…just to screw.

Not surprising, then, that he needed something *more.* But he couldn't see himself taking a human mate, the way

Mason and Brody had done. Anything between him and
a human female was simply too risky…too dangerous. So
where the hell did that leave him?

*It leaves you alone, you miserable jackass. So suck it
up and learn to deal with it.*

Yeah, deal. He'd been *dealing* since he was a kid, which
meant he should be damn good at it by now.

Irritated by the uncharacteristic, unsettling train of his
thoughts, Eric turned his attention back to Jillian. As if
she hadn't had enough fun screwing with his head for one
night, she said, "Have you thought that maybe this thing
between you and Chelsea has happened for a reason?"

"What? You mean like fate?" His chest shook with a
breathless laugh. "Open your eyes, Jilly. This is a goddamn nightmare. For her *and* me."

"Maybe. Maybe not. I think you're looking at it the
wrong way. The drugs. Her sister. It put the two of you
in a situation where you had to get past your baggage
and be close, intimate. It proved to her that you could be
trusted. Proved the same to you, actually. Maybe that's
why it happened."

"If you're right, then I think fate is a little too keen on
gambling with her safety. How could I ever expect her to
trust me when I don't even trust myself?"

"A little faith. That's all you need. And if you ask me,
the idea of the two of you together makes perfect sense."

"A human and a dark wolf?" He snorted, shaking his
head.

"Look deeper, Eric. And you'll see what I'm talking
about. I have a feeling you and Chelsea are more alike
than you realize."

Look deeper? He didn't think so. No telling what he
might find lurking around inside the twisted depths of
his psyche. "If you really think a human is going to be

the answer to my problems, Jilly, then you've lost your mind. If I listen to you, I might as well have some kind of death wish."

"Why do you say that?"

He gave another gritty laugh. "Because the Runners will be forced to hunt me down like a rogue if I let myself get too involved with her."

And was that the true crux of the matter right there? The reason why he was so attracted to her? Was he trying to punish himself? Did he have some kind of secret desire to end his life? Was that what it was all coming to?

"Eric, that's ridiculous. I meant what I said before. You're not your father. You won't hurt her."

"You don't know that," he argued.

This time, she was the one who snorted. "I know *you*."

"Yeah." His smile was bitter. "And you know what I come from. Bad blood comes through, Jillian. You know that as well as I do."

"You're wrong, Eric. I don't believe that."

"Others do," he grunted, thinking of the town that had turned its back on him bit by bit since his father's death.

"And you know they're jerks, so they're not important. Just take some time to think about what I've said." She turned and started to head inside, then stopped and gave him a cheeky grin. "And trust me to know what's best for you. Okay?"

Eric waited until the crazy woman had shut the door behind her, then turned and made his way over to his cabin. Expecting Chelsea to already be in bed, he was surprised when he came inside and found her perched on the edge of a sofa, apparently waiting for him. He had no idea what kind of expression she wore as he shut the door and turned around, resting his shoulders against the dark wood. But whatever it was had her pulling her lower lip through her teeth, her scent spiking with a sudden surge of adrenaline.

"You don't need to be afraid of me," he said in a low voice. "I would never hurt you."

God, he wanted that to be true—which was why he needed to stay the hell away from her. But he didn't know if he could do it. Even now, the force pulling them together was like a static charge against his skin, lifting the hairs on his body, hardening his muscles. He wanted to break her open. Get inside her. Stay there, steeped in her, for as long as he could.

"It's okay, Eric." Her voice was a little husky, her blue eyes clear and bright. "You don't have to keep looking at me like you're expecting a meltdown. I've decided to be sensible about…this."

He fought back a lopsided smile, even while his insides were being ripped to shreds with the primitive need to take hold of her. And if he touched her, he had no doubt that he'd end up keeping her, satisfying one craving after another, for as long as it lasted. Which he knew damn well wouldn't be long, if he lost control.

The urge to smile fled as quickly as it'd come.

Jillian believes in us, the wolf hissed, prowling beneath his skin.

He sucked in a deep breath…so tempted to give in to that belief. To have faith in it.

"Now that I know the truth," she said, licking her lips, "I wanted to tell you again that I'm sorry for giving you such a hard time on Friday night."

"Meaning you'd have left Wesley like I told you to if you'd known what you were getting into?"

"No. I need to find Perry now more than ever."

It wasn't easy, but he managed to keep his expression

neutral. "Why? Because now you know she's probably bedding down with a monster?"

"I'm not judging, Eric. I don't know enough about your world to do that. But I know she's in a situation that might well be out of her control. Did she know what she was getting into? If she wants out, will he let her go? Is he protecting her? Were her actions based on some weird side effect of the drug, if it was even given to her? These are answers I need before I can just let this go. There are too many unknowns for me to just walk away, even if my life wasn't in danger."

"You're right," he admitted, blowing out a rough breath. "I'm sure I'd feel the same if I were you."

Getting back to her original topic, she said, "What I was trying to tell you is that I understand now what you were trying to warn me about. You really were just trying to keep me from getting hurt. And then, when I didn't listen to you and went back to the club, you risked your life to get me out. So I'm sorry I acted like such an ungrateful bitch."

"You don't have to keep apologizing, Chelsea."

"I just wanted you to know that I'm sorry."

"Fine," he muttered under his breath, thinking that all these apologies were getting damn uncomfortable.

She moved to her feet, her hands a little restless at her sides, until she crossed her arms over her chest. Then she carefully said, "You killed him, didn't you? That bald guy in the hallway at the club?"

He gave a slow nod. *Well, hell.*

"Why?"

"He threatened you," he explained in a low rasp. "Said they'd see you dead before they let me have you."

"Oh."

He wasn't sorry for killing the bastard. Hell, he'd have killed the blond one, too, if she hadn't been watching him.

He thought she'd ask him more about the killing, but instead, the next thing she said was, "That whole attitude thing you had going when we got here this afternoon. What was that about? Did you think I'd blame you for what you are?"

He snorted, shaking his head. "You blame me for being a guy. What was I meant to think?"

She made a low sound of frustration, as if he was being thick. But it made perfect sense to him. She judged men without getting the facts, so why should he think she'd react any differently to the unsettling news about his species? How the hell was he meant to know she wouldn't freak and try to nail his ass with a silver bullet? Not that it would kill him, but she wouldn't have known that.

She took a deep breath, looking as if she was savoring the air in her lungs, before she slowly released it. Then she quietly asked him if he gave off a scent. When asked what she meant, she said, "An attractant? Something that causes desire? Because you smell…really good, Eric."

He nearly exploded on the spot, knowing exactly what she was getting at. She wanted him, and was trying to learn if the attraction was chemical…or real.

Christ, in a past life he must have been such a bastard, because this was a torment of biblical proportions, standing there and hearing her say his scent made her hot, but not being able to do anything about it.

"Eric?"

"Um, no," he muttered. "No special scent."

"Oh. Okay." She frowned. "I just thought that might explain why Perry ran off, chasing after this guy. I thought that maybe he…affected her or something."

"She might have a taste for the danger he represents.

OFFICIAL OPINION POLL

Dear Reader,

Since you are a book enthusiast, we would like to know what you think.

Inside you will find a short Opinion Poll. Please participate in our poll by sharing your opinion on 3 subjects that are very important to all of us.

To thank you for your participation, we would like to send you **2 FREE BOOKS** and **2 FREE GIFTS!**

Please enjoy them with our compliments.

Sincerely,

Pam Powers

YOUR OPINION POLL
THANK-YOU FREE GIFTS INCLUDE:

▶ **2 PARANORMAL ROMANCE BOOKS**
▶ **2 LOVELY SURPRISE GIFTS**

◀ **DETACH AND MAIL CARD TODAY!** ▶

OFFICIAL OPINION POLL

YOUR OPINION COUNTS!
Please check TRUE or FALSE below to express your opinion about the following statements:

Q1 Do you believe in "true love"?

"TRUE LOVE HAPPENS ONLY ONCE IN A LIFETIME."
○ TRUE
○ FALSE

Q2 Do you think marriage has any value in today's world?

"YOU CAN BE TOTALLY COMMITTED TO SOMEONE WITHOUT BEING MARRIED."
○ TRUE
○ FALSE

Q3 What kind of books do you enjoy?

"A GREAT NOVEL MUST HAVE A HAPPY ENDING."
○ TRUE
○ FALSE

YES! I have placed my sticker in the space provided below. Please send me the **2 FREE books** and **2 FREE gifts** for which I qualify. I understand that I am under no obligation to purchase anything further, as explained on the back of this card.

237/337 HDL FEQX

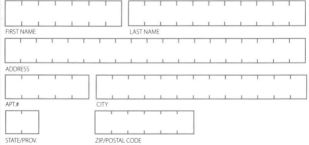

FIRST NAME

LAST NAME

ADDRESS

APT.#

CITY

STATE/PROV.

ZIP/POSTAL CODE

TF-PAR-11
Printed in the U.S.A.
© 2011 HARLEQUIN ENTERPRISES LIMITED

The Reader Service—Here's How It Works:

Accepting your 2 free books and 2 free gifts (gifts valued at approximately $10.00) places you under no obligation to buy anything. You may keep the books and gifts and return the shipping statement marked "cancel." If you do not cancel, about a month later we'll send you 4 additional books and bill you just $21.42 in the U.S. or $23.46 in Canada. That is a savings of at least 21% off the cover price of all 4 books! It's quite a bargain! Shipping and handling is just 50¢ per book in the U.S. and 75¢ per book in Canada.* You may cancel at any time, but if you choose to continue, every month we'll send you 4 more books, which you may either purchase at the discount price or return to us and cancel your subscription.

*Terms and prices subject to change without notice. Prices do not include applicable taxes. Sales tax applicable in N.Y. Canadian residents will be charged applicable taxes. Offer not valid in Quebec. Books received may not be as shown. All orders subject to credit approval. Credit or debit balances in a customer's account(s) may be offset by any other outstanding balance owed by or to the customer. Please allow 4 to 6 weeks for delivery. Offer available while quantities last.

If offer card is missing write to: The Reader Service, P.O. Box 1867, Buffalo NY 14240-1867 or visit: www.ReaderService.com

BUSINESS REPLY MAIL
FIRST-CLASS MAIL   PERMIT NO. 717   BUFFALO, NY

POSTAGE WILL BE PAID BY ADDRESSEE

THE READER SERVICE
PO BOX 1341
BUFFALO NY 14240-8571

NO POSTAGE
NECESSARY
IF MAILED
IN THE
UNITED STATES

The thrill. But I doubt it's more than that." Unless she turned out to be the Lycan's mate, but he wasn't going down that road tonight.

"But you do think she's with another...Lycan, right?"

Nodding, he said, "After what we've learned about that strip club, yeah."

She closed her eyes, looking a little ill.

"If she's still alive, we'll get her back, Chelsea. It's just going to take some time."

"Do you have a plan?" she asked, opening her eyes again.

"Yeah." She followed after him as he headed into the kitchen, took a beer out of the fridge and propped his back against the counter. Then he told her about Sophia Dawson. She listened as she sat at the table, her head propped on her hand, asking questions from time to time, until she finally started to fall asleep right in the middle of their conversation. With a grin on his lips, Eric set his beer down and walked over, thinking he ought to carry her to the bed, when she suddenly woke up with a startled shriek, flinching when she found him standing right next to her.

"I'm sorry," she panted, pressing one hand to her chest as he took a few steps back, giving her more space.

"Don't worry about it," he grated, crossing his arms over his chest so that she wouldn't think he was getting ready to grab her. "And this seems as good a time as any to tell you that despite what happened between us last night, you don't need to worry that I'll try anything with you while you're here. You're not really my type."

She blinked, some of the wild color fading from her cheeks. "I'm not?"

He knew this was for the best, but it still made him feel like an ass. Forcing himself to go through with it, he said, "Naw. I prefer to bed things I don't have to worry about killing."

He'd already walked out of the room, and was making his way down the hall, when she said, "You're lying."

He stopped in his tracks and slowly turned around. "What?"

She lifted her chin and whispered two soft, husky words. "First time."

His heart started to pound a little harder. "Chelsea, what the hell are you talking about?"

"In the motel, when I was…asking you for sex, you said you weren't taking me like that for our *first time*. Thereby implying that we would eventually be having sex with one another."

Eric deliberately arched a brow. "You should know by now that men say lots of things they don't mean when they're in motel rooms."

She lifted her brow to mirror his. "When they're in their homes, too, I guess."

Shit. She was too smart for her own good. And he was so screwed. "I'm not talking about this."

"Then I guess this is good night." Then the little human just turned her back on him and walked into the guest-room, shutting the door behind her.

Eric didn't know how long he stood there, staring at that closed door…wondering what he was going to do. And hoping like hell that he found the strength to stay away from her.

Chapter Nine

The next morning, after her shower, Chelsea stepped out of the bathroom wearing her last pair of clean jeans with another short-sleeved button-down shirt, and nearly ran right into Eric.

"I'm sorry," she said, quickly stepping back to put some space between them, until her spine was pressed against one side of the hallway. She was painfully aware of her wet hair hanging in ropes around her face—a freshly scrubbed, slightly bruised face that unfortunately didn't have an ounce of makeup on it. *Damn.* "I didn't…I didn't think you were here. I heard you leave earlier."

"Just got back." He watched her with the predatory intensity of a hawk. Or rather, a wolf, she corrected herself, finding his Lycan heritage easier to believe when he was standing right in front of her. While he was out, she'd been hoping to use his computer to do some research on Lycans, eager for any additional information she could dig up on his species. But if she got lucky, maybe he would simply answer some of her questions for her.

"You sleep okay?" he asked.

She gave him a tight smile. "Great, if you can believe it."

Something moved through his dark gaze—something hot and primal—and she reacted with a shiver, chill bumps racing across her bare arms. Last night, when they'd been talking, she'd actually argued that he wanted her. But that had been more pride and temper than actual confidence. After she'd gone to bed, her old doubts had crowded back into her mind, making her feel like a fool for the things she'd said to him. She didn't recognize herself around him. Didn't know this woman who looked and wanted and hungered with such visceral craving, as if she were starved for him. Who could say things that she never would have dreamed of saying to another man. She didn't know if it was because of what had happened between them after she'd been drugged, or if it was just Eric. But she liked the way he made her feel, every bit as much as she hated it.

No, she realized, sorting through the chaotic tangle of her thoughts. It wasn't the feeling that she hated. It was the fear. That he could hurt her. That he could make her vulnerable in a way no other man ever had. Not physically, because that was a given. She was human, while he was…something much more primal and powerful. But her fear didn't stem from their differences. It was rooted in this strange attraction that held such a strong emotional element. That held so much power. It was as if he vibrated with a raw, sexual frequency that pulled on her, making her crave him with an intensity that was unlike anything she'd ever known. Such a heady, wonderful feeling, and yet, it made her feel so lost. Threw her even more deeply into new, uncharted territory than the knowledge that werewolves were real, walking the streets around us.

"How do you feel this morning?" He rubbed his palm across the rugged angle of his jaw, the sleeve of his T-shirt shifting to reveal the bottom edge of that sexy tattoo wrapping his thick biceps, and his voice got even lower. "Are you sore?"

Her face flooded with color. "I'm fine," she choked out, stunned that he would just lob a question like that right at her, like a grenade, without any warning. The man was a fiend!

His gaze narrowed, and from this close she could see the way his long lashes tangled together at the corners of his eyes. "It might be a good idea to have Jillian take a look at you anyway," he rumbled in that low, rough-velvet voice.

"I told you I'm fine," she said, trying hard to ignore the effect that wicked-as-sin voice had on her, heat spreading through her system in a slow, inexorable slide. "But I do have some more questions for you."

With a grin lifting the corner of his mouth, he rested his back against the opposite wall, his hands placed behind him. "I'd be surprised if you didn't."

Fiddling with the wet ends of her hair, she said, "Jillian told me about Shadow Peak. How many pack towns like that are there here in the U.S.?"

He gave her a higher number than she'd expected, and she shuddered. "I'll never look at small towns the same way again."

"You wouldn't be able to tell which ones are human and which…aren't. Not just passing through. We're good at hiding what we don't want others to see."

Taking a deep breath, she held his dark gaze and asked,

"Will you...show me? A change? Even if it's only a partial one—like maybe just your hand?"

She watched the muscles in his face tighten, his dark brows pulling together as he said, "I don't think that'd be such a good idea."

"Why?"

"Because I don't want to make you more afraid of me than you already are," he bit out in a rough tone. "So drop it."

"I'm not afraid of you, Eric." She might be out of her mind, but it was true.

He watched her through his long lashes, as if he didn't want her to be able to read the look in his eyes. The brackets around his mouth were deeper, his breaths getting deeper, too, and she had the craziest feeling that he was completely focused on her, aware of her every movement, no matter how slight—of her every thought, no matter how crazy.

Finally, he said, "Your adrenaline levels are off the chart right now, Chelsea. Whatever's causing it, I'd rather not add to your tension."

Letting it go, she crossed her arms over her chest and asked, "How did it go with Sophia?"

He explained that the girl had agreed to talk to Brandon, and was going to visit him that afternoon. When he noticed how nervous she was about the plan, he frowned, saying, "I thought you'd be relieved she was willing to do it."

"I am, because I want Perry found. But I hate the idea of another woman putting herself in danger."

"She's not human, Chelsea."

Her chin lifted at his tone. "She's still a woman."

One of his dark brows arched. "So then you don't think we're all monsters?"

She flinched. "I never said that."

With a smirk, he said, "Honey, your face was saying a hell of a lot last night that your mouth never did. Doesn't mean you weren't thinking it."

"You're wrong," she argued, hating that that's how he saw her. "I'm not a judgmental person."

A gritty laugh rumbled up from his chest, and he shook his head. "Hell, Chelse, you're one of the most judgmental women I've ever known."

She scowled. "If that's how you feel, then I'll just get out of your—"

He caught her as she tried to storm past, pressing her back against the wall and trapping her there with ridiculous ease—caging her in with his huge, hard, muscular body. God, she had to tilt her head back just to see his face.

With his fingers still wrapped around her upper arm, he braced his free arm against the wall and stared down into her eyes with a dark, hooded gaze. "You might be a man-hater, Chelse, but it doesn't mean I don't want you so bad I can taste it." His voice was so soft she almost didn't hear the words. But she watched them form on his lips, mesmerized by how such a sensual mouth could belong to such a hard, rugged male.

"Last night, you said I wasn't your type," she reminded him, trying to sound unaffected. But she had a feeling he could see right through her. That he could sense the need and the lust roiling through her system, breaking her down.

There was no doubt that she wanted him—she just didn't want to want him, damn it. Not when he made her feel so out of control. So desperate and needy.

"Yeah, I might have said that, but what the hell do I

know?" he drawled with a crooked smile. "I'm just a stupid alpha jackass, right?"

"You said it, not me. But I'm certainly not going to argue the fact."

She'd expected him to be insulted, but he threw back his head and laughed—another rich, husky, bone-melting rumble of sound—then looked back down at her with a devastating smile kicking up the corner of that beautiful mouth.

She swallowed, feeling as if the entire situation was slowly slipping out of her control.

But for the first time in her life, Chelsea just didn't give a damn.

The memory of the time he'd spent with her in that cheap motel room had tortured Eric through the long hours of the night, but he'd been ready to put it in perspective. To put it in its place. Planned on staying rational, calm, distanced…

But it wasn't happening.

She might drive him crazy, but she was more than just a pretty face—more than just a sexy, mouthwatering body. The force of Chelsea's personality all but shimmered around her, glowing beneath her skin, smoldering in those big blue eyes that reminded him of the summer sky on a blistering hot day, when even the clouds had been burned away. He couldn't get enough of the unique patterns of her speech or the warm sensuality of her voice, pathetically hanging on to her every word whenever she opened her mouth, as if he wasn't coming apart at the seams—wasn't unraveling like a code that'd suddenly been deciphered after thousands of tries. He even admired her devotion to her sister, though he didn't approve of the risks she'd taken in trying to find her.

And she hadn't run screaming when she'd learned the truth about him. Unbelievable.

That thick, carnal burn of desire was building in the air between them, vibrant and sharp, and he knew she felt it, too. Her eyes were going wide…her scent rising with the heat of her body. He knew, instinctively, that he could lower his head and kiss her. Knew that she wanted him to. But he wanted her to admit it, damn it. Needed to hear it from her lips.

"Yes or no, Chelsea." His voice was raw…thick. "Make a decision. Don't screw around with me."

She blinked, suddenly looking a little pale beneath the rosy color in her cheeks. "A decision?"

"Do you want me?"

"I shouldn't." The pink tip of her tongue swept over her lower lip, and she took a quick breath, as if gathering her courage. "But I do. It's…crazy."

"What? Us?"

"The craving," she whispered. "I feel like I've been drugged again. What the hell are you doing to me, Eric?"

She might not like him, but she wanted him. He could see it in her dilated eyes, read it in the flushed angles of her expression, feel it in the provocative heat pulsing from her soft, delicate skin. Physical hunger was all he'd ever expected from the women he slept with, but for some frustrating reason, it wasn't enough now. Not with this one. He needed…damn it, he didn't know what he needed from her. He just wanted to take…and take, until he'd figured it out.

"I know I should stay away from you," he said with a soft growl. "I told myself I would. But I…can't. I can't do it. You're gonna drive me outta my goddamn mind."

His breathing turned ragged as he let go of her arm and lifted his hand to her face, rubbing the corner of her mouth with his thumb, stroking the pad across her lush lower lip. Unable to wait a second longer, Eric pressed down, opening her mouth, and sank his tongue inside, taking possession as if he owned it, owned her.

It was so strange, how after everything he'd done to her when she'd been under the influence of the drug, he hadn't actually tasted her mouth until now. If he'd known what he was missing—how unbelievably sweet she was—he wouldn't have been able to resist. And now he was done for. Her hands curled around his head, holding him to her, her grip as desperate as his own as he sank one hand into her hair, the other moving boldly over her hip and side. She was wild in her passion, her tongue rubbing against his, tasting with hungry, sexy licks that made him feel crazed. Made him feel like the top of his friggin' head was about to blow off. The kiss was hard and raw, flavored with erotic violence and need. With cravings that were unwanted, but undeniable.

Desperate for the feel of her, Eric curved his hand around a firm breast, her nipple deliciously hard against his palm, thick with desire. Pulling his head back, breaths jerking roughly past his lips, he watched as he tore her shirt open and unhooked the front of her bra, revealing the pale, beautiful slopes of her breasts…the berry-red nipples, puckered tight and sweet. Before she could draw her next breath, he lowered his head over her, a deep, gravelly animal sound rumbling in his chest as he took her in his mouth, sucking and licking as if he'd go mad without the feel and the taste of her against his tongue.

Minutes later, he wasn't quite sure how they'd ended up on the floor in the middle of the hallway, but they had. Her shirt and bra were lying open at her sides, jeans around her knees, his hand shoved inside her panties, as if that was where it belonged. He could remember having her sweet little nipple in his mouth, hearing those sexy moans slipping past her lips, and then everything had gone wild. He'd made her come with the thick thrusts of his fingers, her juices drenching his hand, and now he was lying on his side, facing her with his weight braced on his forearm as she lay on her back, her eyes closed, looking more beautiful than any other woman he'd ever known.

This was so wrong, but Christ, it felt so right.

"I thought I must have been imagining it," she whispered, her voice a little breathless and low. "The way you'd made me feel at the motel. Thought it must be the drug. But it wasn't. It was real." Opening her eyes, she turned her head a little to look at him, her gaze full of wonder and a small part of fear. "How do you do that to me? Make me let go like that?"

"Why does it surprise you?" he asked, painfully aware of the fact that if he didn't come soon, he'd probably end up doing some permanent damage to himself.

"It's embarrassing to admit, but I've been called frigid more than once."

His eyes narrowed. "By who?"

"Just a few of the men I've dated," she told him, trying to shrug it off, as if their criticisms hadn't hurt her. But he could tell that they had.

"Then they were all dickless little runts," he muttered, outraged on her behalf, even though he couldn't stand the thought of another man having his hands on her. "You're not frigid, Chelsea." His palm cupped her possessively. "Far from it. You melt me down just by looking at me. God only knows what sex will do. I might never recover."

"Maybe we should stop, then," she murmured, sounding completely serious. He wasn't sure she was actually teasing him until she added, "In the name of good health and all that."

A breathless laugh shook his chest. "Don't worry. I'm willing to risk it."

"Me, too." The soft smile she sent him had his friggin' head spinning. "Though I still think a guy like you should come with a warning label."

She was joking...but the idea sobered him. Made him sharply aware of just how tightly he was leashing the beast inside him.

That's hardly fair, the wolf complained. *I'm being golden.*

Before he could figure out what to say to her—and what he should do—someone knocked on his front door. Pulling his hand out of her panties, Eric turned his head and sniffed the air. "Damn it, that's Cian. I wasn't expecting him till later."

"Who?" She blinked, looking a little disoriented as he sat up and quickly hooked her bra, then helped her pull up her jeans.

"Cian Hennessey," he told her, moving to his feet. "He's Brody's partner. Brody's married to Michaela."

"Oh." And then, "What's he doing here?"

Reaching down for her hand, Eric pulled her to her feet, then steered her ahead of him as he walked to his bedroom. He needed to grab a few things before leaving, and didn't want to let her out of his sight until he had to. That was probably a bad sign, but at the moment he was still in too good a mood to care. Looking around for his wallet and keys, he answered her question about the Runner. "Hennessey's here because he's going out to Hawkley with me. That's the Whiteclaw pack's hometown. The one I told you about last night."

She stood by his dresser, holding her shirt closed and still looking a little dazed. "What? Why? I thought Sophia was going there."

"She is. But I still need to go and smooth over what happened at the club. If I'm lucky, I can get them off your trail without sending up any red flags. Which means I won't be able to let on that I know about Perry."

"Are you worried they'll hurt her if they know you're looking for her?"

"I don't want to take any chances," he said, pulling his weapons case down from the top of his closet. He took out his Beretta and two rounds of ammo.

"You'll be careful?" she asked, casting a worried look at the gun.

"Always," he told her, slipping the Beretta into the waistband of his jeans at his lower back. The Whiteclaw might pat them down, but it would look too suspicious if he tried to go into the town unarmed.

"I just wish I could go with you," she said, doing up the buttons that remained intact on her shirt. "Perry's my sister. I should be there."

Eric walked across the room, not stopping until he was standing right in front of her. "I understand how you feel, Chelse. But you're just going to have to trust me to handle this."

With a sigh, she said, "Eric, I don't even know you." Her voice was tight, strained with worry. "How can you expect me to trust you?"

"Sometimes you do," he said in a low rumble, lifting his hand to her face. He rubbed his thumb over the slick surface of her lower lip, thinking she had the most sinful mouth he'd ever seen…ever tasted. "You trust me when I make you come, Chelse."

Scowling, she knocked his hand away. "And there you go acting like an ass again."

Despite how much her lack of trust bothered him, he enjoyed riling her. His chest was still shaking with a muffled, gritty laugh as he headed toward the front door and pulled it open.

"Did I interrupt anything?" Cian asked from his perch on the porch railing. His pale gray eyes glittered with humor, since he could no doubt scent the lust that was still surrounding Eric like a cloud.

Ignoring the question, Eric said, "I didn't expect you here this early."

The Runner grinned like a jackass as he caught sight of Chelsea coming up behind him. "Obviously."

"I'd watch your mouth if I were you, Hennessey."

Cian laughed. "It does tend to get me into trouble, doesn't it?"

"Wow," Chelsea murmured, joining him at the door. She slowly slid her gaze over the Runner, blinked, then shook her head. "I didn't think it was possible, but you're exactly how Torrance described you."

Eric scowled, thinking now would be a good time to wipe that suggestive smile right off the Irishman's pretty face, when Chelsea gripped his arm, drawing his attention back to her. "I don't like this, Eric. If you're on bad terms with the Whiteclaw, why do you even think they'll let you onto their land?"

"Let's just say it's a hierarchy thing," Cian drawled, before Eric could respond.

He cut the Runner a sharp glare and warned him to stop right there.

"How about let's not stop," Chelsea muttered, "and you actually tell me the truth?"

With another low laugh, Cian hopped down from the railing. "I'm not sure you can handle the truth, honey. But I will say that Eric here is like werewolf royalty. It would be an extreme insult for a pack leader to turn him away."

Eric had had enough. "Go wait in the damn truck," he snarled, tossing the smirking Runner his keys. "I'll be there in a minute."

Cian shot Chelsea a mischievous wink before walking down the porch steps and disappearing around the side of the cabin. Giving Eric a curious look, she asked, "Do you normally work with him?"

"Not if I can help it." He shoved one hand back through his hair, appearing irritated as hell. "But this is Mason and Jeremy's way of trying to make the two of us get along better."

She couldn't help but smile at his grumbling tone, and he sent her a playful look of warning. "Laugh and I *will* get even, woman."

"Oh, yeah?" She was more than a little surprised by how flirtatious she sounded. "Will it be something I'll like?"

With a deep, guttural groan, he dropped his head in his hand and rubbed his eyes, his tone wry as he muttered, "It shouldn't be this easy for you to get me hard."

Biting her lip, Chelsea reached down and lifted the hem of his shirt, and sure enough, there was a big, distinctive ridge behind his denim fly. She swallowed, then lifted her gaze to find him staring down at her with a dark, smoldering look that made her breath catch.

"You're determined to send me away with a boner, aren't you?"

"If I am, it's nothing less than you deserve," she murmured, wondering if his voice always got rougher when he was aroused, the husky sound giving her chills. The good kind.

The look in his eyes somehow got darker, a slow smile curving the edge of his mouth. "You're a cruel woman, Chelsea Smart."

Knowing he'd think it was funny, she said, "You probably won't be surprised to learn this, Eric, but I hear that
a lot."

She enjoyed the sound of his laughter as he pressed a
quick kiss to her lips, then followed after Cian. As she
shut the front door behind him, Chelsea only hoped to
God she'd get the chance to hear it again.

The drive to Hawkley took a little more than an hour,
and Eric and Cian were allowed into the town without any
issues. Eric parked the truck on one of the side streets, and
they walked over to Crate's Avenue, following the directions they'd gotten from the scouts who had given them
clearance on the main road into the town. As the two men
made their way down the sidewalk, it was obvious they
were being watched. Unlike Shadow Peak, Hawkley had
the look of a well-to-do militarized zone, armed Lycans
watching the streets from rooftops and front porches.

"Is it just me," Cian murmured under his breath, "or
does this place give you the creeps, too?"

"I've got a bad feeling," Eric replied, wondering what
the hell the Whiteclaw and Donovans were up to. Even the
air tasted off, as if something rotten had eaten its way into
the core of the town, contaminating it from the inside out.

They knocked on the wide double doors of the colo-
nial-style house where they'd been told they could find
the pack's leadership, and waited for someone to answer.
It didn't take long before the door was opened by a young
man Eric recognized as Sebastian Claymore, son of the
man who basically ruled the Whiteclaw with an iron fist.
Eric told Seb why they were there, and they were asked
to wait on the porch.

While Cian paced from one end of the porch to the
other, Eric took a seat on one of the white benches, elbows braced on his parted knees, and thought about Chel-

sea. Yeah, he should have had his mind on the coming meeting—but he couldn't get the stubborn woman out of his head.

And he wasn't the only one…

He didn't know what was happening between them, but it was becoming painfully clear that his animal half had started to think of her as something it wanted to possess. A definite problem, since he knew that the more he touched her, the more his wolf would crave her submission, and that was something he couldn't see a woman like Chelsea Smart ever giving a man—especially one like him. Given the situation, he didn't trust how the animal would react.

You should have a little more faith. I know what's at stake.

Did it? Or was it just telling him what he wanted to hear? Earlier that morning, Jillian had told Eric that if he were going to lose control with Chelsea, it would have already happened when she'd been drugged. But he was still afraid to believe.

That isn't fair, the wolf argued. *Didn't I just prove myself again this morning? We gave the human pleasure. No pain.*

"You're a million miles away." Cian's deep voice cut into his thoughts, dragging him back to the moment. "It's time to get your head in the game, Drake."

"I'm fine," he muttered.

The Irishman pulled a pack of cigarettes from the pocket of his jeans, placed one between his lips and cupped his hand over the tip as he flicked open a silver lighter. He took a long, deep drag, then looked at Eric. "You gonna claim her?" he asked as if it was the most casual question in the world.

Eric shook his head. "No. She isn't meant for me."

The Runner arched a brow. "You sure about that?"

"I'm sure it's time to change the subject," he shot back, lighting his own cigarette. They smoked in silence, studying the town, taking in everything they could. Careful to keep his voice low, Eric exhaled a stream of smoke, and said, "You see that blonde over there walking down the street?"

"The one with the legs that go on for a mile? What about her?"

"She was stripping at the club on Saturday night."

Cian sniffed the air. "She's human."

While they watched, one of the Whiteclaw males took the girl's arm and led her into what appeared to be some kind of office building.

An ugly suspicion started burning in Eric's gut. "I've got a bad feeling," he said for the second time that morning.

Dropping his cigarette butt into the ashtray sitting on the end of the bench, the Irishman said, "You're not the only one."

Eric had hoped they might catch sight of Perry Smart, if she was even there, since Monroe had called on their way to Hawkley with the news that the trace on Perry's phone had turned up nothing—but although they spotted two more human girls walking down the street, neither of them looked like the photograph he'd seen of Chelsea's sister. After another few minutes of waiting, the door to the house finally opened again, and the spectacled Sebastian came out onto the porch, saying, "Roy is ready to see you now."

"Where's your father?" Eric asked, wondering why Clive Claymore wasn't the one they'd be dealing with. Roy was Clive's younger brother, and a complete jackass.

Something flickered in the younger man's eyes. "My father passed away several months ago."

"Our condolences," he murmured, sharing a look with

Cian. It was common protocol for packs to report any changes in leadership to their neighbors. The fact that the Whiteclaw hadn't informed the Silvercrest of Clive's death struck them both as another bad sign.

They followed the younger man through the house, which was decorated in dark woods and rustic furniture. At the back of the first floor, they were shown into a large study, where Roy Claymore was perched on the front edge of a massive oak desk, waiting for them. He was a big, brawny man, with thick black hair and a crooked nose. He'd always been known as a bruiser, more concerned with his questionable business dealings than with his pack, while his brother Clive had been the more politically motivated. Though the Whiteclaw had a League of Elders that was similar to the one Eric's father had destroyed in Shadow Peak, their League served as little more than a ceremonial fixture, without any real control. For the past thirty years, the pack's power had sat with Clive. Now, it seemed, Roy had slipped in and taken that power for himself.

"I thought Seb and his brother had been living out West for a few years now," Eric remarked, after they'd all exchanged greetings and Seb had left the office. He and Cian seated themselves in the two sturdy leather chairs situated in front of the desk.

"That's right," Roy said with an easy smile, while the look in his eyes made it clear that he wanted to know why they were there.

"What brought them home?"

The older Lycan regarded him with a shrewd gaze. "They didn't always see eye to eye with their father. Different ideologies and visions for the pack. But it's my goal to see the Whiteclaw embrace a more progressive track than we have in the past. To be blunt, my brother lacked vision. I don't."

"So you called them home," Eric murmured, wondering what the hell Roy was up to, and willing to bet that his nephews were somehow involved.

"I requested they return to their family, where they belong," Roy said, giving Eric a thin smile. "Surely you know what it's like to want to have your family close by?"

Eric knew the bastard was talking about Eli, and he had to struggle to control his temper, not wanting to give himself away with his scent. He had a feeling Roy Claymore could smell aggression from a mile away.

Cian filled in the strained silence. "We couldn't help but notice that you have quite a few humans in town."

Roy shifted his gaze to the Runner. "That's right. Unlike the Silvercrest, many of our males have come to enjoy the pleasures that can be found with a human." Lifting a shoulder, he said, "It was inevitable, really, with so many of them working near the girls at the club we own in Wesley."

"Sounds to me like you're playing a dangerous game," Cian offered.

The Lycan lifted his brows. "Why? We're not eating them." He slid a sly glance toward Eric. "We're just...*enjoying* their company."

"Hennessey," Eric rasped, following the plan that he and Cian had discussed on the drive over, "do you mind waiting for me outside?"

The Irishman moved to his feet. "Not at all," he said in a somewhat deferential tone, wanting Roy to believe that he followed Eric's orders. "I was just thinking that it's time for another smoke."

The instant Cian was out of the room, Roy looked at Eric with a heavy scowl. "I didn't want to say anything in front of the Runner, but you caused quite a disturbance at my club the other night, boy."

"That wasn't my intention," he murmured. "I just wanted the girl."

"Why?" Roy demanded.

With a shrug, Eric said, "I picked up on her scent and couldn't let it go." He flashed the older man a hard smile. "You know what that's like, Roy. I'm sure you can still scent her on me. Not easy to resist something that smells that good."

"Did she mention why she was there?" Roy asked, obviously fishing to learn how much Eric knew.

"She didn't mention anything." He slid Roy a telling look. "Just did a lot of screaming and groaning."

The Lycan laughed. "So it was like that, was it?"

"She was fun for a while," he said with a smirk. "But she didn't last long."

Roy's brows lifted. "You killed her?" he asked with obvious surprise.

Eric gave another shrug. "Didn't think you'd mind. The guard I fought at the club said you were putting her down anyway. I'm sorry he had to die as well, but he was trying to take something that belonged to me."

Snorting, Roy said, "You barely knew the girl."

Careful to keep the disgust he felt for Roy Claymore hidden, Eric casually cocked a brow. "I knew enough to know she needed to be taught a lesson."

For a moment, Roy just stared at him, studying his eyes—then he threw back his head and roared with laughter. "Hell, you really are as ruthless as your old man, Drake. I'd had my doubts, after hearing about your new friends in the Alley. But I get it now."

"We all have our public roles to play, and sometimes it's best to keep our enemies close," Eric drawled, moving to his feet. "I'm sure you understand that better than most."

Roy's only response was a smooth smile.

"To be honest," Eric said, "the Runners were more than

a little surprised to learn of your involvement at the club. It seems the Whiteclaw and the Donovans have found a common interest."

With that perfect politician's smile still in place, Roy said, "Like I mentioned before, we're all about progress now."

"Not a bad thing," Eric agreed. "The old ways are too archaic."

Roy nodded. "That's true—but changes are coming, Drake." He reached out to shake Eric's hand. "It's good to know there's a voice of reason up in Shadow Peak. I'm sure you and I will have the chance to talk again, soon."

Still feeling as if his skin was crawling, Eric closed the door to Roy's office behind him, turned and nearly collided with the last person he wanted to see. Not because he didn't want anything to do with Curtis Donovan. He'd have liked nothing better than to wipe the floor with the son of a bitch who had drugged Chelsea. But until they had Perry out of whatever nightmare she'd gotten herself into, he had to tread carefully.

Unlike most of the Donovans, who were tall and blond, Curtis was a short, stocky guy with shoulder-length brown hair and a goatee. He had small, kinda beady brown eyes, and a nose that looked too long for his face. At first glance, he seemed harmless enough, until you got to know what a ruthless little bastard he was.

"You've got a lot of nerve coming here," Curtis said. "I lost one of my best men because of you, and had to fire another."

Eric snorted. "If they were your best, Donovan, then you need to do some new recruiting."

"You always were a smart-ass," the younger man sneered.

With a gloating grin on his lips, Eric said, "I just

stopped by to let Roy know that the human is no longer your problem."

"You think you just get to keep her?"

He sighed and shook his head. "'Fraid there's nothing left to keep."

"Bullshit," Curtis snarled, his beady eyes narrowing with disbelief. "I smelled that little bitch. No way in hell would you let something like that go without getting some use out of it first."

Though he was burning with rage inside, Eric lifted his shoulder in a lazy shrug. "What can I say? She wasn't nearly as sturdy as she looked."

Curtis gave a cocky laugh. "So I'm supposed to believe that Shadow Peak's once golden boy has now gone to the dark side?"

"I don't really give a shit what you believe," Eric said with a sharp smile, shoving past the little jackass as he made his way back to the front of the house. He joined Hennessey on the porch, and they made their way down to the street in silence, heading back to the truck.

They'd only just started down the side street where they'd parked, when a golden-haired, good-looking Lycan male came around the back of a parked van, coming face to face with them on the sidewalk. Eric knew from his scent that the male was a Youngblood Lycan. He also caught a lighter scent on the guy that reminded him of Chelsea. Not an exact match, but similar enough for him to be sure that this male had recently been in close contact with Perry Smart.

"You're a Youngblood," Eric said, blocking the male's path when he tried to go around them. "I'm Eric Drake," he added, holding out his hand.

The guy gave him a wary look as they shook. "Jason Donovan."

Shit. Perry Smart's boyfriend—if that's what this guy

was—wasn't just associated with the Donovan family. He was one of them.

Carefully watching the Lycan's expression, Eric said, "I've just come from a meeting with Roy Claymore."

Jason's nostrils flared. "Is that right?"

He lowered his voice, not knowing who might be watching…listening. "Despite what she might hear, let your girlfriend know that her sister is safe in the Alley."

He'd taken a chance in trusting Jason Donovan with that information, but knew from the look of relief in the younger man's eyes that he'd made the right choice.

"She doing okay?" Eric asked.

Jason gave a curt nod. "She's being looked after," he said. "Nothing and no one can change that."

"Yeah? Then it might be a good idea to let those who are worrying about her know."

"Time to go," Cian growled. "We're drawing attention from one of the rooftops."

Jason turned and walked into the nearest shop without looking back, and Eric and Cian crossed the street. They'd just reached the truck when his phone rang. He listened to Jeremy as he started the engine and headed out of town, then disconnected the call and pulled out onto the main road, going in the opposite direction from which they'd come.

"Change of plans," he grunted when Cian sent him a questioning look. Then he hit the gas, steering the truck toward Shadow Peak.

Chapter Ten

After Eric left, Chelsea spent the morning worrying about him while she dealt with her laundry, since she was down to the last of her clean clothes. She'd just put her things into the dryer when Jillian and another pretty blonde who introduced herself as Carla Reyes stopped by to check on her. When Jillian found out that she still hadn't eaten breakfast, she ran back to her cabin for some pastries, while Chelsea put on some coffee and talked to Carla, who was a riot. She listened, fascinated, as Carla explained how she was the only female Runner for the Silvercrest pack, her partner a man named Wyatt Pallaton. When Jillian came back, they sat around the kitchen table with their pastries and coffee, spending the time just getting to know each other.

"How are things going with Eric?" Jillian finally asked, before taking a bite of her cinnamon roll.

"Um…complicated."

"I'm not surprised," Carla drawled. "I've always thought he'd be a handful. He's got so much alpha in him, I'm surprised he doesn't…" She suddenly jumped in her seat, a startled expression on her face as her words trailed off. Though neither woman said anything, Chelsea would have bet money that Jillian had just kicked Carla to shut her up.

Wondering what that was all about, she leaned back in her chair and said, "Cian mentioned something this morning about Eric belonging to some kind of werewolf royalty. What did he mean by that?"

It was Jillian who answered. "Just that Eric's bloodline is one of the purest in the pack."

"That's it? From the way Eric was glaring at the guy, I thought it was going to be something…bad."

"Only if you think power is bad," Jillian said, watching her carefully. "Eric's still feeling the burn of his father's betrayal. So he's a little biased against himself at the moment."

Betrayal? She wanted to ask for an explanation, for more information about his father, but it didn't feel right. The answers to her questions should be coming from Eric, not his friends. If he wanted to tell her, he would. If he didn't, then it wasn't any of her business.

Resting her chin in her hand, Jillian gave her a knowing smile. "You've decided to hear the rest from him, haven't you?"

Chelsea laughed. "Did you read my mind?"

"I don't need to. It's obvious you care about him."

"As a…friend," she murmured. "He risked his life to save me. Helped me when I needed it. And now he's trying to find Perry for me. He deserves my respect."

"He does," Jillian agreed. "But he wants more than that. And I think you do, too."

Shaking her head, she said, "I'm not looking for a relationship. And I don't want an affair." In truth, she didn't actually know *what* she wanted, except to get this crazy need for him out of her system.

Jillian reached across the table and patted her hand. "I understand your fears, Chelsea. God knows I had my share of them when things started to heat up with Jeremy. But my sister, Sayre, gave me a good piece of advice that I'm going to pass on to you. She said that the one who protects her heart from fear of loss ends up with no heart at all. Just an empty chest, because she has nothing to lose."

The words resonated inside her, but she swiped them away with a mental hand, knowing damn well that it would be stupid to get hung up on a guy like Eric. He might want to have sex with her—which she was still finding a little hard to believe—but he wasn't looking for love any more than she was. "I'm sure your sister's right, but it's not like that with Eric."

"You don't think he's interested in mating?" Carla asked, reaching for the carafe and pouring herself some more coffee.

Face on fire, Chelsea looked at the Runner. "You mean sex?"

"She's talking about a Lycan mating," Jillian explained.

Lycan mating? "What the hell is that? I mean, I'm afraid I don't understand."

Carla snorted. "Then count yourself lucky, because it's a pain in the ass."

Jillian sent the Runner a sympathetic look, then brought her gaze back to Chelsea. "A Lycan bond is about commitment, fidelity and a metaphysical union of the souls. In a lot of ways, it's like a human marriage. Just…deeper."

Fascinated, she asked, "Are you mated with Jeremy?"

Jillian nodded. "We're a mated pair. And so are Mic and Brody, and Torrance and Mason."

Taking another sip of her coffee, Chelsea was torn between wanting to know more, and fear of what she might learn, too many questions crowding her thoughts. How did a Lycan know who was their mate? Was it a fate kind of thing, or did they get to choose? And what exactly did the bonding entail? How was it done? Before she could decide what to ask them, they heard a vehicle roar into the Alley at full speed. Seconds later, the tires squealed as it skidded to a violent stop.

With a worried look on her face, Jillian made her way over to the front window. She peered through the glass, her brow furrowing at what she saw outside. "Oh, shit," she whispered, quickly heading for the door. Sensing the healer's urgency, Chelsea and Carla took off after her.

"It's not Eric, is it?" she asked, running down the porch steps.

"No. It's one of the women from the pack!" Jillian's breath sucked in with a shocked gasp as they neared the car. A beautiful, blood-covered woman who looked to be in her early twenties climbed out from behind the wheel, her expression dazed as her legs crumpled and she fell to her knees in the grass.

"Casey, what happened?" Jillian shouted, crouching beside her.

"D-Davis," the woman stammered, just before she passed out.

"That no-good son of a bitch," Jillian muttered while Carla looked at Chelsea and mouthed "her husband."

Together, the three of them got Casey inside the Burnses' cabin, taking her to the spare room that Jillian said she often used for her patients. As they began cleaning away the blood with warm cloths so that Jillian could assess the damage, which appeared to be a multitude of bruises and brutal, painful-looking claw marks, Casey came to. Speaking in a halting, broken rasp, the woman explained how her husband, Davis, had come home that morning in a drunken rage after staying out all night at his favorite bar in town. Apparently, there had been some younger Lycans in the bar making lewd comments about Casey flirting with them, and instead of just talking to her about it, Davis had gone off the deep end. From what Chelsea could gather, this wasn't the first time Davis had knocked Casey around, but Jillian promised the abused woman that it would be the last.

Once the wounds were cleaned, Jillian used her healing powers as the pack's Spirit Walker to close them, then gave Casey something to help her sleep. They left her resting in bed, and went into the kitchen, where Jillian called Jeremy, who was training some new scouts. She let him know what had happened, then made a few more calls, before checking on Casey again. When she came back to the kitchen, the three women sat around the table with glasses of iced tea, the atmosphere rife with frustration and anger over the abuse that Casey had suffered.

"I can't believe how much damage he did," Chelsea murmured, rubbing her hands over her chilled arms. "Is that kind of reaction normal in Lycan males?"

"God, no!" Jillian said, giving her a look of horror. "Jeremy and the others, they can get possessive and jealous, but they would never do anything like that. No real man ever would. But like any group, there are always going to be a few bastards who need some sense knocked into them."

They were still talking about how Casey's husband needed to have his ass kicked, when they heard another vehicle pulling into the Alley, and Chelsea hoped it was

Eric. It was crazy, but her heart immediately started thumping in her chest, her pulse rushing, just from the thought of seeing him again.

They went out to the porch, and as she watched Eric climb out of his truck she remembered how her craving for him that morning had been so instant and overwhelming she'd barely been able to breathe through it. It'd consumed her like a flame—like a hungry set of jaws coming up from the dark depths of the ocean and locking her in its grip.

More than once that afternoon, Chelsea had wondered if she'd feel like that again when he returned to the Alley—doubting that she could. It'd been so unlike her, it couldn't possibly happen again. But she'd been wrong. She wanted him so badly it was all she could do to keep from rushing toward him and throwing herself into his arms. She stood rooted to the spot, breath jerking in her lungs, until he came closer and she realized that he'd been in a fight. His knuckles were bloodied and bruised on his right hand, his left cheek scraped raw just beneath his eye.

"What happened?" she gasped, stepping onto the top porch step just as he reached the bottom one. "Did you get in a fight with one of the Whiteclaw?"

"Not exactly," Cian replied before Eric had the chance. "He insisted on paying a personal visit to Casey's husband on our way home."

She stared at Eric, distantly aware of Cian and the others heading into the cabin behind her. "How did you know?" she asked.

"Jeremy called me." He cut a worried look toward the cabin, then brought his gaze back to hers. "How's she doing?"

"Better. Jillian's amazing."

A grin briefly touched his lips. "Yeah, she's pretty special."

Moving down a step, she asked, "How did it go in Hawkley? Did you see Perry?"

"No, but I ran into a young guy named Jason Donovan when we were making our way back to the truck. I'm positive he's the one Perry ran off with, Chelse. He had her scent all over him." Before she could get too excited, he held up his battered hand and said, "I couldn't say much to him, since I didn't know who might be watching us. But I asked him if she's okay, and he said that she is."

"Then what?"

"Then Cian and I had to leave."

"That's it?" She shook her head, her voice thick with confusion. "You just let him walk away?"

"I didn't have any other choice. I don't know what's going on with this Jason guy, or what he's having to deal with in that pack. If we make it obvious that we're interested in Perry, they might try to move her, even get her out of the state, and then our chances of getting her back go to hell."

She nodded, trying to understand, but it was impossible not to question his decision. She didn't care about Jason Donovan or the Whiteclaw. She just wanted her sister back!

As if he could sense her wariness, he lowered his voice. "I know this is difficult, Chelse. All I'm asking is that you trust me."

Crossing her arms over her chest, she took a deep breath. "I'm trying, Eric. But it's not…easy."

A sharp, angry look of impatience hardened his expression. "You either do or you don't, Chelsea."

"It's not that simple!"

She waited for him to say something more, but he just

kept staring, his gaze locked hard and tight on hers, and his dark irises began to burn with a primal, provocative light. They shimmered like pools of metal reflecting the searing heat of the sun, making her feel deliciously warm.

Cursing under his breath, he lowered his head and pressed the heels of his palms to his eyes, clearly struggling for control. "I don't believe this shit," he forced out through his gritted teeth.

"What?"

"Even when you irritate the hell out of me, I still want you," he growled. "You are bloody dangerous."

She fought the urge to smile, knowing it wasn't funny. But, God, it felt good to be so wanted.

When he lifted his head again, his lashes were lowered, banking the molten glow, and he took a sharp breath. "Let's go in and wait for the others. I need to tell them what Cian and I learned."

They went inside, waiting for those who could make it to arrive, and once they were all gathered in the Burnses' kitchen, Eric quickly introduced her to the ones she didn't know, then sat beside her at the table. Mic and her husband, Brody, had gone down to the town of Covington for the day with Torrance, but Jeremy had joined the group, along with Carla's partner, Wyatt, and Torrance's husband, Mason.

Leaning against one of the counters, Mason slid his dark gaze toward Eric. "So what did you guys learn?"

"First of all, Clive Claymore's boys are living back at home."

Mason scowled. "Seb and Harris?"

Eric nodded. "Seems their old man died a few months back, giving his psychopath of a brother control of the pack. The first thing he did was send for his nephews."

"Shit," the Runner muttered.

"That's exactly what we were thinking," Cian drawled, sitting with them at the table.

"Why?" Chelsea asked. "What's wrong with them?"

The sinful-looking Irishman gave an eloquent shrug. "Seb seems fine. It's Harris who was always a problem. But it sounds like his uncle thinks they're both golden."

"So Roy Claymore's running things now?" Mason asked, scrubbing a hand over his rugged jaw.

Eric nodded again, before relaying something Roy had said about the Whiteclaw males enjoying the company of the human girls they knew from the club—and how they'd spotted several of the girls in the town.

"How did you explain what happened on Saturday night?" she asked, since the question had been worrying her all morning.

With a grimace, he said, "I told them you were dead."

"What?" she gasped.

"Until we can go in and get Perry, it's best if we don't have them sniffing around for you."

"Not that you're not lovely to sniff," Cian offered with a wicked grin that had Eric shooting him a warning glare. After a few colorful exchanges, the verbal skirmish ended with Cian laughing, while Eric muttered under his breath about the Runner always acting like a jackass.

They finished up the discussion, making plans to meet up again later for dinner before the others headed out. Touching Eric's arm to get his attention, Chelsea said, "I need to switch my laundry around and make a few phone calls. Do you mind if we head back over to the cabin?"

"You go ahead. I'll be right behind you."

Eric watched silently as Chelsea stood up from the table. He didn't like her leaving without him, but he needed to talk to Jillian.

"You did great today with Casey," Jillian said, giving her a warm smile. "Thanks so much for your help."

"I just wish I could have done more. Your abilities… they're incredible. If I could, I'd take you home with me. The women at the shelter where I volunteer would love you."

Jillian's brown eyes sparkled as she glanced at Eric, then brought her bright gaze back to Chelsea. "And here I was thinking that we should just keep *you*."

"Come on," Jeremy drawled as he moved to his feet, obviously sensing that Eric wanted a few moments alone with his wife. "I'll walk you back over."

The moment he heard the front door close behind them, Eric looked across the table at Jillian and growled, "What the hell were you thinking?"

Her eyes went wide. "Excuse me?"

"Why would you let her see what happened to Casey?"

"What do you mean? She's tough. She can handle it."

"You think letting her see a woman who'd been ripped to shreds by her husband is going to make it easier for her to accept what we are? What *I* am?" he snarled, his voice getting louder. "Christ, Jillian. She's already distrustful where men are concerned. Now she probably won't even let me come near her."

Jillian rolled her eyes, as if he was being ridiculous. "She's not an idiot. She knows you weren't responsible for what happened to Casey."

"She might know it, but she'll still—"

"Eric," she said, cutting him off, "you're underestimating her. Again. She's tougher than she looks. And you're strong enough to make this work."

"It's not me that I'm worried about. It's the parts I don't always control." And thinking about what Davis had done to Casey was really screwing with his head. It just put into perspective how much more fragile Chelsea was than him. How breakable. "I can't afford to make any mistakes, Jillian. This is a woman's life we're talking about."

"That's right. *Your* woman."

"I never said that," he growled.

"You didn't have to," she snapped, her dark gaze glittering with frustration. "She means something to you. I know she does. But you won't ever know what that could be if you don't take a chance."

"Chances are for fools," he grunted, shoving away from the table.

"That's not true," she argued, moving to her feet as soon as he did, looking as if she was ready to chase him down if he decided to run. "What the hell happened to you, Eric? Aren't you the same guy who once told me that when you find love, it's worth taking a risk or two?"

His heart was pounding, pulse rushing hard and fast. "That was different."

"Oh, yeah? How?"

Swiping his hand through the air, he said, "Jeremy loved you. You loved him."

"And you don't love her?"

Losing his tenuous hold on his temper, he roared, "Damn it, Jillian! Did I ever say that I did?"

"Hey, now. Don't make me kick your ass for yelling at my wife," Jeremy drawled, walking back into the kitchen. Eric had been so caught up in their argument that he hadn't even heard Jeremy come back into the cabin.

"Sorry," he grunted, scrubbing his hands down his face. God, he felt like such a mess.

After offering a quick apology to Jillian, who told him to stop being stupid and get his head out of his ass, Eric let himself out. As he walked down the Alley, his thoughts remained focused on Chelsea, working over all the things that he'd learned about her. She was funny, loyal, coura-geous. She was also obviously devoted to those she cared about—the situation with her sister the perfect example. And now there was Casey. He couldn't help but wonder what it would be like to have a woman give him that same level of worry and care. Women had always come easy to him, but what they'd wanted from him had always been just as easy.

That'd always been enough for him. Until now. Another shitty bit of irony, considering Chelsea wasn't someone he could have a future with. All he could hope for was to get as much of her as he could while they were still to-gether, before necessity tore them apart.

He wished like hell that he knew what she was think-ing. If she felt anything at all for him, or if it was just phys-ical on her part. If he was any man but himself, he'd have done everything he could to forge a lasting connection between them. But without the call of her scent, he had no claim on her. And it was really starting to piss him off.

He didn't see her as he walked into the cabin and headed into the laundry room that was connected to the back of the kitchen. But she appeared in the doorway just as he was taking off his bloodied shirt, the look on her face a priceless mix of surprise and desire. Shock and lust.

"Oh, sorry," she said in a rush, apparently flustered to have caught him getting undressed. "I was, uh, just going to ask if you want me to put on some coffee."

"That'd be great. I just need to grab a quick shower."

She stepped out of the doorway and back into the kitchen, so that he could get past. But he didn't move. He just stood there…staring at her…drowning all over again. Then her gaze dropped, her breath coming a little faster as she checked out his chest, and Eric went hard.

* * *

"Sorry again," Chelsea whispered, painfully aware that she was staring. "I know this is rude, but I'm…" She had to swallow before she could get the words out. "I'm just not used to men like you."

"What kind of men do you usually date?" he asked, taking a step toward her.

Her lips twitched with a wry smile. "Not ones like you, that's for sure. You're just…*more*. More height. More muscles." She shot him a telling look from under her lashes. "More attitude."

"I'm curious, Chelse." He was standing right in front of her now, and he lifted his hands, sinking his fingers into her hair and tipping her head back. With his gorgeous face right over hers, he asked, "Hasn't anyone ever told you that more is better?"

"Sometimes," she said, surprised by the way her voice sounded all breathy. "And sometimes it's just…superfluous. Like having too many vibrators to choose from when you only need one. I have a friend with that problem. By the time she finally makes a choice, she's usually so tired she just goes to sleep."

He threw back his head and laughed, his strong, corded throat mesmerizing to watch. And then he was looking down at her again, the lopsided grin on his lips making him seem softer…more tender. Which made his next words that much more jarring, since she'd been expecting a playful seduction, instead of a psyche eval. "You don't have a very high opinion of men, do you?"

Pulling out of his hold, she wrapped her arms over her middle and said, "I try not to judge, but it's hard, after a lot of the cases I've seen at the shelter. Human males can be just as cruel as Casey's husband was. Some are even worse."

* * *

Eric had the feeling that she was talking from personal experience, and wondered just how much of a bastard her old man really was. "Did your father hit your mother? Or you and Perry?"

Her expression tightened, but she shook her head. "He never physically abused any of us. But there are other ways of breaking a woman down."

"I know."

"Abuse comes in a lot of different forms," she muttered, sounding like she was trying to convince him. "My mother's so controlled, she can't even think for herself. She wears his opinions like they're a part of her. It's sick. And he tried to do the same with me and Perry, like we were his little puppets to control. It might not have been physical, but it was definitely mental abuse."

"Chelsea." Though he was seething with rage for her father, he somehow managed to keep his voice gentle. "I'm not disagreeing with you."

For a moment, she only held his stare with those big blue eyes. Then she slowly shook her head again. "I keep trying, Eric, but I can't seem to figure you out."

She sounded so disgruntled about it, he couldn't help but smile. "And you're usually good at figuring men out, aren't you?"

Her shrug spoke volumes. "Men are simple creatures."

"Not all of us," he said softly.

She gave a slow blink, and whispered, "I think I'm beginning to see that."

Eric took a deep breath, then stepped close to her again. "And what else are you starting to see?"

A nervous flick of her tongue over that lush lower lip. "What do you mean?"

"Can you see *me,* Chelse?"

"I see you." Pulling her lower lip through her teeth, she ran her gaze over his bare chest and abs again, and trembled. "Eric, you really are too much for me."

He hadn't meant if she saw him in a physical sense— but he wasn't going to argue about it. He wanted her so badly, he'd take whatever he could get.

"I'm not too much," he rasped, reaching down and hooking one hand under her thigh. Bending his knees a little, he pulled her against him, letting her feel how incredibly hard he was for her. Then he fisted his other hand in her hair and took her mouth with a long, drugging kiss, taking more than he ever had from any other woman, just from the hungry touch of his lips against hers. From the deep, explicit tasting, his tongue moving against her own in a blatantly seductive rhythm that mimicked hot, slick sex. But it backfired and trapped him just as deeply, pulling him in, his heart beating to such a hard, hammering rhythm he could feel it pumping through every cell of his body, pulsing inside his brain.

"When I'm finally inside you, I promise you won't be complaining, Chelse. We'll take it nice and slow—" his lips touched the warm curve of her cheek, trailing toward her ear "—until you're sinking your little nails into my back, begging for more. For *all* of me. I might be bigger and heavier than you are, but I'll *always* make sure you're ready for me."

Oh, God, she thought, clinging to those hard, muscular shoulders, loving the way he felt beneath her hands. She was so primed she was amazed she hadn't already melted into an embarrassing puddle on the floor. "Eric," she gasped, "if I get any more ready, I'll be done."

"Then consider this just for me," he growled, picking her up and laying her down on the kitchen table. Before she could so much as blink, he undid the zipper on her jeans and ripped them off, leaving her lower body clad in nothing but a tiny black pair of panties. "I've been thinking about your taste all damn day," he groaned, rubbing his rough hands along her thighs until his thumbs met at her center. "It's driving me crazy."

She blinked, wondering if his hunger for her was a Lycan thing...or an Eric thing. Then her brain was wiped clean as she watched him tear off her panties, shove her legs apart and lower his head.

Oh, God. Oh, God. Oh, God...

The instant the heat of his mouth touched that most intimate part of her, it shook her apart inside. Melted her down. Brought stupid tears to her eyes that she couldn't stop, couldn't control. It was too good, too...real and raw and beautiful. He held her open with his thumbs, while his wicked tongue did things to her body that made her cry out, the sexy, gravelly sounds he made telling her he was enjoying it every bit as much as she was. She'd never thought a man could be so desperate for her, but Eric licked at her sex as if he was starved for her taste, his tongue thrusting and lapping until she felt ready to come out of her skin. It didn't take long for her to fall into a shattering climax, the deep, rhythmic pulses of pleasure jolting through her body like violent, crashing waves, the sensation lush and tight and breathtaking. Mind-blowing. And he stayed right there with her, tonguing her drenched, sensitive flesh until she felt herself swept up in another wild, devastating wave...and then everything went black and dark and hazy.

When she came back, her lungs were still heaving, struggling to draw in enough air, her body still buzzing with soft, residual spasms of pleasure. She felt full inside, her lashes fluttering as she realized Eric had two big fingers inside her, slowly working them deeper. Opening her eyes, she found him leaning over her, his face close to hers, and her breath caught. She'd never seen so much dark, possessive hunger, so much need.

"One more," he said in a raw voice—and she realized he was trying to work a third finger inside her.

"Can't," she gasped. "It's too much."

"They'll fit, Chelse." Grabbing her hand, he pressed it against the thick, rigid bulge of his cock, his jeans straining to contain it. "They *have* to."

She blinked, gasping again as comprehension dawned. He was big. Bigger than two fingers. Bigger than three. That's why he was pushing her...stretching her. He'd promised he'd get her ready so that he wouldn't hurt her when he put that massive thing inside her, and that's exactly what he was trying to do.

He must have read the panic in her eyes, because he leaned down and pressed a tender kiss to her lips. "It's okay," he whispered, keeping his mouth against hers as he gentled his touch. "We'll take as much time as you need. I won't hurt you. No matter what happens, I swear I'll never hurt you."

Eric meant every word. He just hoped to God it was a promise he could keep.

"Don't stop," she whispered, her scent telling him that her panic was fading. "I want you, Eric. But I...I just—"

Slipping his fingers from her body, he drew back his head so that he could see her eyes. "What is it, honey?"

Face still flushed with color, she licked her lips. "I need you to promise that you won't bite me. Or try to hold me down. I need...I need to feel like I still have control."

He buried his hot face in the smooth curve of her shoulder, choking back a frustrated growl. He was walking such a fine line…and he knew he couldn't go through with this without making her understand. "I won't bite you, Chelse. But I don't know how much control I can give you. It's not in my nature. I like to take charge in and out of bed." Lifting his head, he said, "That need is even more intense with you."

"Because I'm human?"

"To be honest, I've never done this with a human before."

Her eyes went wide. "You mean slept with one?"

"No. I mean anything. I've only ever touched pack females."

"Oh." She paused for a moment, that deep blue gaze searching his face…his eyes. "Is it different?"

"Maybe not for everyone. But it is for me."

"I don't understand."

"Because of my bloodline, I sense things…deeper. Sharper. The way you smell, the way you feel. The way you taste. It's all…magnified."

"And is that a bad thing?" she asked. She looked so incredibly beautiful lying there beneath him, with her long, dark hair spread out over the table, that it made his chest hurt.

He swallowed the lump of emotion stuck in his throat, and forced himself to give her the truth. "If I lose control…it could be."

"Eric," she murmured, brushing her fingers through his hair. "You're the same man who refused to have sex with me when I was drugged, no matter how much I begged. Either you just weren't interested, or you have better control than anyone I've ever known."

"It definitely wasn't for lack of wanting you," he said in a low voice, knowing that she still didn't understand. Not completely. But she was looking at him with so much tenderness, so much passion and need, that he couldn't stop himself from leaning down and taking her mouth again, the warm, addictive taste of her driving him wild. His fingers slipped back inside her, his thumb finding her clit, and he made her come twice more, hard and fast, knowing that the more times he got her off, the easier it would be for her to take him.

Taking her breathless, keening cries of pleasure into his mouth, Eric felt them move through his body like a force of nature, powerful and violent. One that he wished had the power to change him into something...different. Something new. Something that had a chance in hell of keeping her.

Yes, the wolf hissed. *That's right. I want to keep her, too...*

Desperate, his hands shaking, he started ripping at the buttons on his fly, when he realized the annoying buzz coming from his pocket was a text alert on his phone. But he didn't care. Nothing could be more important than doing exactly what he was doing at that moment, only seconds away from getting inside her.

Chelsea, however, didn't see it that way. "Eric, you need to check that."

Dropping his forehead against her soft breasts, he grunted, "Please, Chelse. I'm *begging* you. Just ignore it."

"I know this is crappy timing, but it might be something important. Someone might be trying to get in touch with you about Perry."

He cursed something foul under his breath, but moved away from her. It wasn't easy to take his eyes off the tempting, mouthwatering sight of her half-naked body, but he pulled the phone from his pocket and read the text. "Shit. I just can't catch a bloody break," he muttered a few seconds later, pulling his hand down his face.

"What is it?" she asked, sliding off the edge of the table. "Did something happen?"

"It's from my sister," he told her, quickly buttoning his jeans back up while she pulled on a pair of panties from the laundry basket she'd left on a kitchen chair. "I need to go up to town and make sure she's okay."

"What's wrong?"

"I'm not sure." He grabbed a clean shirt from the laundry room and pulled it on. "It sounds like she thinks someone might have been in her house."

"Could it be someone from another pack?"

Eric shook his head. "Not with the security we have in place. More than likely, it was one of our own trying to freak her out."

"That's awful," she said as she pulled on her jeans. "Would it be okay if I went with you?"

"You sure?" he asked, surprised that she'd want to see the town.

"I'm sure." Slipping her shoes on, she slid him a kinda shy, sincere, beautiful smile. "I want to see where you're from. And I'd love to meet your sister."

So long as they were careful, Eric knew she wouldn't be in any danger. Especially when it was still daylight out. And hell, when she looked at him like that, there was no way he could say no.

"Okay, then," he said, grabbing his keys. "Let's go."

Chapter Eleven

As they made their way up one of the private roads that ran from the Alley to Shadow Peak, Eric found himself wondering what Chelsea would think of his hometown.

As if she was reading his mind, she asked, "What is the town like? And how do you keep it hidden—I mean, what do you do if humans find it?"

"To humans, Shadow Peak looks like any other small mountain community, but we don't get a lot of unwanted visitors." He shot her a quick glance. "As you discovered for yourself the other night, we have scouts posted throughout the forest, who alert us to any humans traveling the mountain roads."

"And what about the pack's land? Is it really privately owned, like you told me before?"

Nodding, he said, "Both the Alley and Shadow Peak are built on private land that has belonged to the eldest pack families for centuries, with access only by private roads that are clearly marked."

"Or not so clearly," she pointed out, her tone wry.

Eric smirked as he glanced her way again, unable to keep his damn eyes off her. "You just weren't paying attention."

"This isn't getting us anywhere," she said, the husky sound of her laughter making him hot. But then, he was still so wound up from their time together in the kitchen, he figured she could blow him a kiss and he'd probably lose it. "So tell me something else about your…people."

Taking it as a good sign that she wanted to know more about him, Eric braced his elbow on the door, his fingers stroking the stubble on his chin, and gave her some facts. "Well, we're good at blending in when we have to, and we all have driver's licenses and Social Security numbers, so we have no problem moving around in the human world. Even our genetic makeup cloaks what we really are, so there's nothing in our DNA to alert a doctor if one of us ends up in the hospital. The only real threat to our secret and our way of life are the rogues."

"The ones who…hunt humans?"

"Yeah. And then there are the other packs. They could become a serious problem for the Silvercrest."

"You mean like the Whiteclaw?" she asked, shifting around a bit in her seat so that she could face him.

With another nod, he said, "We have three packs who border our land, on the north, west and south. After what happened five months ago, they see us as weak."

"What happened five months ago?"

Since there was a chance she might hear something about his father while they were in town—though he didn't plan on taking her around anyone but Elise—Eric figured it was time to tell her about what had happened. He just hoped like hell that it didn't blow up in his face.

Shoving his fingers back through his hair, he tried not to snarl as he said, "We, uh, had a bit of an uprising."

Silence followed, and then she gave a soft, confused laugh. "That's it, Eric? That's all you're going to tell me?"

His throat worked on a hard swallow. "Actually, there are some things that I need to explain before we get there."

Another pause, as if she could sense his tension. And then a simple, encouraging, "Okay."

Pulling in a deep breath, Eric finally bit the bullet and told her about his father's maniacal plan to take over the Silvercrest. A bloodthirsty plan that had resulted in a significant loss of life, had shattered the pack's sense of safety and left an entire group of teens…as well as most of the residents in Shadow Peak…emotionally traumatized. As a result, the town had been left without its leaders, and he described how he'd been trying to set up an interim government based on free election. He also explained that the Runners were now handling all elements of security for the pack, though a few of the residents had set up an auxiliary security unit inside the town itself, since there were still Lycans who were too biased to go to the Runners if there was an issue they needed help with.

Then he told her about Elise's history, so that she would understand what they were heading into. It wasn't easy to convey the brutal story of how his sister had been raped by three Lycan males several years ago, the trauma of the nightmare still affecting her today. He told her about Eli, as well, and how his older brother had been banished from the pack after managing to track down and kill one of the wolves involved in the rape. Because the League of Elders who had governed the pack at the time hadn't sanctioned the kill, Eli had been exiled. The other two Lycans who had attacked Elise had never been found.

"Torrance told me that Lycans are incredible trackers," she said when he was done, her quiet voice thick with emotion. "Why couldn't the pack find the ones who were responsible?"

"The night Elise was attacked, it was storming. The rains washed any traces of scent away, and there was nothing to track. It was just pure luck that Eli managed to find one of them."

"Was he one of the Silvercrest?"

Working his jaw, he said, "No. He was from some pack out in Wyoming. We never could find any connection to any of the packs around here to explain what he was doing in the area."

"So the trail stopped cold." She reached out, placing a comforting hand on his rigid shoulder, rubbing a little at the knotted muscle. It felt so good, he wanted to demand she put it back when she took her hand away. Wanted to insist she keep touching him. But she wrapped her arms around herself, as if she was cold, and added, "No wonder Elise lives on edge. I would, too."

He turned off the cold air blowing in from the vents, and heard himself telling her things that he'd only ever discussed with Jillian—and only then because they'd been in the middle of the nightmare with his father. But he wanted Chelsea to know. Knew, without any doubt, that she would understand. "When she was raped, my father told Elise that it was her fault for being weaker than they were. Then he went and used her in his twisted games, breaking her down even more. If I didn't already hate him for what he did to the pack, I'd despise him for how he treated Elise. For what he put her through."

As they pulled into the town, she said, "I'd feel the same way, Eric."

"So that's the whole ugly story," he grated, scrubbing his hand over his mouth as if he could somehow wipe away the taste of bitterness that still lingered. "My father wreaked havoc on this place, and the pack is still trying to piece itself back together. The teens who were targeted are still going through a rough time, but Max, Michaela's brother, has been doing a great job of working with them."

"She told me about how he was turned and is going to train to be a Runner along with his friend Elliot."

"Yeah, they're some good guys. Since they spend more time in town nowadays than I do, they've been keeping an eye on Elise for me." He steered the truck into a small alley between two closed offices, and turned off the engine. "But from her text, it sounds like neither of them was able to follow her home from work today."

He took his gun out of the glove box, where he'd stowed it before paying a visit to Casey's asshole husband, and then they climbed out of the truck, meeting up at the tailgate. Looking around, she said, "I thought we were going to Elise's house."

"We are. She's just a few blocks over." As they started down the sidewalk, he added, "I thought it might be better if I didn't draw any attention to the fact that I'm in town." At least not when Chelsea was with him. The last thing he wanted was her having to listen to some of the bullshit that got tossed his way these days.

The walk took only a few minutes, the streets thankfully quiet. They made their way up Elise's front steps, but before Eric even had the chance to knock, his sister opened the door, looking as beautiful as ever, though it was clear she was upset. Her dark red hair, which had come from their mother, looked as if it had been combed with nervous fingers, her pale face tight with strain, her scent a heartbreaking mixture of rage and fear that made Eric want to destroy whoever was responsible.

For so many years, he'd put up with his father's bullshit to protect her, make things easier for her, and look where it'd gotten them. If she wasn't hiding out at her office, she was hiding here in her home, both of them now treated with suspicion by the townspeople who had once been their friends.

Damn it, he should have gutted his old man when he had the chance.

Elise stepped aside to let them into the house, managing a small smile for Chelsea, who Eric knew she'd heard about from Jillian. "Hey, El. I've brought someone with me." He took Chelsea's hand, pulling her to his side. "Elise, this is Chelsea. Chelsea, my sister, Elise."

Chelsea said that it was nice to have the chance to meet her, and his sister's smile got a little brighter. "It's nice to meet you, too."

"What exactly happened?" he asked, shutting the door behind them as Chelsea followed Elise into her living room.

Perching on the arm of a loveseat, Elise clutched a throw pillow against her chest and slid him an apologetic look. "Eric, I'm sorry I texted you. I just got a little... spooked. But I'm fine now."

Preferring to stay on his feet, he pushed his hands in his pockets. "You don't need to be sorry, El. Just tell me what happened."

Elise explained how she came home from work to find her back door ajar, when she was certain she'd locked it before leaving. Not wanting to check the house by herself, she tried to get someone from the new security service in town to come over, but they refused, which had Eric saying a few choice things under his breath. He told her that if something like that happened again, she was to call him first, then Max or Elliot, since the younger men were usually close by. Then he asked why the hell she hadn't gotten out of the house. Lifting her chin in a way that reminded him of Chelsea, she told him that she *did* call Max, but wasn't able to get in touch with him. While she was explaining that her neighbor Eddie came home just as she was getting ready to leave and did a walkthrough to make sure no one was inside, Max showed up at the front door and Eric let him in. The two men searched the house themselves, taking different routes, then met up in the living room, where his sister and Chelsea were quietly talking.

"I didn't pick up the scent of another male," Eric said, scraping his palm over his jaw as he stood near the fireplace. "Just Max and Eddie."

"I must have just forgotten to shut the door behind me this morning," Elise murmured, sounding as if she was trying to convince herself it was true.

"Did you tell him about the calls?" Max asked, which earned him a glare from Elise.

Getting the feeling he wasn't being told the whole story, Eric struggled to hold on to his temper. "What calls?"

Elise shook her head, then nervously tucked a dark strand of hair behind her ear. "It's nothing, Eric."

Frustration roughened his tone. "Damn it, El. I can't help you if you won't be honest with me."

"It was just some asshole trying to scare me," she burst out, surging to her feet with the pillow still clutched against her chest. "It's nothing new. After everything that's happened, we've been expecting it."

"That doesn't make it right," he growled.

The conversation went downhill from there, with Eric

trying to convince her to come back to the Alley with him
and Chelsea, and Elise firmly refusing, saying that she
wasn't going to be scared out of her home. Both of them
refused to back down, until Max offered another solu-
tion, saying that he could crash there for the night so she
wouldn't be alone.

Eric shot his sister a look that said she'd either accept
Max's offer or get dragged down to the Alley with him,
so she did. After cutting a hostile glare toward Eric, she
gave Michaela's brother a tight smile. "Thanks, Max. I
really appreciate it."

"Guys, I hate to interrupt," Chelsea said, leaning forward in the chair near the window, her attention focused
on something outside, "but it looks like there's a crowd
gathering in front of the house."

Hell, Eric thought, rubbing his eyes. This was all they
needed. "Wait here." He looked at both women. "I mean
it. The last thing I need is the two of you getting caught
in the middle of whatever's going on." Then he told Max
to keep an eye on them, and walked outside, shutting the
front door behind him.

There were about twenty people gathered in the street,
and in the front of the group, standing on the sidewalk,
was Glenn Farrow. Glenn had been petitioning for Eric
and Elise's banishment ever since their father had gone
all apocalyptic on the pack. He was a social climber of
the worst sort, and he'd zeroed in on Eric's bloodline and
his tie with the Runners as a platform he could use to gain
attention. He spouted nothing but a load of bullshit—and
yet, there were those in town who were listening.

Wearing a smarmy smile that matched the slicked-back
style of his thinning hair, Glenn locked his pale gaze with
Eric's. "Your sister really has to stop bothering our security officers here in town, Drake. You and the Runners

might patrol our borders, but the private security team we've put together is out of your control."

Eric kept his hands loose at his sides as he came to a stop a few feet away from the Lycan, wanting to be ready in case the idiot tried anything. Farrow was shorter than Eric by a good five inches, and scrawny as a sapling—but he wouldn't put it past the guy to fight dirty. "You need to mind your own business, Glenn. This has nothing to do with you—unless you're the one causing the trouble."

"Trouble? What trouble?" the Lycan sneered. "You know she's making it all up."

Beyond Glenn's shoulders, Eric saw several of those in the crowd nodding their heads in agreement. Once, these people had looked up to him—but now he was a prime example of just how far someone could fall in their eyes. There was a time when it would have bothered him greatly, but that was no longer the case. With a sharp little jolt, he realized that the only opinions that mattered to him these days were his own…Chelsea's…Eli's and Elise's…and those of his friends in the Alley. The rest, he was starting to feel, could all go to hell.

He wasn't looking for a fight with Glenn and his cronies. But he wasn't going to let them drag Elise's name through the mud, either. "You need to watch your mouth, Glenn."

"I'm only saying what a bunch of us are thinking."

"I won't tell you again," he warned in a chilling tone. "Get your ass out of here."

"Make me," the Lycan shot back as if they were school kids facing off on a playground. Shaking his head at the pathetic loser, Eric started to turn and head back inside, knowing the last thing he needed to do in front of so many witnesses was give in to his need to knock Glenn on his skinny backside. But the idiot didn't know when to leave well enough alone. Drunk on his little power play, the jackass came up behind him and shoved Eric in the shoulder. "You runnin' now, Drake?"

His fingertips burned as deadly claws pricked just beneath the surface of his skin, but he fought back the urge to release them. Glenn was just looking for a way to add more fuel to the fire, and Eric was damned if he was going to give it to him.

Rubbing his tongue over his teeth, Eric slowly turned around and regarded the Lycan with a look of disgust.

"You and your friends can't keep running things," Glenn snarled, his voice rising. "The pack doesn't want their help."

"Maybe a few bigots feel that way. But I think the majority are finally seeing the Runners for what they are." It was ironic, really. In his bid to destroy the Runners forever, his father had brought the pack closer to acceptance of the half Lycan, half human hunters than they'd ever been before, since it was the Runners who had saved the town from Stefan Drake's psychotic plans. Yeah, there was still a lot of progress to be made, but at least the lines that separated the Runners and the pack were starting to blur.

"What they are," Glenn echoed with a gritty laugh. "You mean a bunch of embarrassing half-breeds?"

"More like heroes!" someone called out from the crowd.

"They're mongrels!" Glenn shouted, turning red in the face. Then he took a deep breath, regrouping, and slid Eric a taunting leer. "There might be a few who misguidedly support the Runners, but you should know that there are a lot of us who will do whatever it takes to stop them from assuming control here." His voice got lower. "And there are a lot of us who believe that your family will finally get what it deserves. Including your sister."

It took no more than a second for Eric to have Glenn's throat in his grip, then slam him down backward on the hood of the nearest parked car with a bone-jarring thud. "You so much as even look at my sister," he said in a low, deadly rasp, leaning over and getting right in the bastard's face, "and I'll take your fucking head off. We clear on that?"

He didn't wait for an answer. He just left Glenn sprawled on the hood, turning back toward the house just in time to catch Chelsea and Elise rushing down the front steps, their expressions of worry nearly identical.

"Sorry!" Max called out, following after them. "I tried to keep them inside, but your woman kneed me." Judging by the way Max was walking, Eric had a good idea of *where* Chelsea had landed the blow, and he was privately thankful he hadn't been the one trying to stop her. She fought dirty!

"Are you okay?" she called out, running up to him.

"I'm fine," he told her just as Crissy Cowell came around the edge of the crowd, a derisive look on her face when she spotted Chelsea.

"A human, Eric? Are you kidding me?"

He cut the female Lycan a dark look from beneath his brows. "Stay out of it, Crissy."

Laughing, showing a catty side of her personality that Eric must have been blind to miss, she asked, "Isn't she a little too much like prey for a guy like you?"

"I'd watch what you say, bitch." The snarled words came from Elise.

Crissy smirked. "So the little human doesn't mind that he likes to use his fangs and claws in the sack?"

Chelsea might have paled, but she didn't cower. "Do you have any idea how jealous you sound right now?" she snapped.

The Lycan looked at Eric, her rouged lips curled in a sneer. "Dark wolves and humans don't mix."

"For the last time," he growled, wondering how he'd ever been stupid enough to get involved with this woman, "mind your own damn business."

"But she's right!" Glenn shouted, pressing one hand against the back of his head as he staggered away from the car where Eric had flattened him. "You're threatening this whole community by bringing her here!"

Everyone started shouting at the same time, his supporters well outnumbered by those who were quickly jumping on Farrow's bandwagon. *"When they find her body, he'll bring the cops down on us!...He was just fooling us for years!...He's just like his father!...This is going to end in another catastrophe!"* In the middle of it all, someone threw a clump of mud at his chest, splattering his T-shirt and arms. Eric growled, scanning the crowd for the guilty party, but all he saw was a sea of angry faces.

"I don't know about the rest of you," Glenn's brother, Mark, muttered, puffing up his chest as he came toward them, "but I think a night in lock-up might do him some good." He started to lower his hand toward the hip holster he always wore for his gun, but Eric beat him to the draw. He whipped his Beretta from his waistband behind his back, aiming it point-blank at the center of the Lycan's forehead.

Slowly releasing the gun's safety, Eric narrowed his eyes on the younger Farrow. "You need to walk away, Mark. Right now. Because I am done with this shit."

"Glenn's right about you," Mark snarled, moving his hand away from his weapon. "You really are as crazy as your old man."

"He's not crazy, Mark. You're just a jackass!" The set down came from Brian Everett, who came to stand beside Chelsea just as Eric was slipping the Beretta back into his jeans. Brian was one of the guys who Eric had worked with on the new housing development he'd started before everything went to hell because of his father. He and Brian had always gotten along, but it was still a surprise to hear him publicly going against Glenn. There'd been such a negative push against him lately that Eric had lost sight of those who still supported him.

They waited until some of the others had dragged Glenn and Mark away, apparently deciding that retreat was their best option at this point. With a small sigh of relief to see a red-faced Crissy leaving, as well, Eric turned his attention to Brian. They talked about how Elise, who was still standing near her front steps with Max, had thought someone had been in her home. "If El has any trouble again," the older Lycan told him, "you let her know that she can give me and Meryl a call, night or day. She's always welcome over at ours."

"Thanks, Brian." He shook the other man's hand. "I really appreciate it."

"I'd like to thank you, as well," Chelsea murmured, still glaring at the few stragglers who remained on the far side of the street. She looked so enraged on his behalf, and it put a kinda warm feeling in Eric's chest that he liked far more than he should.

They said goodbye to Brian, who told them he'd clear away the remaining members of the crowd, then headed over to wrap things up with Elise and Max. Though Chelsea apologized for hurting him, Max still gave her a wide berth—not that Eric blamed the guy. He'd give any woman who kneed him in the nuts a wide berth, too.

After Eric had made Elise promise to call him the next day, his sister and Max went inside the house, talking about what kind of pizza they should order for dinner, and he and Chelsea started back down the blessedly quiet street. "Now I really need that shower," he muttered, scrubbing his hands over his arms to wipe off the splatters of mud that still covered him.

"Do you want to stop by your house while we're here?" she asked.

He slid her a questioning look. "You wouldn't mind?"

"I'd like to see where you live," she said with a little smile.

"It's not far, so we can walk," he told her, thinking it would be a good chance for him to pick up some of his things. And for some reason that he didn't quite understand, he liked the idea of having her in his home.

They turned at the next corner, heading left, and passed a group of children who were playing in one of the yards, running through a sprinkler. The kids waved at Eric, and he started to wave back, until one of the mothers sitting on the front porch of the house caught sight of him and started shooing the kids inside.

Unable to believe what she'd just seen, Chelsea said, "I don't understand this place, Eric. Doesn't it drive you crazy when they act like that?"

He shrugged. "You can't make people trust you, Chelse. They either do or they don't."

"But you haven't done anything to lose their trust!"

The look he slid her was dark and piercing. "That doesn't always matter, does it?"

She flinched, knowing damn well he was thinking about the conversation they'd had earlier about Jason Donovan and Perry. Which wasn't fair. "I've given you more trust than I've ever given any other man. And I've only known you for a few days. So cut me some slack."

He was quiet for a moment, and then he said, "Sorry. This place just sets me on edge."

She was about to tell him that she could understand why, when his phone rang. Eric took the call, his mouth tilting in a frown as he listened, then said goodbye and slid the phone back in his pocket.

"What's wrong?"

Rubbing at the back of his neck, he said, "That was Jeremy. They've found some tracks on our land that don't belong to the pack. From the scent, they think that five or more males from the Greywolf pack up north of us must have been sniffing around, doing reconnaissance on the town."

"Do you really think one of the other packs might attack the Silvercrest?"

"It's always been a possibility, but especially now that we're so vulnerable. And if one tried to invade our land, you can bet the violence would spread. The idea of an all-out pack war is a huge concern for a lot of reasons, the least of which is the threat of exposure."

"You mean to humans?" she asked.

"Yeah." He gave a tense sigh. "But sometimes I think we're lucky it's held together this long."

Before Chelsea could lecture him about having a defeatist attitude, they reached his home—a beautiful two-story on a picturesque street lined by towering oaks. As they made their way inside, she changed the subject, saying, "Crissy was an interesting woman."

He shook his head and made a rough sound in the back of his throat. "She acted like a total bitch."

"She's the one from the other night, isn't she? The one you were with when the scouts called you about me?"

Eric grimaced as he shut the door. "Why the hell would you think that?"

A wry smile twisted the corner of her mouth. "Same hideous shade of lipstick."

He slid her a sharp glance, then slowly shook his head again. "You women are scary," he grumbled under his breath.

"I think the word you're looking for is *perceptive*."

He switched on a lamp in the spacious living room, then rolled his shoulder in one of those purely male gestures of unease. "Yeah, well, it wasn't anything…serious."

Chelsea lifted her brows. "So you were just sleeping with her?"

"Once." His voice was rough, and maybe just a tad embarrassed.

"You must have made quite an impression," she said, trying to keep her tone light. "It's obvious she wants a repeat."

Eric snorted as he headed into the kitchen through an archway. "Doesn't mean she's getting one."

He asked if she wanted anything to drink, bringing her back a cold bottle of water. She thanked him for it, then said, "You never know. You might feel differently about Crissy when things have calmed down and I'm not crowding your life anymore."

He froze with his water bottle halfway to his mouth, his eyes dark with shifting emotions. Anger, frustration and what looked like a sharp, intense burn of desire. It made her toes curl in her shoes, even as her heart gave a painful lurch in her chest. Then, very quietly, he said, "Don't."

She didn't know what she'd expected him to say, but it wasn't that. Just a lone, raw, emotion-rough command. She wanted so desperately to surrender to the relief that was slipping through her veins, easing the tightness in her chest, but couldn't quite find the courage to do it. "I'm just being realistic, Eric. I won't be here forever. Crissy will."

The hard line of his jaw told her he was pissed, but he didn't argue. He just said, "I'm grabbing that shower now. Make yourself at home while I'm gone."

Then he set down the water and pulled off his shirt, and she was stunned once again by how gorgeous his body was. God, his shoulders were huge. His arms, too. Every inch of him seemed to be ripped with muscle, but he didn't look bulky. Just sharp and fast and sleek. She loved watching his biceps bunch beneath that sexy tattoo as he hooked his shirt over his shoulder. Loved the way his muscles shifted and flexed beneath his tight skin.

As if he knew just how devastating he was to her senses, he shot her one of those cocky, crooked grins before turning around and walking away. She watched him until he disappeared through another archway, unable to take her eyes off the beautiful lines of his back and his muscled backside, loving the way his faded Levi's hugged his ass. The fiend knew exactly what he was doing to her, flaunting his gorgeous body at her, and it was working. Big-time.

It was embarrassing, how long she just stood there, staring all dreamy-eyed at the now-empty archway, but she finally shook herself out of the lust-induced trance and started looking around. The house was beautiful, though she preferred the more rustic look of the cabin. But she enjoyed walking through the living room and looking at the books and DVDs on his shelves, as well as the photographs hanging on his walls. There were a lot of pictures of him with Elise and a man who looked so much like them that she knew it must be Eli. Chelsea pored over each photograph, enjoying the different smiles on Eric's face. It was clear he was a guy who liked to have fun, and who loved his family.

This was what she'd been hoping for when she'd suggested they stop by—an insight into his life, into who he really was.

And what she found made her like him even more.

Wearing a clean pair of jeans and running a towel over his head, Eric stood in the archway to the living room and watched Chelsea studying his photographs. It felt strangely right, having her in his home. For so long he'd felt as if there was something he needed to be searching for, something he needed to find, that he couldn't get his hands on. And for the moment, at least, he felt like he had it.

"You're trying to figure me out, aren't you?"

She jumped, startled by the sound of his voice. "Does that bother you?" she asked, turning to face him.

He tossed the towel onto the back of a nearby chair, crossed his arms over his chest and propped his shoulder against the side of the archway. "No. But it won't be easy. Hell, half the time *I* can't even figure out who I am."

"You've never quite fit in here, have you?"

He gave a harsh crack of laughter. "How did you get that from looking at a bunch of photos?"

"Because it's always just the three of you," she said, pushing her hands in her pockets. "I think you have more in common with the Runners than you even realize."

Curious, he asked, "How do you figure that?"

"Because I have a feeling your father made sure you were always set apart. That he never just let you fit in. You might have been at the opposite end of the spectrum from the Runners, but it had the same isolating result."

Shaking his head, he said, "You're too damn smart for your own good sometimes."

She gave a soft laugh. "Do smart women intimidate you?"

"Not at all," he rasped, giving her a slow, intense look-over, his heavy-lidded gaze snagging on the beautiful sight of her nipples pressing against her pale gray shirt. "In fact, I think it's incredibly hot."

She snorted.

"But then," he said, flashing her a sharp smile as he brought his gaze back up to her face, "I pretty much think everything about you is hot."

He loved the husky sound of her laughter. "You wouldn't say that if you ever heard me sing. I'm always off key. Can't carry a note for love or money."

"I bet it's cute." He pulled away from the wall, lowering his arms as he started walking toward her, enjoying the way her eyes went a little wide and her cheeks turned an adorable shade of pink. "Damn cute."

"I'm also competitive at games," she said a little breathlessly.

With a slow smile, Eric rounded the back of the sofa. "I'm competitive at *lots* of things."

"What did Crissy mean, about you being a dark wolf?"

Her question stopped him dead in his tracks. "That woman needs to learn to keep her mouth shut," he muttered.

"Eric, just tell me. Please."

Needing a drink to go with this particular conversation, he turned and padded into the kitchen. A moment later, he came back into the room and handed her a beer, taking a long sip from his own bottle as he paced a few feet away, staring out the front window. After taking another swallow of the icy brew, he cleared his throat, then said, "I'm not exactly known around here for being the gentlest of lovers."

"Oh."

Tension pulsed through his body like a ramped-up,

gnawing ache, but he forced out his explanation, his fingers gripping the bottle so tightly he was surprised it didn't shatter. "It's because of my bloodline. My family and I are what our race calls dark wolves, meaning our blood is purer than most. Because of that, we're considered the highest of the pack hierarchy. It also means that we're stronger and more dominant than the other males." He ground his jaw, then shoved out the rest. "And when it comes to sex, our more visceral natures are often difficult to control."

"Oh," she said again, and he could practically hear her thinking it through. "That's why you never get involved with human women, isn't it?"

He nodded, hyper-aware of every inch of her body as she came to stand beside him.

"And so Crissy was implying that you're dangerous to me?" she asked, setting her beer down on the window ledge.

The sound surging up from his chest was rough and thick…somehow damaged. But then, it was a kind of physical pain, to be so close to something that he wanted this badly and not be able to touch it.

"Eric?" He could feel the warmth of her gaze against the side of his face.

With a hard swallow, he said, "I could be, if I lost control. That's what I was trying to tell you this afternoon."

Her response was soft. "Well, I still think it's ridiculous."

"Is it?" he growled, turning and locking his gaze with hers.

"It is." A small smile flirted with her lips. "You've never hurt me, Eric."

His voice was almost a snarl. "We haven't had sex yet, either."

Her head tilted just a bit to the side, her eyes watchful and bright. "Are you worried?"

"No." He gave a stiff shake of his head. "I won't allow myself to lose control with you."

Lifting her brows, she asked, "Then why are we arguing?"

A few seconds went by, and then he felt the tension in his coiled muscles slowly draining away. He snorted and gave her a lopsided grin. "Hell if I know."

She laughed, the sexy sound rolling down his spine like a lick of flame, making him burn. He wanted her so badly he couldn't see straight, his hunger like another living, animal thing in his body, keeping company with the wolf. It punched against his skin, starved for the feel and the taste of her.

God, there were so many ways he could screw this up. He could make a mistake, a stupid miscalculation. Or even just open his big mouth and say the wrong thing, which would be nothing new. He was an ace at pissing people off.

But, damn it, he wanted to make this work. Wanted her time with him to be something she would look back on later and...*hell,* he didn't know. Think of fondly? What a crock of shit. He didn't want to be a bloody memory.

You don't have to be...

No! He knew damn well that he couldn't give in to temptation. As time went on, it would be too difficult to keep himself balanced on that razor's edge of control. Without the power of a blood bond tying them together, the odds were too great that he'd topple off. Especially given the wolf's need for submission, and her reluctance to give it to him. He might last a week or a month, but no way in hell could he go forever without needing her complete surrender. Without needing to sink his fangs into her tender flesh and take her blood into his body.

Without needing to drive her wild with the darker, more carnal pleasures he wanted to give her again and again, until she was lost in them. Lost in *him*.

Damn it, he wanted to take her, here and now, but one look outside the window told him it was too risky. Finishing off his beer, he wiped his hand over his mouth and said, "It's getting dark out. We should get going."

"What happens after dark?"

"Nothing, usually. I'm just paranoid where you're concerned," he admitted with a frown, wondering when this woman had become so bloody important to him.

She looked out the window for a moment, then brought her sparkling gaze back to his. "You don't need to be so worried. I won't run screaming if I see something scary. I mean, I'm pretty tough. I watch *Dexter* every week and don't even have to close my eyes."

"That *is* pretty tough," he agreed, going along with her playful tone. "But you'll be happy to know that we're not all psychotic serial killers here."

"Psychotic?" she gasped, pretending to be offended. "Don't bad-mouth Dex, you jerk. I happen to think he's a swell guy."

Eric gave her a cocky smirk. "You would."

"Hey! What's that supposed to mean?"

Shaking his head, he said, "Just that you're strange, Chelse." *And funny and sexy and incredibly wonderful.* "I mean, we're talking *seriously* abnormal."

"And this from a werewolf?" She was laughing as she shot him a threatening scowl, then grabbed a pillow from his sofa and threw it at him. He ducked to avoid the soft missile, a goofy grin on his face and a kinda warm feeling in the pit of his stomach as he turned to go and collect his things.

Eric didn't know what that warm feeling meant—but he was starting to suspect it might be something remarkably close to happiness.

Chapter Twelve

By the time they reached the Alley, late afternoon had given way to early evening, darkening the sky as long, indigo-hued shadows spread through the forest. While Eric grabbed his bag from the back of the truck, Chelsea took a deep breath of the pine-scented air, enjoying the way it filled her lungs.

"Come on, you two!" Jeremy shouted from his front porch. "We're having dinner here tonight. It's almost ready."

Eric ran the clothes he'd brought back with them up to his cabin, and then they joined everyone in Jeremy and Jillian's living room, where extra chairs had been put out to accommodate the crowd. It was the first time that Chelsea had met Michaela's husband, and the first time she'd seen all the Runners together in the same place. With the exception of Carla Reyes, they should have been a formidable sight, considering their battle-honed bodies and rugged looks—but it was hard to be intimidated by a group who smiled and laughed as much as they did.

The meal turned out to be a loud, festive affair, with everyone joking and sharing stories. While she and Eric had been gone, they'd all pitched in to make barbecue chicken, three different kinds of salad, sautéed zucchini and fresh baked bread. Chelsea's mouth was watering from the scrumptious smells by the time the food was laid out buffet style on the massive dining-room table, the roughhewn pine a perfect fit for the rustic, luxurious cabin.

"Where's Casey?" she asked, taking a seat beside Eric on one of the two leather sofas. She balanced her loaded plate on her lap, her glass of chilled white wine sitting beside his Corona on the low coffee table. Michaela sat on the other sofa with Brody, who had his thick, auburn hair pulled back from his scarred face with a band. They were a striking couple, the tenderness the big guy felt for his wife shining in his green eyes every time he looked at her.

Taking a seat in the chair to her right, Carla answered Chelsea's question. "Her parents came and picked her up while you were in Shadow Peak."

She couldn't stop a worried frown from settling between her brows. "She isn't going back to her husband, is she?"

"If she does," Cian murmured, "I think Eric made it pretty clear what will happen to him if he ever lays a finger on Casey again."

"And if he survived that first pounding," his partner drawled, "I'm sure you told him that he'd be dealing with you next. Am I right?"

A slow smile curved Cian's mouth. "Let's just say he knows we're watching him."

Chelsea didn't know what it was, but there was something a little different about the sexy Irishman. Something that was even a little darker, and maybe even a little deadlier, than the others, and she made a mental note to ask Eric about him later.

Looking at Eric, Wyatt asked, "How was Elise?"

While he told everyone what had happened with Glenn Farrow, explaining that he wanted to have some protection set up for his sister at her home, Chelsea couldn't help but watch him from the corner of her eye. Even in a room full of outrageously good-looking men, he really was the sexiest thing she'd ever seen. She loved the way the tendons in his strong throat worked when he tilted his beer bottle up to his mouth and swallowed. Loved watching his forearms as he set the bottle back down on the table, remembering how the muscles and sinew had flexed beneath his golden skin that afternoon when he'd been working her with his fingers. It'd been so erotic. So impossibly...

"Chelse, are you okay?"

His deep voice pulled her back to the moment and she blinked, managing a quick nod as she reached for her wineglass, her face feeling like it was on fire. She didn't know what would happen when they left and went back to his cabin together. Did he think they were going to pick up right where they'd left off that afternoon? Did she want them to?

Seriously? I might be out of my depths here, but I've never wanted anything more.

It was hard to admit, but she'd been so wrong about him, her first impression completely off base. Yeah, he was tough and rough and as alpha as they came. But he was a good man, a good friend, a good brother. She'd seen how he was with Elise, supportive without being controlling. And he had a great sense of humor, holding his own with his friends whenever they started ribbing him.

Most surprisingly, though, was the fact that she didn't care he was a Lycan from a dark wolf bloodline. She didn't even care that they hadn't known each other for all that long. They'd already been through more together than she'd ever shared with any other man. She might not be the kind of woman who could ever completely surrender to a relationship, opening herself up to disappointment and heartbreak. But for the first time in her life, Chelsea felt the wild, uncontrollable need for connection with a man, and she was going to take it.

No matter what happened, she was going to grab on to this unbelievable experience with both hands...and enjoy every moment of it that she could.

While the room buzzed with conversation, Eric found himself having a hard time focusing on anything apart from the woman sitting at his side, enjoying watching the way she interacted with his friends. He'd expected her to shy away from Brody, seeing as how he was massive and scarred. Granted, Brody wore an easy smile these days, his expression that of a man who had more than his fair share of happiness. Still, he would have thought a human female would find the Runner intimidating, but Chelsea didn't avoid him. She smiled and laughed with the auburn-haired giant, seeming to like him even more than the other pretty-faced Runners. Was it because she sensed the vulnerability beneath Brody's gruff exterior? He wouldn't be surprised if that was the case. She was always studying people, trying to figure them out.

Looking back on Friday night, he didn't know how he'd thought her only attraction was her looks. There was so much more to it than that. He enjoyed talking to her, just being close to her, as if it was where he was meant to be. And watching her interact with his sister and standing up to the others in town had been like a slap upside the head. She was so much more than just a beautiful face and body. She was fiery hot, brimming with passion, ready to fight for what she thought was right. Even though she didn't quite trust him, she'd stood up for him. Even in the face of a town that had to terrify her, she'd held her chin high, shoulders back, ready to take them on because they'd dared to insult him.

She was…well, incredible, and he'd have to be a blind, senseless fool not to be head over ass for her. The more time he spent with her, the more desperate he became for the whole damn package. For every complicated, stubborn, at times aggravating inch of her.

Taking another long swallow of his cold beer, he realized that there were so many things he wanted to ask her about, so many aspects of her life that were still a mystery to him. He still didn't know her favorite foods…or movies…or what she liked to do for fun, and it drove him crazy. He wanted to know it all, damn it. Everything.

From the moment he'd set eyes on her, Eric had been telling himself he needed to keep his distance. But he couldn't do it. He was drawn to her, like a force of gravity—one that was about more than mere lust, though the physical hunger he felt for her was stronger than any he'd ever known. But he liked her, too. Respected her. God knew she was obstinate, but she was fiercely loyal to those she cared about. And she enjoyed laughing, the sexy, husky sound always warming his blood. With all the baggage she carried from her childhood, he hadn't expected her to have such a wonderful sense of humor, but then he was hardly traveling light. And maybe that was the point of a relationship, of getting close to someone, since it meant that you were no longer alone. That you could ease the other's burdens, carrying the load together.

At least until they had to go their separate ways.

His wolf chuffed at the thought, the beast growing a little more restless every time he shoved that inevitable conclusion in its face. But there wasn't any way around it. She wasn't meant to be theirs, which meant they didn't get to keep her.

The thought had Eric draining the last of his beer. As he leaned forward to set the empty bottle on the table, Michaela smiled at him and Chelsea, and said, "I love the story of how you two met."

Beside him, Chelsea sat up a little straighter and blushed.

Jillian grinned. "Is it true that he asked you to leave and you flipped him off?"

Chelsea slid him a laughing look, then shifted her gaze back to Jillian. "It's true," she replied, lips twitching with humor. "I pulled a gun on him, too. But in my defense, he was being *really* annoying."

"Sounds like Eric," Jeremy drawled, chuckling when Eric flipped *him* off.

"He also had red lipstick smeared all over the side of his mouth," she added, her blue eyes bright with amusement as she glanced his way again.

"Thanks," he muttered drily, while the whole group roared with laughter.

"Aside from the lipstick part," Torrance said, "it reminds me a bit of mine and Mason's beginning."

Jeremy grinned as he looked at Chelsea and explained. "Mase got one whiff of her in a crowded café down in Covington and panicked. Big-time."

"What'd he do?"

"He tripped her while she was carrying a tray of food,"

Jeremy said completely deadpan, while Mason turned a
little red in the face, muttering something under his breath
about faithless friends.

"Are you serious?" Chelsea asked, sounding as if she
thought the Runner might be pulling her leg.

Jeremy laughed. "Swear to God. It was the funniest
damn thing I've ever seen."

Eric wondered if Jillian and the others had told Chelsea about the mating bond and how a Lycan recognized
his mate through scent. If they had, she didn't remark on
it, and he wasn't about to bring it up himself. If she asked
him about what effects her scent had on him, he wouldn't
have a clue what to say. How did he explain the strange
reaction he had to her? The way her scent affected him in
a way that no other ever had, and yet, wasn't something
that called to him as *his?*

Best just to leave that particular can of worms closed,
so that it didn't blow up in his face.

Everyone helped clean up after coffee and a mouthwatering batch of homemade brownies that Carla had
brought over, and then they finally said good-night.

"Did you have a good time tonight?" he asked as he
and Chelsea made their way up the sloping glade.

A soft smile touched her lips. "You know I did. This
place is great." The wind surged, and as she caught her
long hair over her shoulder to keep it in place, she added,
"I don't know why you don't just stay here permanently."

Eric pushed his hands in his pockets. "As tempting
as the idea is, I can't run away from the problems in the
pack, Chelse. That's not the answer."

"But you belong here," she argued, looking impossibly beautiful in the silvery glow of moonlight. "Sooner
or later, the Lycans in Shadow Peak are going to realize
what a righteous guy you are. And when that time comes,

you can help bridge the gap between the Alley and the pack. Until then, nothing is going to be right here, Eric. And your pack will never know balance."

"What about Elise? I can't just leave her up there on her own."

"Bring her here to live, too. Not just for visits. It would do her good to be around friends, in a place where she felt comfortable."

"Maybe," he murmured, but in his mind he could see it so clearly. Elise would be able to find a sense of peace in the Alley that she'd likely never have in Shadow Peak. He didn't know why he hadn't thought of the idea before, except that his heart and mind were still having a hard time accepting everything that had happened. He was still trying to function within a framework that no longer existed, but it probably *was* time to make a change—and he had the remarkable woman walking beside him to thank for the idea.

Unable to stop himself, Eric suddenly swung her up into his arms, holding her against his chest. Then he lowered his head and took her mouth in a blistering kiss that was hungry and deep and invasive, making it clear just how badly he wanted her.

"Wh-where did that come from?" she gasped, when he finally let her come up for air.

"I couldn't wait any longer," he growled, keeping her in his arms as he headed for his cabin with a long, purposeful stride. "And as soon as we reach a bed, I'm going to kiss you that way between your legs again, Chelse. I can't stop thinking about it. About how unbelievably good you taste."

And it was true. Her scent was unreal, but her taste was somehow even better.

"Before we go inside," he said, setting her down on

the porch since he had to get his keys out of his pocket to unlock the front door, "I want you to know that I won't hurt you. I would never risk you that way."

Running her palm down his arm, she laced their fingers together when she reached his trembling hand. "Your dark side doesn't scare me, Eric. I might have a problem with dominating males, but it won't keep me from enjoying you. I'm not afraid of you."

Shit. When she said things like that, she should be. Because they just made the wolf want to force her submission that much more.

"Now get moving," she said with a grin, pushing him toward the door. He gave a low, excited laugh as he got out his keys with one hand, still clasping her hand with the other.

Eric was just about to open the door when someone shouted his name. Wondering what was going on, he stepped over to the edge of the porch. "Yeah?"

Jeremy came running up the glade. "Some girl just called us using Sophia's phone. She said that Soph's in bad shape, but she's still alive."

"What?" Sophia wasn't meant to check back in with them until the morning, since she'd planned on staying overnight in Hawkley at Brandon's. "What the hell happened?"

Jeremy reached the porch steps, his golden eyes burning with fury. "One of those sons of bitches put a bullet in her."

It took Eric and Cian no more than five minutes to load up on weapons and ammo, then they were ready to go. After a quick discussion, it'd been decided that they would head up together to Miller's Ridge, a bluff near Hawkley where the caller had said she'd taken Sophia, with Mason and Jeremy holding back, ready to move in if needed. Brody, Wyatt and Reyes were staying at the Alley, ensuring that Chelsea and the others remained safe.

After arguing with Chelsea about why he had to be in the team going to collect Sophia, she finally relented. "Okay. I understand that you're going to run off and be all heroic and everything. Just…be careful. I mean it."

He started to say something flip, like he would to Jillian or Elise. But the glib response wouldn't form. Instead, he pulled her into his arms and took her mouth in another scorching, brain-melting kiss.

When she was breathless and trembling, Eric forced himself to let her go and step back. For one searing moment, their gazes held, an electric charge in the air as a thousand messages transmitted between them. Then he turned and climbed into the truck, hoping like hell he had good news to bring her when he made it back.

When they were close, they left the truck parked on the side of a dirt road, then went the rest of the way on foot. As soon as they reached the bluff, they found a human female in her late teens, dressed in jeans and a sweater, kneeling on the ground beside Sophia's body. The girl didn't notice their approach, her focus on the balled-up sweatshirt she was pressing against the bleeding bullet wound in Sophia's right side.

Eric knew exactly who the human was from the first whiff he got of her scent. "Perry?"

Her head whipped up at the sound of his voice, her gaze wary as she watched their approach. "How do you know my name? I didn't give it to the guy on the phone."

Eric held his hands out so that he wouldn't spook her as he came closer. "I'm a friend of your sister's."

She didn't look like she believed him, but then, she didn't look like she believed in a whole lot anymore. She didn't have any of her sister's vitality or freshness, her pretty face already telling a story that was too rough for a girl her age.

She backed away from Sophia as Cian knelt down beside the girl, his deep voice hard with anger. "What the hell happened to her?"

"I don't know," she told him, wiping her bloodstained palms on her jeans. "I was home by myself tonight, sitting out on the back porch having a smoke, when I saw her trying to make it into the woods behind the house. She asked me for help, said that she'd gotten shot trying to get information for some friends of my sister's. But I don't know who shot her. She hasn't been able to talk much. I just helped her get here and called the number she told me to call."

Cursing under his breath, Cian lifted Sophia into his arms, then started heading back to the truck.

Eric looked at Perry. "Are you coming with us?"

Instead of answering his question, she chewed on the corner of her lip, then asked two of her own. "What's my sister doing? I heard that she showed up at that club in Wesley. Is she okay?"

"Why the hell should I tell you? You don't care about her." His voice was rough, thick with disgust. "You've been sitting here for the past hour with Sophia's phone, and I bet you haven't even called her, have you? Do you have any idea how worried she's been?"

"Excuse me for not being in the mood for another one of her boring lectures about what a screw-up I am," Perry sneered, sounding like a snotty teenager. "I didn't ask her to come chasing after me. It's not my fault she ended up in trouble."

"You selfish little bitch!" he snarled, angry enough to put his fist through a wall—and he was quietly thankful there wasn't one around. He had enough problems to deal with without adding a broken hand to the list.

Struggling to get a hold on his temper, he took a deep breath and said, "Look, are you coming with us or not?"

Crossing her arms over her chest, she lifted her chin in a way that reminded him of Chelsea. "Whether you believe it or not, I'm sorry that Chelsea's caught up in the middle of this. And I'd go with you if I could. But I—I can't. Jason is in trouble because of me. I can't just abandon him. They've already threatened to strip his ranking if he screws up again—which is exactly how they would see my disappearance. I can't let that happen."

"Has he said that he'll get you out of here?" he asked, wondering what in God's name he was going to tell Chelsea.

"He's going to try, because he wants us to go somewhere and start a new life together. He…he says that he loves me."

"For your sake," Eric muttered, "I hope it's true."

"What about you and Chelsea?" she asked, stepping a little closer. "What's going on between the two of you?"

"It's…complicated."

She almost smiled. "That sounds like my sister."

"Perry, I know you think you're doing the right thing, but it's dangerous for you in Hawkley. The best thing you—"

"The best thing I can do is stay with Jason," she said, cutting him off. "It's where I belong."

He wanted to keep arguing, but could see that she wasn't going to change her mind. Apparently love trumped danger, which left him in a goddamn mess. Short of throwing her over his shoulder and taking her out of there kicking and screaming, there wasn't a whole lot he could do.

With a frustrated sigh, he said, "If you change your mind, you can reach me on your sister's number. Day or night."

"Okay. And...take care of her."

He didn't know if she meant Chelsea or Sophia, and he didn't have time to ask. He could hear Cian revving the truck's engine, signaling him to get moving or be left behind.

Muttering every foul word he could think of, Eric left Perry Smart standing on the bluff and ran back to the truck. He made sure that Sophia was okay in the backseat, then climbed in on the passenger's side, and Cian drove like a demon, getting them back to the Alley in record time.

Chelsea and the others were all waiting for them in the center of the Alley when they arrived. "What happened?" she and Jillian both asked at the same time, the second Eric climbed out of the truck. Cian grabbed Sophia from the backseat, carrying her to the Burnses' cabin, and Eric explained as they followed after them.

"She hasn't been able to tell us much. Only bits and pieces. But it sounds like Brandon wasn't being cooperative, so she got him drunk and started questioning him. The plan was working, until his roommate came home and overheard what Brandon was telling her. He tried to drag Sophia over to Roy's, but she managed to get away. The bastard got her with a bullet as she was running."

As soon as they were inside, Jillian headed back to the guestroom, where Cian had taken Sophia, and Eric sat down on one of the sofas, scrubbing his hands over his face. Chelsea sat down beside him, and asked, "Did Sophia say anything about Perry?"

"I'm afraid not," he told her, which was technically the truth. He was the one who'd asked Sophia not to mention anything about Perry Smart until he'd figured out the best way to tell Chelsea that her sister had chosen Jason Donovan over her.

By the time Jillian came back into the living room an hour later, it was crowded with people, everyone gathering at the cabin to find out how Sophia was doing. From Jillian's troubled expression, they all feared the worst, since Sophia had lost a significant amount of blood. But Jillian said that she was actually doing a lot better, and had even been able to talk about what she'd learned from Brandon—and it wasn't good.

Looking at Eric, Jillian said, "You were right to have a bad feeling about the Whiteclaw and the Donovans. They're not dating the humans who work at that club. They're using them in private sex shows up in Hawkley. Clients are paying a fortune to rape the girls, sometimes up to ten males at a time. The men are all Lycan, and they're allowed to take the girls in whichever form they choose."

Eric felt the color drain from his face. "Son of a bitch," he grated, while the others muttered their own outraged curses.

Jillian went on. "From what I understand, they have a drug that they give the girls. It acts as a high-powered aphrodisiac, making them mindless with lust, then leaves them with no memory of the event. That way, they can use the same girls over and over. They keep stripping at the club, until a client hires them out, and then they're taken up to Hawkley. The rapes can last up to two days, and then the girls' injuries are healed by the pack's Spirit Walker, and they're returned to the club with some fabricated story about a drinking binge."

"Those men are monsters," Chelsea breathed out, her eyes glistening with tears.

Eric completely agreed. He'd thought that maybe there'd be some rough play involved. Maybe even wolves getting off on the fear factor. But he hadn't expected anything like this. They might not be feeding like rogues on those girls' bodies, but they were feeding on their spirits, and that was just as evil. No matter what he had to do to make it happen, he was going to bring their sadistic operation down.

Chelsea wiped her eyes, then looked at Jillian. "Do you think it's the same drug they gave me on Saturday night?"

There was a low sound in his throat, Eric's fury rising as he made the same connection Chelsea just had. But there was a significant difference. "You still had a lot of your memories, Chelse. They must have given you something different."

"I wondered the same thing and asked Sophia," Jillian explained. "She talked to Brandon about it, and he said the drug Curtis gave Chelsea was part of a new batch they recently had created for clients who are interested in a long-term arrangement with the girls."

"You mean like sex slaves?" Cian demanded in a near shout. "Those dirty motherfu—"

"Cian!" Jillian said, cutting the Runner off. "I know you're angry, but we need to keep it down out here for Soph, okay?"

"Right," he muttered, shoving both hands back through his hair as he paced the floor. "Sorry."

Leaning forward in his chair, Mason braced his elbows on his parted knees. "We need to come up with a way to put a stop to this. The sooner, the better. But until we do, I'm worried they might try to move the girls now that they know Brandon talked. In addition to the surveillance group that's been set up at the club, we need something on the roads going in and out of Hawkley."

Brody moved away from his place by the wall. "I'm on it."

Cian headed out with his partner, and while the others went to the kitchen for coffee, Eric stayed on the sofa with Chelsea.

"I'm worried about Perry," she whispered. "I hate the thought of her being there in that town."

Eric squeezed her hand, letting her know he understood, but then Torrance and Carla came back into the room, and the conversation turned to Sophia and how her family was going to react when they found out she'd been hurt. As the hour grew later, the Runners started heading back to their cabins, and he finally said, "We should get going, Chelse."

They said their goodbyes, then made their way out into the crisp night air. Eric put his arm around her shoulders, sharing his warmth as she huddled against his side.

"I don't think I'm going to be able to fall asleep," she murmured. "I'm too worried."

Despite the gravity of the night, a low, husky laugh rumbled in his chest.

Tilting her head back, she gave him a disgruntled look. "You think my worrying is funny?"

"Not at all, sweetheart. I was just thinking about how much fun it would be to wear you out."

"*Oh.* Okay," she whispered. "I'm still game if you—"

He didn't give her a chance to finish, her words choking off with a gasp as Eric lifted her into his arms...and started running.

Chapter Thirteen

Eric set Chelsea on her feet as soon as they were inside his cabin, then turned and locked the door, making sure they wouldn't be disturbed. Her scent was all over him, all around him, making him feel like a live wire. Making him furious that it didn't *call* to him. That he couldn't sink his fangs into her tender throat and claim her for his own.

He knew of others who had committed without being able to make a bond. It could be done. But *he* couldn't risk it. Not when he was dark wolf and she was human. Only the claiming would ease his wolf completely and balance its hungers. Without it, there was too much risk of disaster.

"Remember, no biting," she reminded him in a soft voice. "And no holding me down."

Lifting his hand, he pushed her hair back from her face, and said, "You can trust me, Chelse. I won't bite. Won't hold you down, either." Grinning a little, he added,

"Though someday you might actually like the idea of being at my mercy."

He didn't give her a chance to respond, suddenly pulling her close and taking her mouth in a hard, relentless, ravaging kiss. And his heart damn near exploded when she wrapped her arms around his neck and started kissing him back, her tongue rubbing against his, telling him that she accepted him. That she wasn't going to turn him away.

As he lost himself in the warm silk of her mouth, his hands moved over her body, pulling and ripping at her clothes, needing the feel of her smooth, bare skin with a desperation that shook him to his core. Hunger clawed through his system, his blood rushing so hard and fast it was all he could hear, and with a guttural growl vibrating in the back of his throat, Eric lifted her against his chest.

Then he carried her to his bed.

One moment Chelsea was lost in the dark, succulent taste of him, and in the next she found herself lying on Eric's massive king-size bed, in the shadowed darkness of his room, while he tore away what was left of her clothes. When she was naked beneath him, he took a deep breath and pulled away, moving back to his feet. She tracked his tall, broad-shouldered form as he reached down and turned on one of the bedside lamps, casting a wash of warm, golden light through the room. For a split second she thought about reaching for the edge of the bedspread and pulling it over her, but then he pulled off his shirt, and she forgot to be embarrassed or shy.

Then he started undoing the buttons on his jeans, and she had to prop herself up on her elbows just so she could get a better view, the flexing of muscle in his arms and across the broad expanse of his chest making her mouth water. But it was the thick ridge trapped behind the fly of his jeans that stole her breath. "My, God, Eric. You're so beautiful."

"You're the beautiful one," he groaned, taking down his tight black boxers with his jeans, then kicking them away. Her eyes went wide and her jaw dropped as she got her first look at him. With his muscular thighs braced apart, he wrapped his hand around the heavy, vein-ridged shaft, and stroked it with a few long, strong pulls that had her panting…melting. It was the most masculine, erotic sight Chelsea had ever seen.

But what she loved most was the way he stared down at her, his glittering, molten gaze burning with heat, warming her blood until she didn't care about being too short or curvy or pale. When Eric gave her that hot, primal look of hunger, she felt like the most beautiful woman in the world. One who didn't have a single frigid bone in her body.

She wanted to touch him…taste him. Wanted to run her mouth over the burnished, satiny skin of his chest and abs, feel the tight stretch of golden skin over powerful muscles that thrummed beneath her lips. She wanted to eat him alive. Gobble him up like something she could hold in her mouth, savoring for years. For…ever. Like something she could keep.

"Spread your legs for me, Chelse."

She licked her lips, surprised by how badly she craved him. "No way, Eric. I want you in my mouth first. It's *my* turn tonight."

"No."

Her eyes went wide again. "Why not? I thought guys like getting head."

"Liking it isn't the point. When I think I can get through it without you killing me," he growled, "*then* you'll get a turn."

She couldn't believe he'd just said that! "Hey, I'm not *that* bad at it."

"That's what I'm afraid of," he grated, his eyes going heavy and dark. "You could breathe on me and it'd probably stop my heart. And I'd rather not die before getting inside you."

"Fine. But I'll get my turn eventually," she grumbled. "You can't put it off forever."

Hearing the word *forever* on her lips made him crazed. Made him want to throw back his head and howl.

"Just do what I said and spread your damn legs, Chelsea." The words were rough with command, satisfaction pooling thickly through his veins when she slowly let her thighs fall open. Yeah, he could have done it for her, but he wanted this. Wanted to know that she was hungry for him. That she needed it as badly as he did.

Crawling onto the bed, Eric braced himself on one arm as he leaned over her lower body and ran two fingers through the pink, glistening folds of her sex. He brought them to his mouth, sucking them clean, savoring the succulent juice as it sat on his tongue. He might not be able to figure out her scent, but her flavor called to every primitive, possessive instinct he possessed.

"Your taste, Chelse. It's unreal."

Lowering his head, he pressed his open mouth to the tender skin just beneath her navel, laving it with his tongue.

"Stop teasing me!" she gasped, trying to pull him up with her hands on his shoulders. "I thought we were finally going to—"

"We *will,*" he growled, pressing a kiss lower, to the silky curls on her mound. "But I'm still getting you ready. So shut up and let me eat."

"Eric," she groaned. "You're obsessed!"

"You got that right. I can't get enough of you."

She gave another soft, breathless gasp. "Are you always like this? Is it a wolf thing?"

He hoped the look on his face made it clear what he thought of her questions, as if she was just another girl he liked to go down on. Yeah, he'd done it to lovers in the past, even enjoyed it. But he'd never *needed* it. Never ached for it so bad he thought he'd go out of his mind if he didn't get it.

"No, it's not a wolf thing," he told her, his voice raspy and low. "It's a *Chelsea* thing." He lowered his head again, licking the satiny folds, and then pushing inside, letting her feel him licking her from the inside out. Slow, deep. He licked his lips, licked her, trying to get as much of that honeyed sweetness in his mouth as he could. "You taste like you were made for me."

"Really?" Her back arched, that lush lower lip caught in her white teeth.

His voice rumbled with satisfaction. "Oh, yeah." He braced himself over her, holding his weight on one hand, while he reached down with the other and pushed two thick fingers back inside her, working them deep. "Feel like it, too."

"God, Eric, now. Stop torturing me!"

Feeling just as desperate, he quickly grabbed the box of condoms from his bedside drawer, ripped open one of the foil packets and sheathed himself in the thin latex. Then he crawled back over her, caging her beneath him. "I'm not going to stop this time, Chelse. I don't care if the damn mountain starts crumbling down around us. Flashfloods, earthquakes, hurricanes—they won't stop me. I'm seeing this through to the end."

She stared up him, panting and flushed, her blue eyes

dark with emotion. "I know. Just don't…don't hold my arms down."

He knew he shouldn't be surprised, but he tensed.

"Please," she whispered, "don't be insulted, Eric. I've given you more trust than I've ever given any other man. I just…I don't like feeling trapped."

It was ironic, how they were both so alike in their need for control. But it was all an illusion. He could no more master his fate than she could hold her own with him if he went too far. She wanted her arms free to hold him back if he tried to bite her, but if that were what he wanted, she wouldn't be able to stop him.

He wanted to tell her that the day would come when she would look up at him and ask for him to hold her down. When she would want to know what it felt like to give every part of herself to him. To know that she could use him as something to break against when she needed an anchor. But he held the words inside, because that day was never going to be theirs.

He didn't know how long they had together, but he intended to make every damn moment of it count.

Reaching down, Eric positioned himself at her tender entrance, his gaze locked on hers as he held still. Her breath caught, a warm flush of color building beneath her skin, her eyes like a window into the very heart of her soul. He could see her need and desire, her vulnerability, her strength, her courage and her fear. He'd never thought about how significant this moment was with the women he'd known before, how intimate. Never cared, really, which just made him an ass. But then, he knew they'd never cared about him, either.

But Chelsea…God, she was different. Yeah, she drove him crazy with her stubborn pride, but she enthralled him even more. Made him desperate, hungry, needy. Made him

ache. Made him *want*. It was such an easy, simple word
that had such huge meaning. Such force.

"Yes or no, Chelse?"

Her whispered *yes* made his pulse roar, his heart threatening to slam its way out of his chest as he started to push
inside. Rocking his hips, he tried to go slow as he worked
himself in, but it got away from him and he went too
deep, too quickly, and she gasped. "Damn it, I'm sorry,"
he growled, somehow finding the strength to hold still,
though it just about killed him.

She reached up and touched his face with her fingertips, trailing them over his hot skin, her sky-blue gaze
staring deep into his mind…into those dark, dangerous
places he didn't want touching her. He tried to turn his
head, but she cupped his cheek, stopping him. "It's okay,"
she whispered. "I won't break, Eric."

She took a deep breath, and those tight, plush muscles
clamping down on him eased a little, letting him sink an
inch deeper. He muttered something really dirty under
his breath about how good she felt—how slick and tight
and hot—and as he worked his hips, she took another
inch…and then another. She was taking him, moaning,
her storm-dark eyes glazed with passion, and with a deep,
grinding thrust, he nearly made it all the way in. Fisting his hands in the bedding, he pulled back his hips and
gave her another hard thrust that took him to the root, her
throaty cry echoing in his ears as he held there, packed
up tight inside her. His eyes nearly rolled back in his head
from the feel of her, and he reached down with one hand
and grabbed her ass, grinding up tighter against her, until
not a fraction of space separated them. Then he waited,
his muscles locked, skin misted with sweat, giving her
the time she needed to get used to him.

"Eric," she moaned.

"Yeah?"

Her head went back, neck curved in a beautiful, feminine arch as her nails dug into his shoulders, her legs wrapping around his hips. *"Move."*

"Are you sure?" he asked, making a thick, serrated sound in his throat.

Chelsea was sure he was going to drive her out of her mind. He was buried deep inside her—heavy, hot, thick. She could feel the throbbing pulse of his heartbeat, the sensation the most intimate thing she'd ever experienced. But she needed him to let go. Needed to see that look of strain on his face replaced by one of pleasure.

"Either you start moving, Eric, or you let me be on top."

His chest shook with a low, deliciously male laugh as he pulled back his hips, and he gave her the most sinful smile she'd ever seen as he suddenly pushed back in with a thick, powerful thrust that pushed the air from her lungs. His eyes went heavy, hers went wide, and he pulled back again, a sexy curse on his lips as he gave her another one of those heavy lunges, forcing his way inside. The rhythm got faster, his powerful muscles flexing beneath his dark skin, while the primal, provocative scent of hot, wet sex filled the room.

"You like that, Chelse?"

"Love it!" she gasped. "Give me more, Eric. Don't hold back."

He took her at her word, riding her with a hard, hammering rhythm that had their bodies going steamy and slick. She was with him all the way, until her third orgasm left her trembling and cracked open, all her defenses crumbling around her. "This isn't me," she choked out, her throat tight with emotion. "I'm not like this."

He lifted his head, his jaw hard, and there was a thin,

stunning rim of golden amber burning around the metallic gray of his eyes. "I thought you weren't afraid of me."

"I'm not! But that doesn't mean I have to like losing control. Because I *don't!*"

"That's not true." The raw, husky timbre of his voice was just another level of heat that glowed inside her, melting her down. "You might not have liked it before—but you like it with me. You told me not to hold back, remember?"

"You just…you have to let me keep my balance."

He shook his head. "No way. That would bore you to tears. You might not trust me about a lot of things, but you can trust me about this, Chelse. I know how to make you feel good."

"I don't doubt your ability to make me orgasm!"

The corner of his mouth curved with an adorable grin. "Hell, I don't want some run-of-the-mill orgasm. I want to keep making you come so hard you see God." He touched his mouth to hers, nipping her lower lip, before adding in that dark, devastatingly sexy murmur, "I want you to scream and scratch and shout dirty things at me, demanding I ride you harder. Longer. Deeper."

"You want too much."

"I want *you*. Every damn part of you," he groaned, the possessive words sending her spiraling into another screaming, bone-melting orgasm, and this time he was right there with her. He came down over her, his hands in her hair, holding her still for the hard, demanding hunger of his kiss as he drove inside her with a strength that didn't seem human. She could feel the breathtaking, explosive force of his release as it tore through him, a rough growl vibrating deep in his chest, his hips grinding against hers in sharp, urgent pulses, until he finally stilled inside her. But his lips stayed on hers, the kiss gentling into a poignant melding of breaths and sighs, their lips rubbing and sipping, and then they both…smiled.

It was the last thing she would have expected after such incredibly wild, aggressive sex—but knowing that she'd brought a smile to his lips, that she'd made him *happy,* was the part that meant the most to her. The part she'd always hold close to her heart.

Somehow, they found the strength to pull themselves onto the pillows, facing each other as they lay on their sides. Their hands and lips stroked and explored, learning the other's body through taste and touch. She traced the swirls of his tattoo with her finger, then moved on to one of the scars on his chest, trailing her fingertips down to another long scar that slashed across his ribs. "Where did you get this one?"

Eric felt his lips twitch with a smile. "Believe it or not, Eli."

"Your brother?" she asked, shifting up on an elbow. "How?"

"We were goofing around, playing too rough. We were always like that. Drove my old man crazy. He'd go off the deep end whenever he caught us, but Eli always stepped in and took the brunt of his anger. He protected me, every damn time." He glanced down at the scar. "The day I got this, I'd been teasing him about his new girlfriend. I was being a shit, egging him on. We started wrestling out behind our barn and I ended up cutting myself open on some metal that was sticking out of the ground. Eli freaked out, carrying me like a damn baby all the way to Jillian's mom, who was our healer at the time. I kept telling him it was no big deal, but I'd never seen him so upset. He looked worried until she finally got the wound closed."

"You miss him, don't you?"

"Every damn day," he said in a low voice, covering the dip at her lower back with his hand. He spread his fingers, splaying his hand over her skin, loving how soft she was. "I wanted to send for him the moment the League was destroyed, but I can't do that to him. Bring him back into this mess. If I told him we needed him, he'd come. But he doesn't deserve to get caught up in this shit."

"He might feel differently. He might feel that it's worth it, if it means having his family back."

"You think so?" he asked.

Caressing the grain of stubble on his jaw with her fingertips, she said, "I think you need to give him the choice."

He sighed. "We'll have to find him first."

Her eyes widened with surprise. "You don't know where he is?"

Pulling in a deep breath of her mouthwatering scent, Eric took a moment to enjoy the way a gleaming lock of hair draped over her feminine shoulder, the ends curling against one of those deliciously small, berry-red nipples. He wanted to take that sweet little nipple into his mouth and suckle until she came again. But he knew she probably needed a little more recovery time, so he forced his attention back to the conversation. "Not exactly," he murmured, lifting his gaze back to hers as he answered her question. "Eli works with an…interesting group of people. They travel around a lot."

"What do you mean by interesting?" She looked more than a little curious.

"Think non-human mercenaries," he offered drily, "and you'd be pretty close."

"Mercenaries!" She muffled her *well-that-certainly-wasn't-what-I-was-expecting* laugh with her hand. "Sorry I asked."

Eric grinned, loving the lyrical sound of her laughter. "They're good guys. Just a little rough around the edges."

"I can imagine." Her tone was wry.

He stroked her hip, but as his hand started to slip toward her sex, she stiffened, grasping his wrist. "I should, um, go and tidy up."

"No, don't. Please," he begged, quickly cupping her in his palm. After so many orgasms, she was slippery and warm, drenched in her juices.

Her face turned crimson. "But I'm…soaked."

"I know," he groaned, loving the way she arched when he found her clit with his thumb. "It's so perfect, Chelse. You feel so good. No way in hell am I letting you wash this away."

He hadn't paid any attention to her beautiful breasts before, but he intended to make up for that now. While his fingers played through her slick, swollen folds, he spent long moments feasting on her nipples, loving the way they felt in his mouth…against his tongue, until his control finally snapped.

"Damn it," he growled, quickly sheathing himself in another condom and pulling her beneath him. "I know you're probably too sore, but I can't wait. I just need…I need to be inside you."

She gasped as he worked himself in, thrusting his hips against hers until she'd taken every inch of him, the fit tight and perfect and slick.

"Hurt?" he asked, his chest heaving with the ragged force of his breaths.

"A little. But it feels too good to stop." She reached up, smoothing her fingertip over his brows. "Your eyes are glowing."

His voice was a whisper. "Are you scared?"

She shook her head. "No. I know you won't hurt me."

He closed his eyes and lowered his head, pressing soft kisses along the tender column of her throat.

"Just…don't bite me." There was a catch in her voice.

Eric slowly lifted his head, watching her with a hard, penetrating stare, frustration riding his body like a second skin. "You can trust me, Chelse. If I feel myself losing control, I won't stick around and take the chance of hurting you." He drew in a shuddering breath. "Just give me a chance. That's all I'm asking."

She gazed up at him as she curved her hands over his shoulders, her own stare deep and measuring. Then she drew him down to her until their lips were touching, their breaths soughing together, and whispered, "I'll…try."

When it was over, their passion-wrecked bodies collapsed like the victims of a violent storm, bruised and exhausted, but it'd been worth it. He didn't know how long they lay there, waiting for their breathing to return to normal, but he finally worked up the energy to deal with the condom. Then he came back to the bed, turned off the light, and for the first time in his life, Eric wrapped his arms around a woman and held her close after sex, unwilling to let her go. Clinging to her for all he was worth. "Don't go."

Her breath tickled his chest. "You want me to stay?"

He buried his face in the silken mass of her hair, breathing her in, and rasped a husky response against the shell of her ear. "Just try to leave me."

Eric opened his eyes to the silvery glow of moonlight playing over the gentle curve of Chelsea's cheek, her long hair spread out over the pillow. He wanted to press his face into that silken mass and breathe the scent of her into his lungs, keeping it there for as long as he could. Keeping her close, beneath his hands…his body, so that he could be there to see to her safety, sheltering her from the dangers of the world.

Just don't forget that you're a threat to her, too.

"Shut up," he muttered under his breath, no longer willing to listen to that destructive voice. Old fears? His conscience? Whoever it was, they could mind their own damn business. He had no use for them tonight.

He knew she still didn't trust him. Hell, he still didn't completely trust himself. But they could work around it for however long this thing between them lasted. The idea of an ending made him want to snarl, so he shoved that irritating thought from his mind, as well, focusing instead on the moment. He'd spent the night in her arms, and he hadn't lost her. Lost some of his control…yeah. He'd taken her hard and rough and raw, but he hadn't hurt her. Judging by the number of times she'd come screaming in his arms, the primitive, visceral craving she incited in him worked for her.

He'd always been an aggressive lover, but never like he'd been with Chelsea. His hunger for her made his past experiences with women seem like child's play. Her soft skin probably bore the marks of his fingers from where he'd gripped her hips and thighs in a hard, possessive hold, but she'd never complained. She'd simply given as good as she got, his own body bearing the marks of her nails, and he loved it. Would wear them with pride, the marks healing too quickly for his liking.

Just have her make new ones.

He smiled, his wolf and him for once on the same page. It was a hell of a plan. But first, as much as he hated to cause her pain, he knew he had to come clean with her.

As if she sensed his disquiet, she stirred beside him, a sleepy smile curving her kiss-swollen lips as she stretched and cuddled closer. "Hey, you."

"I didn't mean to wake you."

She reached down, curling her soft hand around the rigid length of his cock. Her eyes sparkled. "I think maybe you did."

"Chelse," he murmured, bracing himself on an elbow, "there's something we need to talk about."

"What's wrong?" she asked, obviously sensing from his tone that she wasn't going to like what he had to say. She pulled her hand away and sat up, clutching the sheet to her chest as she stared down at him.

"Nothing's wrong." He climbed out of the bed and turned on the light, then grabbed his jeans and pulled them on. Lifting his hand, he rubbed the back of his neck as he turned to face her. "I just…there's something I need to tell you about Perry. It isn't going to be easy for you to hear. The only reason I didn't tell you earlier is because I—"

"What is it? Is she hurt?" she asked, cutting him off.

"No, she's fine." He blew out a frustrated breath. "Hell, I know I'm screwing this up, I just don't know how to—"

"Eric, just say it."

"The girl that helped Sophia make it up to Miller's Ridge—the one who called Jeremy on Sophia's phone—it was Perry."

"You saw her?"

He gave a brief nod. "I also talked to her."

Her eyes went wide with disbelief. "And you just left her there?"

"Not by choice," he grunted, not liking the way she was looking at him. "Damn it, I tried to get her to come with us, Chelsea. She refused."

"That doesn't make any sense, Eric. If you're telling the truth, she must not have been in her right mind. They'd probably drugged her!"

He braced his hands on his hips. "She didn't smell drugged. I would have known, Chelse. She said she couldn't leave because Jason is in some kind of trouble that has to do with her. She's afraid that if she runs out on him, he'll lose his ranking in the pack."

"His ranking?" she choked out, shaking with fury. "You expect me to believe that she's worried about his stupid ranking? That's impossible. She wouldn't risk her life because of his goddamn social status. She's childish and selfish, but she wouldn't be that stupid! She wouldn't act just like our mother!"

"I know this is hard to hear, Chelse." His voice was deep and low. "But I'm telling you the truth."

"No...I can't—I refuse to believe this." Her long hair streamed over her shoulders as she shook her head, her pale skin flushed with anger. "You probably just didn't want to have to deal with her."

Eric narrowed his eyes. "That's bullshit and you know it."

"And what about Cian?" she snapped. "Why didn't he say anything to me about Perry being there?"

"Because I asked him not to," he ground out, knowing this particular truth was going to piss her off even more. But he refused to lie to her. "I wanted the chance to tell you myself. When it was the right time."

"Well, you should have done it before!" she shouted. "Because now I don't believe anything you have to say. All you've done is prove that you're just another selfish, controlling bastard who isn't worthy of—"

There was a screech, followed by his guttural curse, and then she was panting, saying, "Let me go, Eric. Now."

He blinked, surprised to find her trapped beneath him on the bed, her wrists bound in the hard grip of his hands. He released her as he reared back, bracing himself on his knees, terrified by the thought of what could have happened. His throat was tight, a burning lump stuck in the middle that made it hard to talk. "I was afraid you were going to react like this," he panted, his voice little more than a croak. "I was hoping that after what happened between us, that you might…hell, I don't know. Have a little faith in me."

"That was your plan?" she snapped, using the sheet to cover her body as she rose up on her knees in front of him, ·both of them kneeling in the middle of the bed. "Were you hoping that I'd be more inclined to believe your lies about Perry after you'd screwed me?"

He ground his jaw so hard that it hurt. "You know that's not true. I tried to get her to leave with me, Chelsea. But she was determined to stay."

She snorted, still not believing a word he'd said. "Like I told you before, she might be selfish, but she isn't stupid. She isn't a doormat. If you'd really offered her the chance to get away from that place, she would have taken it."

Keeping his gaze locked on hers, he took a deep breath and said, "I'm not saying I agree with her, but did it ever occur to you that she might actually be in love with this guy? That as upset as it makes you, you should support her decision to stay with him?"

Her breathing got a little harder, her mouth trembling. "You really are a manipulative son of a bitch, aren't you? I can't believe I let you get close to me."

"You didn't let me, Chelsea." His eyes narrowed with a visceral jolt of anger. "You *begged* me."

The next thing he knew, his head was snapping to the side, the imprint of her hand burning in his skin. He took a deep, rattling breath, and knew the wolf was burning in his eyes when he brought his gaze back to hers. Its fury seared through him, scorching his veins, his muscles bulging as he stared her down.

She paled, her scent spiking with the heartbreaking threads of fear. She actually thought he was going to hurt her. Thought he was going to be just like all the other bastards who had treated their women like shit. Battered and abused and psychologically tormented them.

Yeah, he was pissed. Furious. Hurting at her lack of trust. He'd known the truth was going to be hard for her to take, but he hadn't expected this. Hadn't expected her to throw it all back on *him*.

There was really only one thing left to do.

Moving off the bed, Eric reached into his jeans pocket and pulled out the set of keys that Wyatt had slipped him earlier at dinner. Then he padded on his bare feet across the room, set the keys on the dresser and turned toward the door. "The keys are yours," he said, keeping his back to her. "They belong to the gray Rav4 that's parked beside the cabin."

"Wh-what?"

"I had Wyatt pick it up for you this afternoon, while we were in Shadow Peak."

"I don't understand," she breathed out. "Are you…are you saying that you bought me a car?"

A humorless laugh rumbled in his chest. "What can I say? It was all a part of my master plan to turn you into a doormat," he drawled sarcastically. "It might have failed, but you still get to keep the bait."

Softly, she said, "I can't accept it, Eric."

He gave another gritty laugh. "Yeah, I figured you'd

say that. Just use it to get back to Virginia, and I'll send someone down to collect it."

Then he opened the door and got the hell out of there, since there wasn't any point in staying. He had nothing left to say.

Chapter Fourteen

The first thing Chelsea realized as she walked onto the front porch of Eric's cabin the following afternoon was that she'd never seen so many bitter, determined expressions. It seemed that almost everyone was there to see her off—the sooner the better seeming to be the collective opinion. The only person she didn't see was Eric.

Either someone had been watching the cabin for signs that she was awake, or they'd been waiting a long time. After Eric had stormed out on her, it'd taken her hours to fall back into a restless sleep. One that had left her drained and exhausted. She didn't have nearly enough energy to deal with the coming argument. Unfortunately, it was pretty clear that no one in the Alley gave a damn. A line had been drawn, and they were all on Eric's side.

"Give the word when you're ready to leave," Jillian said in a tight voice, her arms crossed over her chest. Her normally pleasant features were pinched with anger and disappointment as she stood near the bottom of the porch steps. "Cian's agreed to let you follow him down to Wesley."

It wasn't easy for Chelsea to stand her ground in the face of such hostility from a woman she'd considered her friend, but she somehow found the strength. "That's not necessary, because I'm not leaving."

"You don't get that choice," Carla called out, sitting on the steps of her cabin, a steaming cup of coffee in her hand. "Go stay with some friends, since it probably isn't safe for you to go home. But there's no point in you staying here any longer."

"No point?" she choked out. "My sister is still out there with those monsters. I can't just leave."

"It was her choice to stay with Donovan," Jeremy drawled, walking over to stand beside his wife.

She didn't know how they knew about her and Eric's conversation—if he'd told them, or if they'd been shouting so loudly that they'd simply been overheard—but it was obvious where their loyalties lay. She would have found their united front odd for a group of humans, but aside from Torrance and Michaela, these were men and women who had Lycan blood running through their veins. In their eyes, she'd wronged someone in their own little private pack there in the Alley, which meant she was no longer welcome or accepted.

"You all believe him, then?" she asked, scanning the group. But there wasn't a single understanding face among them.

"Damn right we believe him," Jillian answered. "And you should have believed him, too. However Eric says it happened, then that's how it happened."

Digging her nails into her palms, Chelsea looked at Cian, who was leaning against the back of his Land Rover, and he smirked. "Want my opinion, lass? You're making a big mistake. I might not have heard the conversation Drake had with your sister last night, but she sure as hell didn't look like she was in any rush to come back with us."

"No. That can't be right," she argued, shaking her head. The idea of her sister making such a ridiculous choice was simply impossible for her to accept, going against everything that she believed in. "Either you're lying for him, or there was some kind of misunderstanding."

Standing at her husband's side, Torrance spoke up for the first time, sounding just as disappointed as Jillian. "I hate to say it, Chelsea, but it seems the only misunderstanding was the one we had about you."

She flinched, trying to think of how to respond…to make them understand, when Jillian said, "Do you have any idea what he was willing to do for you? Eric could have left your ass in that club on Saturday night, but he didn't. He went and killed for you, put himself on the line for you, and this is how you repay him? By accusing him of leaving your sister behind because he didn't want to be *bothered* with her?" The Spirit Walker's voice shook with emotion. "Are you out of your bloody mind?"

Jeremy put his hand on his wife's shoulder. "Easy, Jilly."

She bristled as she turned her gaze up to her husband's concerned face. "No! I'm not going to take it easy on her. Why should I? She hasn't taken it easy on Eric. She's done nothing but use him!"

Before Chelsea could defend herself, everyone turned toward the road leading into the Alley. Seconds later, a red Jeep came into view, screeching to a halt in the center of the glade.

"Oh, hell," Michaela groaned, cutting a worried look

toward Brody, who had his arm around her waist. "This is all we needed."

"Who is it?" Chelsea asked, stepping up to the porch railing. She was privately thankful for the diversion, but judging from the group's reaction, she had a feeling she wouldn't feel that way for long.

"It's Todd Dawson, Sophia's brother," Jeremy explained. "He's a total jackass, which means this is bound to get ugly."

Her stomach churned as a tall, dark-haired Lycan climbed out of the Jeep, his face a hard, aggressive mask of rage. "Where the hell's my sister?" he shouted, scanning the group with a belligerent gaze. "I just found out that she's here and I want her out of this stinking Alley. Now!"

"Calm down, Todd. I'm right here."

Everyone turned their heads to see Sophia standing on the Burnses' porch, a heavy blanket wrapped around her, while Eric stood protectively at her side, his hand on her shoulder. Chelsea didn't know how long the two of them had been standing there, but considering what his friends had been saying to her, and *about* her, she hoped it hadn't been long.

"Get your filthy hands off of her!" Todd roared, stalking toward the cabin. "I don't want scum like you anywhere near her! You're worse than the half-breeds!"

"Stop it!" Sophia cried, looking pale and outraged as she marched down the porch steps to confront her brother. "Eric's been nothing but kind to me, Todd. Don't you dare say anything mean about him."

"I just want to get you out of here," he muttered. He put her behind him as he started backing away from the cabin, acting as if she needed shielding from the man still standing on the porch. Eric hadn't moved, hadn't said a word. He just stood there with his hands in his pockets, looking as though he couldn't have cared less what Todd Dawson thought about him. But Chelsea had a feeling his indifferent attitude was just a front.

Todd got his sister in the Jeep, then walked around to the driver's side. He opened his door, but before he climbed in, he turned his angry gaze on Chelsea. "You really think you're safe here, human? With a guy like Drake? He'll probably rip your throat out the second you're alone with him."

"Shut your filthy mouth," Jillian snarled, starting to lurch forward, until Jeremy yanked her back against his chest. She was like an enraged tigress ready to protect her cub, and for the first time since meeting the beautiful blonde, Chelsea began to understand just how strong Jillian's connection to her people really was. And Eric was her friend, which only strengthened that connection.

Todd turned his hate-filled eyes on Jillian and sneered. "I'm just saying what a lot of us are thinking. It isn't right, his kind hooking up with a human. We can't take another disaster at this point."

"You need to mind your own damn business," Mason growled, the sharp bite in his voice sending Todd scurrying into his Jeep, his tires churning up clumps of grass as he sped away.

Though it was a beautiful day, the sun casting golden rays over the verdant glade, Chelsea shivered, feeling chilled to the bone. The Lycan's attitude toward the Runners had been appalling—but it was the things he'd said about Eric that bothered her the most. He'd had such seething hatred and distrust for Eric, simply because of his bloodline…because of the things that his father had done. She knew, from talking to Jillian and Carla, how much good Eric had done for the pack, but the Lycans in

Shadow Peak didn't care. They continued to cast blame and to pass judgment, throwing accusations around like verbal grenades, without any basis or proof.

Just like you've done, whispered a voice in her head.

She shuddered, not wanting to listen, but knew it was true. She'd lashed out at Eric because she hadn't wanted to face the possibility that Perry was acting like their mother, putting a man's interests above her own. Hadn't wanted to accept that Perry cared so little about her own sister, she couldn't even pick up a phone and call to let her know that she was okay. Not even when she must have known that Chelsea was now as caught up in the nightmare as she was.

You really think those are the only reasons? Come on, Chelsea. Man up.

She didn't want to admit it—wanted to ignore that irritating voice—but it was right. There *was* more to the issue. A deeper fear that had nothing to do with Perry and her worry that beneath her sister's reckless acts of independence, she'd really just become a replica of their subjugated mother. No, this reason had to do with her…and Eric…and what had happened between them in his bed.

Like a blind woman who was suddenly blessed with sight, the hours of mind-blowing, breathtaking pleasure they'd shared had made her realize just how hollow and pale her life had been before she met him. In so many ways, he'd awakened her. Had opened her eyes…but to things she wasn't quite ready to face, her armor splintering before she was ready to abandon its shelter. The searing sexual intimacy between them had been so much more than what Chelsea had bargained for—so much hotter and sweeter and more intensely emotional—and when given a way to get out before she was too far gone to care, she'd taken it. In an act of pure, blind panic, she'd used the situation with Perry to drive a wedge between them, without even realizing that's what she was doing.

She'd chosen retreat rather than to take a chance on finding something that was real and strong and beautiful. Something that could...*last.*

Cutting her gaze across the grass-covered glade, she spotted Eric talking to Mason, who had joined him on the Burnses' porch. Eric looked gorgeous, but tired, and she knew that she'd hurt him. That was why Jillian was so angry with her, and she didn't blame the healer. Even though she clung to the hope that he was somehow wrong about Perry, Chelsea knew that she owed him an apology for reacting the way that she had. He'd been taking so many unfair knocks from his pack lately, and all she'd done was add to the bullshit.

Taking a deep breath, she started to make her way down the porch steps, but stopped when her cell phone started to ring in her pocket. She'd been carrying the phone with her every day, in the hopes that Perry might call. But this was the first time it had rung since she'd come to the Alley.

The moment she answered the call, her sister started speaking in a sobbing, breathless rush. "Chelsea, I'm so s-sorry. I should have listened to him."

"What? Listened to who? Perry, where are you?"

Voice cracking, her sister said, "To the guy you're with. He tried to get me to come back with him yesterday, but I wouldn't. I told him I wanted to stay with Jason. But everything's gone wrong."

"Oh, God." She was only distantly aware of sinking onto one of the porch steps, the phone still clutched in her shaking hand as the others gathered around her.

"Perry, where are you?" she asked again, nearly choking on her guilt. Feeling ill with it. "I'll come and get you, but you have to stop crying and tell me where you are."

"I'm calling from the women's shelter in Wesley. I hitchhiked here, because I didn't know where else to go."

"Okay, that's good," Chelsea told her, lifting her gaze to search for Eric, knowing that he'd help her, even though she didn't deserve it. "Just stay there, honey. I'm on my way."

Hours later, Eric still wasn't quite sure how he'd ended up in such a screwed-up situation. One minute he'd been using every ounce of strength he possessed to keep from running across the Alley and grabbing Chelsea up in his arms, the sight of her after everything that had happened damn near killing him. Then her phone had rung, and he hadn't been able to stop himself from going to her when it was clear that something was wrong. The others had all argued that he didn't owe her anything, telling him to stay behind and let them handle the situation with Perry Smart. But he hadn't been able to do it. Instead, he'd climbed into Jeremy's truck with her, and the three of them had driven down to Wesley together.

After a long, drawn-out argument between the sisters at the shelter, Chelsea had finally convinced Perry that the best course of action at the moment, until they had a better understanding of what was going on with Jason and the Whiteclaw, was for them to both go up to the Alley. According to the distraught, nearly incoherent Perry, Jason Donovan had sneaked her out of Hawkley earlier that morning. He'd left her at a rest stop on one of the main highways that cut through the mountains, telling her to find a ride and go back home because she was making things too difficult for him.

The way Eric saw it, either Jason had finally gotten

tired of Perry and wanted her gone—or something had happened and he was trying to get her the hell away from Hawkley because he actually cared about her. Were the Whiteclaw after Perry? Did they know that she'd helped Sophia? Or was it something else that had forced Jason Donovan to let her go? Until they learned the answers to those questions, everyone knew that the safest place for the girl was with the Runners.

When they finally reached the Alley, Eric gave a sharp sigh of relief, thankful that they'd made it back without any problems. But just as he climbed out of the truck, the hairs on the back of his neck prickled, alerting him to danger. He sniffed the air as he cut a sharp look toward Jeremy, the Runner obviously feeling it, too, his golden gaze scanning the glade. Mason and the other Runners were coming outside to meet up with them, one of the truck's back doors opening as Chelsea started to climb out, but Eric shoved her back inside. Slamming the door, he growled, "Stay there!" She shouted something through the glass, but he couldn't hear the words over the menacing howls that suddenly filled the night.

And in the next moment, hell was upon them.

The ambush happened so quickly, there wasn't even time to get Chelsea and Perry inside the safety of a cabin, the two women trapped in the truck while Eric and the others became immersed in the battle. Out of nowhere, he and the Runners found themselves surrounded by at least a dozen werewolves out for the kill. With no time to think of how Chelsea would react, Eric allowed the change to wash over him, cloth shredding as ebony fur rippled over his expanding form. Within seconds he and the other Runners had taken the monstrous shapes of their beasts. They stood at nearly seven feet tall, with wolf-shaped heads and powerfully formed bodies, complete with lethal, claw-tipped hands and long, deadly fangs.

With a collective roar, he and the Runners engaged the enemy. It took only seconds to realize that the wolves they were fighting weren't giving off a scent, which was how they'd been able to infiltrate the Alley without detection. And that wasn't the only disturbing discovery. Though Eric and the others were fighting for all they were worth, these enemy Lycans were unnaturally strong, making them impossible to take down.

"They're doped up on some superdrug," Cian snarled beside him, the guttural words distorted by the muzzled shape of his mouth. The Runner ducked to avoid the lethal claws that were aimed for his throat, then said, "I tasted it when I got a bite out of one. It's made them stronger."

"Trust me, I noticed," Eric grated, using everything he had to hold off the ginger wolf that kept going for him.

"Jason, stop screwing around and take one down!" The shout came from one of the enemy wolves, and Eric could tell by the voice that it was Curtis Donovan. He'd suspected these were Curtis's men, though he hadn't been able to identify them by scent. The "Jason" that Curtis had just commanded to make a kill must be Jason Donovan, which meant Perry's boyfriend had attacked the very men who were trying to protect her. Eric didn't know what kind of game Jason was playing, but it would end tonight, when he died with the others. They just had to figure out a way to bring these bastards down.

Suspecting they were there to either kill the Smart sisters or to kidnap them, Eric did everything he could to keep close to the truck. But it wasn't enough, and he soon found himself being driven away by three Lycans who came after him all at once, trapping him against the side of a cabin. Just as they were getting ready to go in for

the kill, Curtis told them to move aside, a malicious grin
on his wide mouth as he stalked toward Eric. His golden
eyes burned with triumph. "I've got you now, Drake."

"You know that the Silvercrest will consider your actions here tonight an act of war," Eric snarled, flexing his
blood-drenched claws at his sides. No way in hell was he
going down without a fight. Not when Chelsea's life was
in the balance.

Curtis smirked as he rolled his bulky head over his fur-
covered shoulders. "Because of you? I doubt that. Rumor
has it that you're not beloved by your little pack anymore."
He gave a low laugh. "But it doesn't matter. War is coming, Drake. And there's nothing you or I can do to stop it."

"War? What do those sex shows you're running have
to do with war?"

"Wars take money." A slow, cruel smile curved the bastard's black lips. "And those little human bitches in the
truck over there are going to bring in a premium price—
once I'm done with them."

"You're never getting your hands on them!" he growled,
launching himself at Curtis with a bloodthirsty roar. But
the Lycan was too strong. Eric engaged him with every
fighting tactic he'd ever learned, but Curtis was too well
trained to be caught off guard, and the drug seemed to
have made him invincible to pain. Eric was taking a brutal beating, worried that he wouldn't be able to stay on
his feet much longer, when help came from one of the last
places he'd expected to find it. In a blur of honey-colored
fur, Jason Donovan joined the fight, snapping at Curtis
with his slathering jaws.

"You bloody little traitor!" Curtis bellowed, rage fu-
eling his strength as he ripped his claws through Jason's
abdomen, blood spraying in a wide arc as the Lycan went
down. Leaping over Jason's body, Curtis started to launch

himself at Eric with his claws extended, going in for a kill strike, when suddenly there was a furious, harrowing cry behind the Lycan. In the next instant, Curtis's body gave a violent shudder as the sound of gunshot tore through the air, and he dropped to his knees on the ground, a gushing hole torn through the center of his chest. Lifting his gaze, Eric was stunned to see Chelsea standing on the roof of Jeremy's truck, her eyes wide with shock, the smoking gun gripped in her hands.

Holy Christ. She'd saved his life. Had climbed onto the roof of the truck in the middle of a goddamn nightmare, when she should have been catatonic with fear, and fired a bullet for him.

For me... She did it for me.

That stunning thought staggered through his brain. He needed to think it through, decipher its significance, but there was no damn time. Now she was in even greater danger than before, because Curtis's men were closing in on the truck.

No! Not going to lose her, the wolf snarled inside his head, its gravelly voice brimming with rage. *Not today. Not ever!*

Determined to do whatever it took to get her to the safety of one of the cabins before they killed him, Eric started running toward her, when he realized something was happening to him. That he was experiencing some kind of change. He could literally taste the air around him as it crackled against his skin. Smell its heat and life. See everything down to the sharpest point of precision, laser focused with high-octane energy, feeling as if he had a goddamn nuclear-powered well-of-purpose building inside him that was just waiting to be unleashed.

For a single searing moment, he looked at Chelsea, seeing everything he'd been too blind to see before, understanding and recognition slamming into him with jarring, heart-stopping force. He staggered under the impact, the revelation so stunning and bright it hurt his eyes. Then he lowered his gaze to the Lycans closing in on her, his nostrils flaring as his muscles coiled with fury, and he let the primal, visceral surge of energy riding beneath his skin break free. Screams echoed in his ears, accompanied by the sound of shattering bones and the rending, tearing rasp of claws and fangs slicing through flesh. His blood raged as he worked to destroy those who had threatened his woman, annihilating everything in his path.

When it was finally over, Eric's claws and fangs were drenched in blood, and he found himself standing a few feet away from Curtis Donovan's shredded body, while the bastard's men lay mangled and broken on the ground around him.

He'd thought he understood the dark, destructive power that he held inside—thought he'd known what it was capable of. But he'd never had a clue. This had been unlike anything he'd ever known. Violent and unstoppable, an endless supply of strength and speed that he could have never imagined, all held in perfect control, used for one specific purpose: to keep Chelsea alive. To keep her safe. Keep her *with* him.

Forever.

For the first time in his life, his dark wolf had risen up in all its destructive glory, determined to do whatever it took to protect *their* mate.

Eric had heard it said that a dark wolf could only fully awaken, embracing its total power, once it had found its true life mate. Like so many things in nature, the rule was meant to keep balance, since it was a dark wolf's need for its mate that was meant to temper its savage, visceral aggression.

However, the rule no longer applied when that aggression was being channeled toward someone who had threatened the wolf's woman. In that event, all bets were off, and the threat was destroyed by any means necessary. Which was exactly what Eric had done.

Oh, yeah. He got it now. The crazy, stubborn, smart-mouthed little human was *his,* and he wouldn't have her any other way.

The only problem was whether or not *she'd* have him.

The other Runners were eyeing him with expressions that ranged from shock to gratitude, but the only reaction he cared about was Chelsea's. He could sense her behind him, could feel the power of her gaze as it roamed his massive, beast-shaped body, and tried to work up the courage to turn and face her.

She saved us, the wolf growled, its guttural voice thick with possession.

True. But then, that had been before she'd seen the sort of violence he was truly capable of.

Retaking his human shape, Eric wiped a hand over his mouth and headed toward Jeremy, who was standing beside Jason Donovan's human body and calling him over. Though Eric hadn't attacked Jason in his rage, the bleeding wounds that Curtis had inflicted were too severe for Jillian to heal.

As Eric dropped to his knees, Jason opened his eyes. "Curtis wanted…Perry," he rasped, his lungs working hard as he struggled for breath. "He didn't want me to take her from the club, but I had to. Been trying to protect her, but I…I didn't trust him. He was getting Roy on his side, so I told them she escaped today. But Curtis wouldn't let it go—started putting together a search party to go after her. Said he was going to get good money for her, after he'd used her himself. I couldn't…couldn't let that happen, so I told them I'd talked to you. Said that her sister was here. Wanted to…to get him here…so you and the Runners would kill him. Didn't know Curtis would…give us that drug. Just wanted Perry to be…safe."

Son of a bitch. The kid had led Curtis right to their doorsteps, counting on Eric and the Runners to destroy him, so that Perry would no longer be in danger. He hadn't been working with Curtis tonight—he'd been setting him up. Leading him to slaughter. And he'd been willing to risk his own life to see the bastard taken down.

Wishing like hell that Jason had come to him for help before all this shit happened, he asked, "Is Perry your mate, Jason?"

Blood slipped from the corner of his mouth as he gave a pained laugh. "What's it matter if she was? She'll be better off without me. Hell, dying is the best thing I could do…for her." He took a shallow breath, shaking his head as he said, "When we met, I t-told her not to come after me. Knew she'd be in danger, because of what I was mixed up in." His lips twitched with a strained smile. "Crazy girl did it anyway."

Eric lifted his head, ready to call for Perry, who was still in the truck—but Jason's fingers dug into his arm, demanding his attention. "Have to…warn you. Roy's using those sex shows to make blackmail tapes. He's gonna… force others to fight on their side. You have to stop them."

Shit. All this time, they'd thought the Donovans had recruited the Whiteclaw. But they'd been wrong. It was Roy's crazy ass that was causing all the trouble.

"He wants…war," Jason growled, just as his last breath rattled past his lips.

Ignoring the aches and pains in his battered body, Eric pushed back to his feet, his thoughts on everything Jason had told him…and the woman still waiting behind him.

Wyatt tossed him a clean pair of jeans, which he pulled on, before turning to face Chelsea. He didn't know what to expect from her now that it was over. Fear? Disgust? Who knew how she would react to what she'd seen him do…to the monster she'd seen him become.

She stood less than a dozen feet away, pale but beautiful, her tear-filled gaze locked tight on his. "Your eyes are still completely amber," she whispered.

He wasn't surprised, since he now knew the amber coloring was a mark of the dark wolf.

Taking a deep breath, Eric parted his lips, praying he could think of the right thing to say. But he didn't need to.

Before the first word could fall from his lips, Chelsea gave a choked cry and ran straight toward him…right into his blood-covered arms.

It had taken Eric and the Runners a good hour to deal with the bodies that had been scattered over the Alley. They were all feeling more than a little battered and bruised, but by some miracle of fate, they'd avoided any serious injuries in the group. By the time they were finally done clearing away the casualties, it was near midnight. Chelsea and Perry had headed into his cabin as soon as the cleanup had started, and he figured they were both asleep by now. But, as he walked through the front door, he found Chelsea waiting for him.

God, there was so much he wanted to say to her, he didn't even know where to begin. So much that he needed to try and make her understand. He had no idea how he was going to convince her to give him a chance—only the driving need to make it happen.

He finally got it now—the reason his wolf had been so intense about her…as well as why it had hidden the truth from him. The animal had been protecting them.

Had been willing to deny its own nature until it was sure she could accept them both: the man *and* the beast. He didn't even know if it had been a conscious decision on the wolf's part. But he had no doubt that the animal's powerful instincts were the reason the truth had been kept from him until tonight, when she'd proven that she was willing to drill a bullet into another living thing to save his life. And at a time when he was more monster than man. Despite the frustration he'd had to endure these past days, Eric knew it had been the right choice, and now he would never doubt the beast again. It might be darker than the man, but they were the same. Two sides of one whole. He'd live better for that understanding. That acceptance.

But they'd never be complete without their woman.

As she rose from her place on the sofa, he said, "I didn't think you'd still be up."

With trembling fingers, she tucked a lock of hair behind her ear. "I didn't want to go to bed until I had a chance to tell you that I'm sorry. For all the stupid things I said last night." She took a step closer as she licked her lips, her blue eyes wide and bright. "I know I acted horrible, and that I don't deserve it, but I'm hoping you'll give me another chance."

His fingers flexed at his sides, his relief so acute that it hurt. "With me, Chelse, you can have as many chances as it takes," he said in a low rumble, aching to claim what was *his*. What he knew, with every fiber of his being, belonged to him.

He was no longer worried about how she'd fare in his world, because there wasn't any need. Tonight had shown him just how badly he'd underestimated her. She could handle him and his wolf…and even the whole damn pack, if it came to that. The woman was hell on wheels, and he wanted her so badly he didn't know what would happen to him if she walked away from him. Yeah, he was worried about how she would take everything he had to unload on her, but he was determined to find a way to make her understand. He'd never walked away from a challenge in his life, and he sure as hell wasn't about to start now, when it was the most important thing he'd ever had to do.

With his heart beating to a strong, heavy rhythm, Eric closed the distance between them and lifted his hand to her face, his thumb stroking across her lower lip. "Tonight changed everything, sweetheart. Even though it was wrong, I wanted to keep you, to make you mine, whether the wolf accepted you or not. But now that it has, I don't have to worry that I'll slip up. It will protect you as fiercely as I will. Forever."

She blinked. "Forever?"

Taking a deep breath, he dropped his hand and said, "I want to bond with you, Chelsea."

"Wh-what?" she gasped, her eyes going wide.

"I want to claim you in the way of the wolf. Pierce your neck with my fangs and take your blood." His voice was low, rough, stripped down to raw, blistering emotion. "I know it probably sounds scary, but it's meant to be extremely pleasurable for the female."

Confusion creased her brow. "But wouldn't that turn me into a werewolf?"

Very carefully, he said, "If you weren't mine, then, yes. But it doesn't work that way with mates."

Chelsea couldn't believe what she was hearing. She'd waited up to ask him for a chance to keep seeing each other—not to bind their lives together in a way that could never be undone. "Mates?" she choked out, shaking her head. "I…I don't understand, Eric. Why are you saying these things to me *now,* when you've never talked about a future between us before?"

"Tonight, I recognized your scent." He gave her a dark, possessive look, his gray eyes beginning to glow around the edges again with that warm, amber light that they'd had after the fight. "I recognized it as something that belongs to me, Chelsea. It says that you're *mine.*"

Needing to put more space between them, Chelsea took an instinctive step back. "But thatthat doesn't make any sense." Her emotions were in a chaotic jumble that was heading swiftly toward panic. "You smell something good and *poof,* just like that you're ready to take things to the next level?"

"Damn it, you don't get to make me sound like some juvenile pup who doesn't know his ass from his elbow," he growled, the angry thunder of his voice nearly making her jump. "You have no… idea how significant this is."

Tossing her arms up, she shouted, "That's right! I don't. Because you've never bothered to explain it to me!"

With a low groan vibrating in the back of his throat, he pressed the heels of his hands to his eyes, looking as if he was trying to get a handle on his frustration. Breathing hard and rough, he said, "What happened tonight means that my wolf completely accepts you as ours. It means I no longer have to fight to maintain full control over myself when we make love." He lowered his hands, the look in his glittering eyes imploring her to understand. "It means I can finally *trust* myself with you. That I no longer have to be afraid."

He'd been that worried? All this time? Though he'd tried to explain the danger to her, she'd never really believed him.

Shivering, she wrapped her arms around her middle, her voice little more than a croak. "And if you had never had this understanding? This…this *recognition* of my scent? Even if we hadn't argued last night, you still would have just walked away from me? After what? A day? A week?"

His throat worked as he swallowed. "Walking away from you is the best thing I could have done, because my wolf was only growing more possessive of you. But I don't know that I would have been strong enough to make it happen." He sounded as if he was confessing a sin.

Softly, she asked, "And you think our being together now is a given?"

"You can't change the facts, Chelsea." He took a quick, sharp breath, every line in his body and face going hard with determination. "No matter how you look at it, you're *mine*. Do you understand what I'm telling you?"

Oh, she understood. Understood that he wanted things from her she didn't think she would ever be able to give him. How could she, when she simply didn't have the ability to open up and completely put her faith in another person?

Shaking her head, she said, "I'm sorry, Eric. But that isn't the way that it works. Not for me. We don't all get the magic answer."

His eyes narrowed to blazing, piercing chips of gray. "What the hell does that mean?"

"It means I'm still me!" she told him, pressing a hand against the center of her chest. "Still the same woman with the same hang-ups. I'm not ready to submit and give myself to you. Not for forever. I might *never* be."

"I can…be patient," he scraped out, but she knew it was a lie.

"No, you can't. I can see it in your eyes." She took another step back, looking to the side, her face hidden by the veil of her hair. All of this…it was too much, and she could feel her defense mechanisms kicking into gear, working to bury her confusing feelings beneath layers and layers of cold, glacial ice. "It's…it's best to end this now, Eric, before either one of us gets any deeper."

"Any deeper?" He gave a hard, bitter laugh, feeling like she'd reached into his chest and ripped out his heart. "Christ, Chelsea. This isn't something that's going to just go away for me. I only get *one* mate, and that's *you*. I don't get any second chances."

"I'm sorry," she said, her voice eerily quiet and flat. "But I can't do this."

He cursed under his breath, hands braced on his hips, head hanging forward, as he paced the length of the room. The mountain winds howled beyond the night-black windows, mirroring the crushing tension in the air. Finally, he blew out another ragged breath and turned toward her. "I'm not asking you to change who you are. I'm just asking you to start a life with me."

Bringing her gaze back to his, she asked, "And where would we live?"

Because of his bloodline, his family was going to be at the forefront of danger for months, if not years to come. Though Eric knew she was tough, he also knew that only a madman would take a human female to live with the pack right now, when things were still so volatile and unstable, catastrophe waiting to erupt at any moment. But they could build a life together in the Alley. Despite what had happened tonight, she would be safe here. He and the Runners would see to it.

"Eric?"

He took another deep breath, collecting his thoughts, and said, "We'd live here, in the Alley. It would be perfect, Chelse. You would still have your teaching career.

I'm not trying to take that away from you. And you could still devote time to your causes. Hell, the women up in Shadow Peak need your help more than you can even imagine. You could start a shelter for them here, in one of the cabins. Give them counseling and a safe place to go when they need it."

She looked at him with an expression that was nothing short of stunned. "What do I know about werewolves?"

"You know about women—especially ones who have to deal with overbearing, abusive males. Trust me, we've got our share of those. God knows their mates could use a safe place to go when things at home get too rough. You'd be needed, there's no doubt of that." *And I'd need you. So damn much.*

"Eric, I...I don't—"

He couldn't stop himself from taking a step toward her, wanting to hold her so badly it was killing him. "I don't want to change you or force you to be anything other than what you are, Chelsea. I just...I want you to make room for me," he rasped, forcing the words from his tight throat. "I want inside. Want to know every part of you. *All* of them. Not just the ones you feel safe sharing with me."

Chelsea took another step back. "No. I'm sorry, but I can't do that. I *won't*." Her voice shook. "I can't bind my life to you, Eric. I can't be what you want."

She watched his strong, tanned throat work on a hard swallow, but he didn't give her another argument or heart-breaking plea. His jaw was clenched so hard and tight, she wasn't even sure that he could.

Filling the awful silence, she said, "I know I need to leave, but it would be wrong to move Perry tonight, when she's so devastated by Jason's betrayal. But we'll go first thing in the morning." Ignoring the pain in her chest, and the voice screaming in her head that she was making the biggest mistake of her life, she added, "You're a great guy, Eric. The best. You deserve someone who can be what you need."

"I don't need someone to fit a goddamn mold," he snarled. "I just needed you."

"It'll pass," she whispered, trying to keep her voice from breaking.

"Damn it, Chelsea." He looked…shattered, his own voice guttural and bleak. "Don't do this."

"I'm sorry," she said again, sniffing to hold back her tears. "But it's for the best. For both of us. I know you'll come to see that. Probably a lot sooner than you realize."

She turned to go, needing to get away, but he grunted, "Wait!" When she'd forced her gaze back to his, he said, "You should know that Jason was only trying to protect your sister. I think he believed she wouldn't leave him if she knew he still loved her." He gave another one of those hard, bitter laughs that made something inside her feel like it was splintering into a hundred pieces. "Anyway, he knew that Curtis wanted her, so he played the bastard, telling him that Perry had run away. He also told him about meeting me in Hawkley, and that you were here in the Alley. Said this would be the first place we brought her. Instead of betraying Perry, Jason saw tonight as the perfect chance to get rid of Curtis for good, since he didn't think Curtis and his men would be any match for the Runners. But he hadn't banked on Curtis pumping them up with that drug."

"So you got lucky," she whispered, thinking of how his dark wolf had risen and taken control, destroying their enemies.

"Yeah," he rasped, a grim smile on his beautiful lips

as he started to back away. "I'm definitely one lucky son of a bitch."

Then he turned and left the cabin, and Chelsea didn't see him again that night…or the following morning.

As she and Perry loaded up the SUV he'd bought for her and drove out of the glade, Eric remained out of sight. She didn't even know if he was still in the Alley.

All she knew was that she'd lost him.

Forever.

Chapter Fifteen

A day went by, then another, and then more, until it had been over a week since Chelsea had driven out of the Alley. Which meant it'd been over a week since she'd seen Eric.

Over a week since she'd felt…alive.

Standing at her kitchen sink and staring out the window, she thought about how colorless life seemed without him, how placid. Beige and dull, all the hours blending together in a hazy blur of nothingness. There were so many things that she missed about him, it was impossible to name just one. His wicked laugh and those crooked, cocky grins he was always giving her. That exhilarating rush that had swept through her every time he walked into a room. The way he'd always looked at her with so much hunger and heat, as if he saw her in a way that no other man ever had.

Damn it, she missed *him*. So much that it was slowly killing her inside.

Their time together had been such a mess, but it had proven one thing. Even in the midst of a nightmare, something beautiful could be found. You just had to be willing to fight for it, and she hadn't.

She didn't know how long she just stood there, staring at the gray sky through her small window by the kitchen sink, but it seemed as if seasons had passed by the time Perry came shuffling into the kitchen, breaking her out of her trance.

Turning around, she said, "Hey, you."

Perry jerked her chin in acknowledgment, slipping silently into one of the kitchen chairs. She looked awful, her hair tangled around her pale face, dark smudges under her puffy eyes. She was nothing but a shell now. No spark, no fire. And for the first time since everything had fallen apart in their lives, Chelsea realized that a lot of the blame for Perry's depression fell on her shoulders. It had been her choice not to tell her sister the truth about what Jason Donovan had been doing in the Alley with Curtis and the others that night. She'd told herself it would only make it harder for Perry to accept his loss. Convinced herself that she was saving her sister from more heartbreak and pain. But she'd been wrong.

The truth was that she'd been trying to make Perry more like her. Trying to help her build that sturdy, brittle shell around her heart so that nothing and no one could ever hurt her. But that wasn't what she wanted for this troubled young woman who had the rest of her life ahead of her.

"Honey," she said, taking a seat at the table. "We need to talk."

Then she did what she should have done from the very beginning, and gave her sister the truth. Yes, it hurt, but it also proved that Perry had been right to follow her heart.

Jason might have been caught up in something beyond his control, but he *had* loved her—so much that he'd been willing to die for her—and he'd wanted her to be safe... to find happiness.

She hoped that one day Perry would find love again— that she wouldn't be afraid to risk her heart—because in that moment, Chelsea suddenly realized a beautiful truth: no matter how afraid you were of being hurt, it was always better to choose love. To take the risk and cherish the reward, rather than to play it safe and never know love at all. To never have the courage to surrender to its power and simply let it overtake you and reshape you. To let it find the parts of yourself that you never even knew existed.

Knowing what she had to do, Chelsea gave her sister a hug and told her that she'd always be there for her when she needed it. Then she packed a bag, jumped in her car and set off with the burning determination to undo the biggest mistake of her life.

A blood-orange sun hung low in the sky when Chelsea finally pulled her car into the Alley. She'd been lucky enough to avoid any Silvercrest scouts—either that, or they'd decided to let her pass onto their land unchallenged. She parked the Rav4—she was still driving the SUV, since no had ever come to collect it—beside Eric's cabin, surprised that no one came out to see who had arrived. She'd just started to make her way up the porch steps when she heard a deep voice call her name. Without even looking, the Irish accent told her it was Cian who'd called out to her.

"Where is everyone?" she asked, turning around. The Runner was walking over from his cabin, and for the first time since she'd met him, he didn't give her one of those devilish smiles that she'd come to expect.

Flicking the butt of his cigarette into the damp grass, he said, "We decided I'd be the one to deal with you."

Confusion creased her brow. "How did you know I was coming?"

"Hendricks called."

Since he wasn't coming up the steps to join her, she decided to come down them. "Isn't he one of the scouts I met before?" she asked, using her hand to shield her eyes against the vibrant rays of late-afternoon sunshine. "How did he know what I was doing? Has he been watching me in Smythe?"

With a brief nod, he said, "Until this crap is cleared up with the Whiteclaw, Eric wanted to make sure you were protected."

"So he sent the scout?"

"He would have done it himself," he explained, studying her with a dark, glittering gaze, "but he didn't trust himself to be that near you."

Before Chelsea could figure out what to say, the Runner pulled a set of keys from his pocket and jerked his chin. "Come on, we need to hurry."

"Why?" She followed after him as he headed toward his Land Rover. "What's going on?"

"There's something happening up in Shadow Peak that I think you should see," he tossed over his shoulder.

"Is that where Eric is?"

He climbed behind the wheel without responding, so she repeated the question once she was in the passenger's seat and he was starting the engine.

It wasn't until he'd driven out of the Alley, and they were turning onto the same road that Eric had taken when they'd gone up to see Elise, that the Irishman finally gave her an answer. "Eric's been up in town for a while now."

"And?"

His dark brows lifted. "And what?"

His attitude was really starting to piss her off. "Look, I get that I'm not your favorite person at the moment, but at least tell me how he's doing," she snapped.

He slanted her a wry look and smirked. "You sure you want to know?"

Swallowing the lump of guilt in her throat, she said, "Yes."

"Well, to be honest, he's gone a little mad," he muttered, taking the curves in the road so fast that she had to hold on to the door with a white-knuckled grip. "Stubborn jackass has been taking on everyone and everything like he has a bloody death wish."

"What do you mean?" she asked, his words twisting her stomach into knots.

Scrubbing his hand over his jaw, he said, "Let's see, since you left he's gotten Heaven and Hell permanently shut down, had about twenty different fights up in town, and made it his personal goal in life to destroy Roy Claymore."

Oh, hell. "Destroy him how?" she croaked, dreading what she would hear.

"He goes to the borders of Hawkley every day, demanding entrance into the town, because he wants to challenge the bastard in a fight to the death. If you ask me, it's been a way for him to channel all his anger toward you into something useful."

She flinched, thinking he was probably right. "And you've done nothing to stop him?"

Cian shrugged. "We send someone with him wherever he goes. But aside from locking him up, there isn't a hell of a lot we can do. He's a grown man, Chelsea. One who's pissed and hurt and spoiling for a fight."

The words put a sharp pain in her chest, and though

Cian's driving was scaring the hell out of her, she silently willed him to go faster, desperate to get to Shadow Peak so that she could tell Eric how sorry she was and beg his forgiveness. They made the rest of the trip in tense silence, and it wasn't long before they were pulling into the town. But instead of taking her to Eric's house, like she'd expected, Cian parked on a busy street near what appeared to be the town center.

"What's going on?" she asked, looking out the Rover's window at the gathering crowd. "Why are there so many people here?"

Turning off the engine, he said, "There's a meeting going on in front of the Town Hall. All these people are heading over there, because they don't want to miss seeing Glenn Farrow make a formal accusation against Eric. And it's all because of you."

"Because of me? I don't understand. What's he being accused of?"

"Ever since all that shit went down with his father, Farrow and his lot have been looking for a way to get Eric banished," he explained, sliding her a chilling look. "And *you* handed it right to them. They're using your sudden disappearance as a way to get rid of him."

"My disappearance?"

"Farrow somehow learned that you're no longer staying in the Alley, and now he's trying to use the situation as a way to get at Eric. We've told him you went back home to Virginia, but he doesn't care. All he's interested in is pushing for an immediate vote, before we can deliver proof that you're alive."

"Ohmygod," she whispered, her head spinning as she tried to take it all in.

"God isn't going to be able to help with this one," he ground out. "The others are already here to support him, but there isn't a lot they can do. Not if things swing in Farrow's favor. I was planning to drive down to Smythe and drag you back with me, but then we heard that you were already on your way. You need to make an appearance in front of everyone and set the record straight."

"I will," she told him, her voice choked with emotion. "In more ways than one."

Then she climbed out of the Rover and took off running through the crowd.

Son of a bitch.

Without even turning around, Eric knew that Chelsea was somewhere in the growing crowd behind him, her sweet, intoxicating scent wrapping around him like a damn vise—one that had a wrenching hold on his body, as well as his heart. He'd spent the past week in hell because of this woman, and yet, he still wanted her. Still *craved* her. But then, there was no longer any doubt that she was meant to be his. That she belonged to him, body and soul.

"Eric!" Chelsea's husky voice rose above the shocked murmurs spreading through the crowd, demanding his attention. "Eric!"

Knowing he was going to regret it, he braced himself and turned around, his heart giving a painful thump the instant he set eyes on her.

With glaring rays of sunlight burning in his eyes, he watched her break through the edge of the crowd and start making her way toward him. Hating that he could still need her so badly, Eric cursed under his breath.

Behind him, Glenn Farrow and his cronies were standing on the top steps of the Town Hall, only seconds away from pleading their case to the crowd. Since there was no body or evidence of a crime, they hadn't been able to seek his execution. But there was still enough paranoia in the town that they'd hoped to have Eric banished on grounds of suspicion in the trumped-up case of Chelsea Smart's disappearance. It was nothing but a load of bullshit—but then, in times of hysteria and fear, he knew that people could be convinced of ridiculous things.

The Runners were all standing off to his right, ready to plead his innocence before the pack in a unified show of support. The only one who hadn't shown for the event was Hennessey, and Eric had assumed the Irishman was driving down to Smythe to get Chelsea and drag her back to Shadow Peak, providing the proof that no crime had been committed. But there was no way the Runner could have made it there and back already. So what the hell was she doing here?

More whispers started to spread through the crowd as the townspeople began to realize who she was. She was only a few feet away when word of what was going on must have reached Glenn, because he turned away from the group he'd been talking to and started down the steps. "This doesn't change anything!" he snarled, seething with rage. His hand shook as he pointed a finger in their direction. "We're still going to ask for a banishment vote!"

There were a few cheers from the crowd, but the majority remained silent, waiting to see what would happen. The Runners began to form an outward-facing circle around him and Chelsea, making it clear that no one would be getting past them.

"Someone get the human out of here!" Glenn roared, his narrow face mottled with rage as he realized his moment of glory was slipping away from him.

Now that Chelsea was right in front of him, Eric started to demand an explanation for her appearance, but she swept right past him, climbing onto the step behind him and then turning to face the crowd. Voice shaking with anger, she stared down the Silvercrest pack and shouted, "What in God's name is wrong with you people? Eric would give the skin off his back for any one of you, and this is how you repay his loyalty? By whispering about him like a bunch of old women and believing the lies of a man who is obviously more concerned with inciting paranoia than the truth. You should be ashamed of yourselves!"

"What the hell do you know?" someone called out from the far side of the street. "You're just a human."

"I know you don't deserve him!"

"And you do?" Jeremy asked, shooting her a questioning look over his shoulder.

Locking her gaze with the Runner's, she shook her head and said, "No, I don't. I know that I don't. But I plan on doing everything I can to become someone who does."

Wondering if he was dreaming, Eric had to swallow twice before he could say her name. "Chelsea?"

Tears glistened in her eyes as she turned her head to look at him. "I'm so sorry," she whispered, taking a step closer. "I should have been here for you, Eric. I should have never left you. I missed you so much."

"And how do I know that you won't leave me again?" The words were thick…rough, scraping against his throat, while his lungs started to work in a violent rhythm.

"Because I'm madly, desperately in love with you," she told him in a strong, clear voice as if she wanted everyone to hear the stunning declaration. "I left because I was afraid of the way you made me feel, but I'm not afraid anymore. I know I'm not perfect, and that I'll make mistakes. But I'm hoping you'll give me another chance anyway." Then she moved a little closer, and with her passion-dark gaze locked tight on his, she said, "And I really want to go someplace where I can be alone with you."

After that, Eric couldn't get her out of there fast

enough. He knew that Jeremy and the others would deal with the lingering crowd, and with Chelsea's sudden appearance, Farrow's banishment ploy had been destroyed.

Taking her hand, Eric started to pull her along behind him, still half terrified he was going to wake up and find that it'd all been some kind of heartbreaking hallucination, when someone reached out and grabbed his arm.

"Hell of a woman you've got there," Cian drawled, when he turned to see who'd stopped him.

"I know," he rasped, pulling her close to his side.

Cian shot her a playful wink, then smiled at Eric and lowered his hand. "Whatever it takes, just treat her right… and make sure she doesn't get away from you again."

He would have been insulted if any other man had said those words to him, but he knew this was the Irishman's way of offering his congratulations.

With an answering smile on his lips, Eric said, "You can count on it."

"Drive faster, Eric. I can't wait."

As she sat in the passenger's seat of his truck, clutching her seat belt with both hands, Chelsea felt like she was going to come out of her freaking skin if she didn't get him inside her.

When she told him exactly that, his nostrils flared, a muscle pulsing in the rugged line of his jaw. "You mean that?"

"God, yes. I've never meant anything more."

His fingers tightened until the steering wheel nearly cracked. "You want me to find a place to pull over?"

"Please," she whispered, licking her lips. "The Alley's too far away."

He cut her a heated look, his gray eyes blazing with hunger. "I don't have any condoms with me."

Shivering at the thought of feeling him skin-on-skin, she said, "I couldn't care less. I love you. I want you inside me. Now."

He quickly found a private spot where they could pull off the road, hidden by a thick line of trees. Chelsea pulled off her jeans and panties while he let his seat back, and then she climbed over his lap, eagerly straddling him. Their loud, ragged breaths filled the sun-dappled cab, the heat rising from their bodies creating a lush, sensual haze that added to the dreamy atmosphere. Within minutes, they were going to be fogging up the windows, and she couldn't wait.

She helped him get his bloodstained T-shirt over his head, her teeth sinking into her bottom lip as she gently touched one of the healing cuts on his chest. "Cian told me that you've been fighting."

"My mood's been foul," he muttered, running his hands over the front of her shirt and cupping her breasts, his thumbs flicking against her nipples. "You left and it nearly killed me."

Clutching his shoulders, she said, "I'm so sorry, Eric. When you told me that you wanted to bond with me, I didn't feel like I deserved you. I…I don't even feel that way now."

"Chelse." His deep voice was rough with emotion.

"No, let me finish. Please." She took a deep breath, letting everything she felt for him show in her expression, no longer struggling to hold it inside. "You're the most amazing man I've ever known," she whispered. "You were willing to give me everything, even after the way I'd acted—blaming you, instead of believing in you. Judging you. I know I have so much to make up for, and so much to learn about being a good partner, but I'm *begging* you to give me that chance. To give me the beautiful life that

you offered me before, but I was too stupid and cowardly
to take. Because I want that life with you, Eric. I want it
more than anything."

He made a low, guttural sound in his throat and yanked
her closer, nipping her lower lip with his teeth. "You fucking undo me, you know that?" he growled, taking her
mouth in a kiss that was hot and deep and savage in its
intensity. She could feel his fingers working between them
as he tore open his jeans, and then he was pressing against
her, so long and deliciously thick. Her breath caught, everything in her body going soft and warm, and she let
herself sink down, taking him in, at the same time he
pushed up, thrusting hard and deep. The sensation was
piercing, every inch of his hot, massive staff rammed
up tight inside her, reaching into the very heart of her,
and she cried out, her head falling back as her eyes slid
closed. She was snug enough that it hurt, but she didn't
give a damn. Not when it felt so incredible to have him
be a part of her again.

"No, don't close your eyes," he rasped, holding her
head in his shaking hands and drawing it closer. Her
lashes lifted, and their gazes locked, creating a connection that somehow intensified the blissful sensations. "I
need you to look at me, Chelse. I need you to be right
here with me."

She tried to breathe around the pressure, the pleasure,
the overwhelming rightness of their joining and the moment, but it was nearly impossible.

"I know," he whispered, rubbing his lips against hers
until she was finally able to draw in a gasping breath of
air. "I feel it, too, baby."

Unable to hold still, she started to move on him, using
her knees for leverage as she slowly worked her body on his.
"Tell me you didn't touch anyone else while I was gone."

* * *

Eric couldn't fathom touching anyone else…or even thinking about a woman who wasn't Chelsea. "Of course I didn't," he grated. "You're the only woman I want. The only woman I'll *ever* want. And I'm going to be on you night and day, so you'll never have any reason to doubt it."

"When I started falling in love with you," she told him, "it felt like dying."

"And now?" he asked, his hands settling on her hips as she stilled.

"Now I finally know how it feels to be alive. Not just parts of me, but all of them." Her long hair streamed over her shoulders as she shook her head. "I don't how to explain it. It's like you woke me up. Made me open my eyes."

"You did the same thing to me," he groaned, the wolf's fangs hot and heavy in his gums. But he fought their release, not wanting to ruin the moment, still worried about how she would react. Then she shocked the hell out of him by reaching up and pulling her hair over her shoulder, her head turned to the side as she made him an offering of the pale, tender column of her throat.

The instant she whispered, "Make me yours, Eric," his fangs burst into his mouth so hard that it hurt, his fingers reflexively biting into her skin with bruising force.

"Are you…are you sure this is what you want?"

"I'm sure," she said a little breathlessly, the words brimming with lust…and love.

"Christ. I want it so badly, Chelse. I just…I don't want you to ever regret it."

I don't want you to ever regret it. Chelsea knew she never would. "I won't," she told him, bringing her gaze back to his. "I want this, Eric. I want to be as close to you as I can, bound together in every possible way."

She loved feeling the way he pulsed inside her, his beautiful eyes going heavy and dark.

"Please, just trust me on this," she pleaded, "because I love every part of you. I don't want you to ever hold anything back from me, and I promise that I won't hold anything back from you. Not ever again. I don't want any barriers or stay-out zones in our relationship. I just want to be yours, completely, Eric."

"God, woman, I'll take you any way I can have you," he groaned, his arms wrapping around her like steel manacles, yanking her close. His face was buried in the curve of her shoulder, his powerful body vibrating with a fine tremor of emotion that brought tears to her eyes. "Just promise that you won't run from me."

"You mean that I won't leave you again?" she asked, her voice breaking.

He lifted his head, and his eyes were glistening with a sheen of moisture, the same as hers. "If you stay with me, your life isn't going to be easy, Chelse."

She gave him a watery smile, pouring her heart into every word. "I don't care, so long as I'm with you."

He blinked, then slowly started to smile. But it was a cautious sort of smile, as if he didn't really believe he could be that lucky.

Touching the side of his face, she said, "Eric, I'm not naive. I know there are some rough times ahead for your pack and the Runners. But I'm ready to handle whatever they throw at us, because my life is wherever you are. Just think, in the time that you've known me, have I ever given you any reason to doubt my determination?"

With a soft snort, he said, "No, you're the most stubborn woman I've ever known."

Then he lifted his hands to her hair, his breath quickening as he pulled her head a little farther to the side, a rumbling groan on his lips as he leaned in close.

"Chelsea, I've wanted this from the moment I set eyes on you," he growled, and she could hear the animal in each one of those deep, guttural words. But it didn't frighten her. She'd seen the beast in all its feral glory the night it'd saved her life, and she knew it would never harm her. Then she felt the soft touch of his lips against the side of her throat, followed by the strangely erotic scrape of a fang, and in the next instant he sank them deep, piercing her flesh. She cried out from the intense, blistering jolt of sensation, a womanly smile curving her lips as she listened to the raw, animalistic sounds that he made as he worked his jaws, taking her blood into his body and binding them together. For now and through all eternity.

When he lifted his head, his amber eyes blazed with a breathtaking look of possession and love. "You're mine now," he rasped, licking two scarlet drops of her blood from his lips.

"Forever," she moaned, unable to believe how freaking sexy it'd been.

"Forever," he echoed, his gaze shifting to her throat, to the throbbing bite marks that were burning with heat, and she could feel him getting thicker inside her, somehow getting even harder, when he was already hard as stone. "Damn it, I don't want it to end," he growled, his fingers biting into her hips as her body pulsed around him. "But I'm close, Chelse. I can't hold it."

He started to lift her up, as if he intended to spill outside her body, but she threw her arms around him, bearing down with all her strength. "No. Stay."

His body shook, strained to its absolute limit, and his gaze burned even hotter with a primitive, molten gleam.

Softly, she said, "Please don't leave me. I want you to fill me up, Eric. To give me every part of you."

He swallowed, searching her expression. "You want to start a family? *Our* family?"

The hope in his deep voice shattered her, and there was a fresh surge of tears in her eyes as she said, "God, yes. I can't think of anything I'd love more."

With just those simple words, he lost it. His powerful grip locked her in place as he drove up into her—the hard, spearing pleasure hurtling her into an explosive, mind-shattering orgasm. And he was right there with her. His head went back as dark energy roared through him, the blistering heat of his release surging inside her, making her scream. Chelsea had never felt so deliciously female, full of power and strength, as if she could take on the entire world and make it heel at her feet.

But it wasn't the world that she wanted, just one man. *Her* man. And she clutched at his hard, slick shoulders, wanting to freeze this moment in time and never let it go.

"Mmm," she moaned, when she could finally find her voice again. She was draped over him, her cheek plastered against his chest, the stroking of his fingertips along her spine making her shiver. "I've never been ravished in a truck before, but I liked it."

He gave a low, wicked laugh that rumbled beneath her ear. "Given my lack of control around you, get used to it. Your sweet little ass is going to get ravished 24-7. The truck is only one of a hundred new places I plan on staking my claim."

Loving the sound of that, she said, "Just be prepared to get claimed right back."

With his finger curled under her chin, he tipped her face up to him, the look in his eyes making her breath catch. "That's exactly what I'm hoping for. Whatever you want, woman, I'm at your mercy."

It was such a heady feeling to know that he meant every word. To feel the mating bond pulsing between them like a sensual, comforting current in the air, connecting their bodies, their souls, their hearts. "I love you, Eric. So much."

His hands shook as he pulled her closer, her ear once again pressed to the hammering beat of his heart, his lips warm against the top of her head. "Christ, Chelse. You don't know how amazing it feels to hear you say that."

"I should have said it before. But I was too afraid."

"Me, too. But it's true. I love you, Chelsea, and every moment I've spent with you has just made me fall that much harder. I love the way you smile. The way you laugh and taste and feel against me...the way you feel around me. I love the fact that you're strong and smart and always ready to stand up for what you believe in, even when dealing with an arrogant bastard like myself. I love every facet of your personality that I know, and all the ones that I still get to discover. I love you so much that I don't even know how to put it all into words."

"I feel the same way," she whispered, her cheeks wet with the tears she couldn't stop from falling. She was completely undone by his stunning declaration, fully aware that she was the luckiest of women. Eric was all that was good and right and beautiful in her world.

And no matter what life threw at them, she was never going to let him forget it.

Eric had just unlocked the door to his cabin when Brian Everett pulled up in his truck, parking in front of the porch.

After climbing out of the truck, the Lycan tipped back

his cowboy hat, and said, "Elise was talking to me and Meryl after you left town today, and she told us that you're leaving Shadow Peak to become a Runner."

"That's right," he replied, enjoying Chelsea's little gasp of surprise. Hooking his arm around her waist, he held her close to his side as he walked to the top of the steps to hear what Brian had to say.

"We want you back, Eric. Is there anything I can do to get you to change your mind?"

Giving the older man a friendly smile, he said, "I appreciate you coming all the way down here, Brian, but my decision's final."

For a moment, Brian looked like he would argue. Then he shook his head and sighed. "Hell, it's not like I can blame you. But there are a lot of us who think you're the best one to take us into the future, Eric. So we won't stop asking. We need a natural leader."

"The Runners will be here to help, however we can. But this is where I belong." The tight bond he shared with those who lived here in the Alley, as well as their friendship and loyalty, had proven that to him.

"Well, Meryl's making her famous barbecue tomorrow," Brian said, letting the matter go for the moment. "We'd like it if you and Chelsea could come up and have dinner with us. She wants to meet your little lady."

Eric slid a questioning look at Chelsea, who smiled up at him with so much love shining in her eyes, he found it hard to believe he wasn't dreaming. "I think we can manage that," he replied in a low rumble, barely able to take his gaze off her so he could return his attention to Brian.

They settled on a time, and after they'd said goodbye and watched him drive away, Eric grabbed her hand and pulled her with him into the cabin.

"Are you really going to do it?" she asked while he locked the door behind them. "Become a Runner?"

Moving to stand in front of her, he said, "As long as you don't have any objections."

Chelsea couldn't keep the smile off her face. "Are you kidding? I think it's perfect. You're needed here, Eric. And I hope that maybe I am, too." It was hard to keep the worry out of her voice as she said, "So long as I can get the others to forgive me."

Cupping her face in his hands, he said, "We need the hell out of you, sweetheart. And the others love you. They'll forgive you for anything."

For so many years she'd been locked down, her heart frozen into a hard, useless knot in her chest. But no more. Now she was burning with love for this outrageously wonderful man, undone by the breathtaking wealth of love she could feel burning in his own heart, and she knew what she needed to do. In a soft, emotional whisper, she said, "Then I have a question for you."

"Okay," he murmured, looking as if he was already thinking about kissing her again…and *more*.

Gripping handfuls of his shirt to anchor herself, she stared up into his impossibly gorgeous face, and said, "Eric Drake, I love you more than I've ever even known was possible, and I can't wait to spend the rest of my life with you. Will you marry me?"

"Isn't that *my* question?" His tone was wry, but there was an incandescent smile shining in his beautiful eyes.

"You're too much action, too little words," she teased with a soft laugh. "If I want it done, I've got to take matters into my own hands."

With his own husky bark of laughter, he swept her up

into his arms and carried her across the room, heading for the hallway. "How's this for being a man of action?"

"It's pretty smooth. I'll give you that."

He stopped just outside his bedroom door, his eyes blazing with molten hunger as he ran his tongue over the edge of his teeth, and it was so sexy she nearly died. Then he lowered his head, putting his face close to hers. "And what else will you give me?" he asked against her mouth.

"Everything," she whispered, her heart so full she thought it might burst. "Anything you want."

He pulled back a little, searching her eyes. "You mean it?"

Chelsea gave him a slow, wicked smile. "Baby, I've never meant anything more."

* * * * *

Be sure to look for the next darkly sensual installment in Rhyannon's Bloodrunners series this fall, when Elise Drake and Wyatt Pallaton's sizzling battle of wills comes to a head in Dark Wolf Running.

#153 THIS WICKED MAGIC
by Michele Hauf

Possessed by demons, Certainly Jones has no choice but to turn to Vika St. Charles—a powerful witch who serves the Light—to exorcise them. While her powers fill Certainly with a sense of hope, he knows his condition terrifies her, and convincing Vika to help him will require all his skills of seduction. Especially when his actions unleash a host of evil factors that will put *both* of their abilities to the test...

#154 UNDERCOVER WOLF • *Alpha Force*
by Linda O. Johnston

When Sergeant Kristine Norwood is assigned to help Quinn Parran assimilate to the military unit Alpha Force, it's quite difficult for her to retain a professional demeanor around the gorgeous shape-shifter. But when tragedy hits a nearby national park and Quinn's brother and sister-in-law go missing, Kristine must concentrate on solving a case whose clues all point to a wolf. Racing against the clock and forced to go undercover with Quinn as newlyweds, Kristine finds she's enjoying the charade a little too much, and senses that Quinn is, too.

REQUEST YOUR FREE BOOKS!

2 FREE NOVELS FROM THE PARANORMAL ROMANCE COLLECTION PLUS 2 FREE GIFTS!

YES! Please send me 2 FREE novels from the Paranormal Romance Collection and my 2 FREE gifts (gifts are worth about $10). After receiving them, if I don't wish to receive any more books, I can return the shipping statement marked "cancel." If I don't cancel, I will receive 4 brand-new novels every month and be billed just $21.42 in the U.S. or $23.46 in Canada. That's a savings of at least 21% off the cover price of all 4 books. It's quite a bargain! Shipping and handling is just 50¢ per book in the U.S. and 75¢ per book in Canada.* I understand that accepting the 2 free books and gifts places me under no obligation to buy anything. I can always return a shipment and cancel at any time. Even if I never buy another book, the two free books and gifts are mine to keep forever.

237/337 HDN FVVV

Name	(PLEASE PRINT)	

Address		Apt. #

City	State/Prov.	Zip/Postal Code

Signature (if under 18, a parent or guardian must sign)

Mail to the **Harlequin® Reader Service:**
IN U.S.A.: P.O. Box 1867, Buffalo, NY 14240-1867
IN CANADA: P.O. Box 609, Fort Erie, Ontario L2A 5X3

Want to try two free books from another line?
Call 1-800-873-8635 or visit www.ReaderService.com.

* Terms and prices subject to change without notice. Prices do not include applicable taxes. Sales tax applicable in N.Y. Canadian residents will be charged applicable taxes. Offer not valid in Quebec. This offer is limited to one order per household. Not valid for current subscribers to Paranormal Romance Collection or Harlequin® Nocturne™ books. All orders subject to credit approval. Credit or debit balances in a customer's account(s) may be offset by any other outstanding balance owed by or to the customer. Please allow 4 to 6 weeks for delivery. Offer available while quantities last.

Your Privacy—The Harlequin® Reader Service is committed to protecting your privacy. Our Privacy Policy is available online at www.ReaderService.com or upon request from the Harlequin Reader Service.

We make a portion of our mailing list available to reputable third parties that offer products we believe may interest you. If you prefer that we not exchange your name with third parties, or if you wish to clarify or modify your communication preferences, please visit us at www.ReaderService.com/consumerschoice or write to us at Harlequin Reader Service Preference Service, P.O. Box 9062, Buffalo, NY 14269. Include your complete name and address.

SPECIAL EXCERPT FROM

HARLEQUIN®

NOCTURNE™

Craving more dark and sensual paranormal
romances? Read on for a sneak peek of

THIS WICKED MAGIC

by Michele Hauf

Possessed by demons, Certainly Jones needs
the help of an exceptional witch who serves
the Light to exorcise them. Seducing this sexy
temptress will be a pleasure...but dealing with
the evil forces that their actions have unleashed
is a different matter entirely.

Everything about the man tweaked Vika's curiosity. He was
scruffy and pale, while she preferred her men neat and sun-
kissed. When she looked in his eyes she couldn't see beyond
the flat jade there. Most men's eyes gleamed and gave away
their thoughts before they had them. And his unabashed willingness to say what he thought offended her, but only because
she was taking offense.

If she did not take offense, then he had power over her.

Vika shifted into Reverse but didn't take her foot off the brake.

Certainly Jones. What a name. Must be English. He did
have the slightest hint of a British accent. Accents did appeal
to her carnal passions. Yet she was calm and cool when around
an attractive man. A wise woman never gave away too much
too soon.

She didn't need him to find the missing soul. She could
attract a wayward soul on her own, thank you very much.

Not that she'd been successful at it thus far.

"He deserves whatever he's gotten," she whispered.

And yet he'd pleaded for her to help him. He was desperate. The man couldn't go into darkness for fear of a demon taking over his body.

"There must be some spell," she mused. "And if there is, I want to find it." She eyed him in the rearview mirror. "You ready for me, CJ? Because I always accomplish what I set out to clean—I mean, help."

Uh-huh. She'd meant clean.

Vika took her foot off the brake and backed down the alleyway. Shadows glanced off the white hood of the car sandwiched between three-story buildings. When the hearse sidled alongside the man, she rolled down the passenger window.

"Get in. I have a lot of work to do, and the day isn't getting any lighter."

He slid inside but didn't offer a gregarious *I've won* smile, as she expected. Instead, he winced. In fact, he struggled to keep his jaw from opening, or maybe he was fighting a shout. And when he turned a frown on her, his face looked different. Not so slender.

And his eyes glowed red.

Vika heard the lightning crackle the air before darkness swept the sky.

CJ grabbed the steering wheel and slid his boot over on top of her foot. "Let's go for a ride, sweetie."

Will Vika be able to exorcise CJ's demons before it's too late?

Find out in THIS WICKED MAGIC by Michele Hauf, available February 5, 2013, from Harlequin® Nocturne™.

HARLEQUIN®

NOCTURNE

Discover

THE KEEPERS: L.A.,

a dark and epic new paranormal quartet
led by *New York Times* bestselling author

HEATHER GRAHAM

New Keeper Rhiannon Gryffald has her peacekeeping
duties cut out for her. Because in Hollywood, it's hard
to tell the actors from the werewolves, bloodsuckers and
shape-shifters. When Rhiannon hears about a string of
murders that bear all the hallmarks of a vampire serial
killer, she must unite forces with sexy undercover
Elven agent Brodie to uncover a plot that may forever
alter the face of human-paranormal relations....

KEEPER OF THE NIGHT

by **Heather Graham,**
coming **December 18, 2012.**
And look for

Keeper of the Moon by Harley Jane Kozack—
Available March 5, 2013
Keeper of the Shadows by Alexandra Sokoloff—
Available May 7, 2013
Keeper of the Dawn by Heather Graham—
Available July 1, 2013

HARLEQUIN®

NOCTURNE

They never expected to fall for each other…

She's a committed sergeant in a top secret military unit. He's a reluctant recruit—and a shape-shifter. But sparks fly when Kristine and Quinn masquerade as honeymooners on a beautiful island in search of Quinn's missing brother and his new bride. Can the unlikely pair set aside their differences in order to catch a killer bent on destroying Alpha Force?

FIND OUT IN

UNDERCOVER WOLF,

a sexy, adrenaline-fueled new tale in the Alpha Force miniseries from

LINDA O. JOHNSTON

Available February 5, 2013, from Harlequin® Nocturne™.